AF350835

The Ferrymen

Evie Cappelli Book Two

By Sophia Beaumont

Chapter One
Minor Felonies

Do you ever look at your life and think, *What the hell happened? What am I doing? How did I get here?*

I had one of those moments as I stood in the middle of the Boston Museum of History. Less than year ago, I was in a Toronto psych ward after a thorough but ultimately unsuccessful suicide attempt. For all intents and purposes, I was a textbook clinical depression patient, so much as there is ever a "textbook" case when it comes to mental illness.

Back then, I had no idea there was a secret society who wanted to sacrifice me to bring back a goddess. I couldn't see ghosts. I couldn't control fibers with my thoughts.

Back then, a lot of things were different.

For example, I never would have considered breaking into a museum and stealing a priceless artifact.

"Are you sure about this? It's not too late. We could just go back to the airport and wait for the flight to Chicago. No harm, no foul." Though he stood right next to me, Micha was invisible save for his reflection on the display case. The concerned look on his face was superimposed over the lapis and onyx scarab resting inside.

I took a deep breath and nodded, my fingers twitching slightly in his direction. I felt his cool, ghostly hand against my palm.

A crisp female voice came over the loudspeaker. "Attention, patrons. The museum will be closing in five minutes. Please make your way to the exits in a timely fashion. The Boston Museum of History thanks you for your visit. Please come again soon."

"That's my cue," I whispered, turning back to the hallway.

I followed a line of stragglers toward the front doors, but veered left at the last moment and went into the ladies' room instead. One last woman was washing her hands when I entered. I picked the last stall on the end and waited until she was gone and the final announcement was made before drawing my feet up onto the toilet seat.

I crouched there precariously, keeping my balance by pressing my hands against the sides of the stall.

"Breathe deep. Remember our meditation practices," Micha said. He was visible now—to me, anyway—and the stall felt very crowded.

I ducked my head, pulling the hood of my elaborately cabled gray sweater over my head, and fishing a matching pair of gloves from the pockets. Resuming my previous position, I put all my energy into clearing my head, into being unobtrusive and invisible, and my spirit companion did the same.

After several moments, bathroom door opened. The heavy footsteps of a security guard moved slowly from stall to stall, doors banging open one at a time.

The fibers of my sweater shifted against my skin. I could feel the warmth of the fibers, which oozed comfort and protection, wrapping around my hands and wrists. The cables writhed, repositioning themselves. Some people hug stuffed toys or pet animals when they are upset. When I'm upset, the soft things pet me back.

I'm not here. Not here.

The stall door clanged open. I twitched but managed not to jump. Micha and I had practiced this part for weeks, ever since we realized what we'd have to do to get our hands on the scarab.

I held my breath, heart hammering.

The door swung slowly closed and the footsteps became more distant until the bathroom door opened and shut, and I was left alone in the cold, dark washroom.

The breath I'd been holding came out in a rush. I sagged against the metal wall and stiffly dropped my feet down to the floor.

"He's gone. Hallway's empty," Micha reported, appearing once again in the stall.

I nodded. "Right. Let's go."

I wasn't sure how long I'd been hiding in the bathroom. Half an hour, maybe. In that time, the museum had gone dark. My calf length sweater swished around my legs like a cape, but I wasn't sure if I felt like a hero or a villain. I concentrated on staying out of sight, and hoped the magic I spent the summer infusing into every stitch would hold, making me invisible to cameras and watchful eyes alike.

Finally, we made it back to the gallery with the Egyptian exhibit. A metal gate blocked the opening. Through the lattice work, I could see the red blinking light of a smoke detector reflecting on the display case over the scarab.

The gate was padlocked. I reached into my bag and pulled out a 1.25mm double pointed knitting needle and a 1.75mm crochet hook and started picking the padlock.

Micha hovered nearby, occasionally vanishing and reappearing as he checked on the positions of the guards.

The lock snapped open and I slid through the gate.

"It's quarter of nine," Micha said, falling into step beside me. "We need to hurry. If we aren't in a cab in the next twenty minutes, you'll miss your flight."

"Mmhm."

I tried to look at the other cases we passed—jewelry, *shabti*, canopic jars. The eyes of a gold funerary mask, long since separated from its owner, followed accusingly as I approached the scarab.

"Ready?" I whispered.

He nodded, flexing his fingers on the other side of the Plexiglas. "Do you have it?"

This time my bag surrendered a plush toy. Crocheted and stuffed with beans and fiber fill, it was a duplicate of the scarab, but where the hieroglyphic spell for protection in the afterlife was carved into the beetle's wings, mine had an embroidered spell (courtesy of the god Anubis himself) that would fool the eye. Like the spell on my sweater, it wouldn't withstand close scrutiny, but if someone expected to see an ancient scarab, then they would see an ancient scarab.

This was the worst part. I could practice the invisibility spell or the lock picking, but we didn't exactly have a high-end security system for Micha to practice on.

Ghosts and paranormal activity are notorious for disrupting electrical signals—draining batteries, cutting out cell signals, that kind of thing. Micha was really good at stuff like that. Unlike most ghosts, he'd had about two thousand years to practice his haunting technique.

Still, this could go one of two ways. Either he would short out the system just right and nothing would happen, or he would set off the alarm system and I would spend the next twenty-five years in a federal prison.

Please don't screw this up, I thought desperately as he placed his hands on the glass.

Something beeped. Then there was the complete absence of sound that happens when everything electronic stops working at once and all the background noise you didn't even realize was there is cut off.

"Hurry! We've only got a few seconds!"

I was already raising the lid. In went the crocheted scarab, and out came the stone one. The lid dropped back into place just before another series of beeps as the backup power kicked in.

Micha and I had just enough time to share a triumphant grin before there was the unmistakable sound of a walkie-talkie in the gallery next door.

"Power's back up in zone B. What happened?" the guard was saying. I looked through the lattice just in time to catch a flashlight beam in the face.

"Hey!"

I bolted, back the way I had come. I hadn't even reached the open gate when the alarm started going off.

Micha vanished, but an instant later he was back.

"Go left! Down the stairs!"

I did what I was told, but saw a problem before I

even reached the stairwell.

"Keypad lock!"

"On it!"

He teleported to the end of the hall, passing a ghostly hand through the keypad. It beeped manically, but just as I hit the push bar it clicked open.

The alarm seemed even louder now. I pounded down the concrete stairs. I couldn't even hear my own footsteps over the din.

"Incoming! Hide!"

But there was nowhere to hide. I threw myself into a corner on the landing, covering my face and willing the magic to work.

No sooner had I pulled my hood up than I felt, more than heard, two more security guards run past at top speed. I waited until they were on the landing above before taking off again.

Jumping down the last three steps, I landed with a thud. Above, the guards were shouting and coming back down.

The only exit was into the lobby. Through the narrow window in the door, I spotted the guard at the desk and the one at the front door.

But when I paid my entry fee that afternoon, I'd also seen a possible distraction.

The entire first floor was given over to a display of costumes from the Boston Theater.

Dozens of costumes. Hundreds of textiles.

Billions of fibers.

They didn't notice at first. Not until Peter Pan was about to tap the guard at the desk on the shoulder.

He turned around, saw the headless "man" and screamed so loud it could be heard even over the cacophony of the alarm. Peter was soon joined by

Othello, Juliette, a clown and a marching band uniform. The guard at the door ran to help his coworker.

I couldn't hold the invisibility spell and control the costumes at the same time. Peter and Othello restrained the guards, turning them away from the doors.

Micha was already ahead of me, taking care of the automatic locks and cameras. I could feel my control slipping. I'd never done so much at once. The marching band uniform stumbled, crashing into Juliette before crumbling in a heap.

Sirens.

I practically tumbled down the front steps of the museum. The snap of broken thread hit me as I ran down the alley away from the sirens. Gasping, I stumbled. The costumes were just costumes once again.

Racing down the sidewalk, I nearly crashed into a tall, stocky man, veering out of the way at the last moment. It wasn't so much that I *saw* him, but I certainly *smelled* him. Like burned toast and rotten meat.

"Oh—god, sorry." I mumbled, ducking out of his way.

His head swung around to stare at me, and the glow of a streetlamp I saw half his face—burn black, with an empty socket where the eye once was. The remaining flesh had a greyish cast to it.

I sucked in a breath and covered my mouth. For a moment all I could do was stare in horrified fascination at him.

His mouth worked, a guttural grunt squeezing past his swollen lips.

"Evie!"

Reality crashed back into my stunned brain. I checked the time on my phone. 8:51 pm. I took off at a run.

One street over, I stopped and slowed to a walk. Hood up, I tried to catch my breath and blend in with the brick of the storefronts. I ducked into a crowded bar, waiting with some other patrons for a seat.

8:56. *It's a good thing I took up running over the summer.*

8:57. The program on the muted television above the bar was interrupted by a newscaster. The caption announced a break in at the Boston Museum of History.

My stomach dropped.

8:58. Where the hell was that cab?

8:59. Oh, god. I was going to spend the rest of my life in a foreign prison. Would I be considered a terrorist? Why had I googled the penalty for felony theft?

9:00. More sirens. The bar was lit up with blue flashing lights as more police cars raced past outside.

9:01. Where the fucking hell was that cab?!

9:02. *I'm going to be sick. I can't handle this level of anxiety.*

9:03. My phone vibrated.

An automated text from the cab company: *Your ride is here!*

Sighing with relief, I slipped out of the queue and back to the street.

"Where to?" asked the driver.

"Boston Logan Airport. Domestic terminal."

As I climbed into the car, I thought I saw a deformed figure limping toward me in the dark, the glowing intensity of a single eye following my movements from under a blistered, burned brow.

Chapter Two
Welcome to the Night Shift

I had hoped to sleep on the plane from Boston to Chicago, but I was too wired. I'd wanted to be in and out without drawing any attention to myself, but that plan failed spectacularly. I sat on the plane with my foot jiggling madly from the time I sat down until the seatbelt sign came on over Illinois.

What if they knew it was me? What if the cops are waiting for me? What if that guy on the street turned me in, and they find me—

By the time we taxied into the terminal, I was convinced I was going to be deported.

"Evie, you aren't going to be deported."

"You don't know that," I said through clenched teeth as I followed the long, winding corridor to the exit. In the interest of speed, I'd packed light. My only luggage was my messenger bag.

No one waited for me at the gate. There were no announcements about escaping felons, no increased security presence. Well, there was still a lot of security.

I mean, this is O'Hare we're talking about, and America is obsessed with terrorism. But by and large, the world seemed unconcerned with my existence. Generally, I liked the world better that way.

I made it.

The automatic doors hissed open, and I veered around a couple trying to collapse a stroller while their toddler screamed, only to come to a dead stop on the sidewalk.

Or not.

Parked along the sidewalk was a long black limo, circa 1930. The kind of car you only see in BBC costume dramas that involve spunky female detectives, copious amounts of gin, and cigarettes in long, slender holders.

The man leaning against it looked like an extra from one of those movies. No, scratch that. Men that tall and well-built are always the love interest. Or the gangster's body guard, but he didn't have enough scars for that role.

He looked up at me, flicking his cigarette onto the sidewalk and putting it out with the toe of his polished wingtip. The man was *actually* wearing spats with his impeccably cut three-piece pinstripe suit and fedora.

"Evie." He nodded in my direction.

I sighed. "Hi, Mr. Mulhaney. Ian. Sir." I wasn't sure what I was supposed to call him now. He'd saved my life once, but then I'd found out we were related. And now he was kind of—In a roundabout way—my boss.

He grinned a little at my awkwardness, stepping back and opening the door of the car for me. "Let's take a ride."

Merde.

"Pull any heists lately?" he asked casually, once we were settled inside the car. It had squishy leather seats, and a driver in a chauffeur's uniform on the other side of a window.

I winced. "I can explain."

"I'm sure you can. But it was incredibly reckless, drawing attention to yourself like that."

"For the record, I wasn't trying to draw attention. I was trying to stay under the radar. It just...didn't go so well."

"Clearly. I've spent the last two hours on the phone with the Boston office, trying to smooth things over. They're going to have a hell of a time clearing things up with the local cops. Since nothing is technically missing—" he shot me a look out of the corner of his eye "—they're trying to play it off as some kind of gas leak. The guards are already convinced that was what triggered the alarms and caused their hallucinations." He put a subtle emphasis on the last word. I held very tightly to my bag. Beside me, Micha looked just as abashed as I did.

"I'm assuming you were the reason a bunch of empty dresses took themselves off the mannequins and turned on the guards."

"Um...I might have had something to do with it, yes."

Micha and I were both surprised when straight-laced Ian burst out laughing. "Nice work. You've improved a lot since I saw you in June. But in the future, maybe a different course of action is in order. And perhaps not taking lessons in breaking and entering from a children's book."

I blushed. "Are you going to arrest me? I mean, I didn't *actually* break anything." At least, nothing I was aware of.

"No. Not yet. It depends on what exactly you were doing in the museum in the first place."

I bit my lip and looked at Micha, who only shrugged.

I've never been good at keeping secrets. Just one look from Ian's hard, unearthly green eyes, and I cracked like bone china.

When I was done, Ian didn't say anything. The car slowed down. We were in a rundown part of the city, with burned out streetlights and broken bottles on the sidewalk. We turned into a rutted driveway, bouncing along toward a derelict building held back by a crooked chain link fence. A crooked sign read "Municipal Water." Below it, someone had tagged the Night Shift's nine-pointed star.

I decided I liked the cover for the Montreal office better. We had a consignment/antique/resale shop in the Old Port area. Stone building, about three hundred years old. My job mostly involved manning the cash register—selling old clothes helped cover our utilities, and every once in a while something that shouldn't be out in the world would turn up. Last week there had been a cursed teapot, and my first day there was rusty katana with a very angry samurai's ghost still attached to it. Nobody knew the beaded curtain behind my stool went down to a hidden basement facility where Jean and the others tracked down anything that went bump in the night.

My position at the front desk was probably related directly to my boss, Jean Letrec, and Ian and his stunning show of nepotism. I'd been fired from my job at the bookstore a few weeks after Ian and I met, and shortly thereafter I was recruited by the Montreal Night Patrol. Since Ian oversaw international relations between the various Night Shift offices, he had more than enough pull to get me a job with the local office.

But it didn't mean Jean had to like it.

Jean was a well-dressed man of fifty or so. He was also very French, and I wasn't certain if he disliked me more because my first language was English, or because I was a woman. Or because Ian had swooped in and told him to give me a job. Whatever the reason, the end result was a better paycheck, a stable job, and a boss who hated my guts and gave me the most demeaning tasks he could think of.

Even if Jean knew about my powers—and I wasn't sure he didn't—he'd still probably keep me at the front desk. The fates had definitely been high on something when they decided to give me superpowers. Sure, they were kind of dorky superpowers by most standards. I mean, I'm pretty sure Superman would be less than impressed if I told him I couldn't fly or shoot laser beams from my eyes, but I could unravel his cape like a champ.

Of course, it was hard to imagine me, Social Anxiety and Chronic Depression Girl, starting a career as either a superhero or an international cat burglar, but how else was I going to get my hands on two ancient Egyptian artifacts? It wasn't as if I could just politely ask the curators to let me borrow them for six weeks or so.

The driver pulled up to the front door. The windows had been blacked out and the entrance was padlocked shut.

I yawned and stretched as I got out of the car. It was

two in the morning Montreal time, and I hadn't been sleeping well. I never slept well, but it had been worse the past few days as I prepared for my international crime spree.

"It's not really a crime spree, per say…"

I raised an eyebrow at Micha, but didn't say anything. *Well, what would you call flying to Boston to steal a priceless artifact, then going to Chicago to track down and steal another one?*

"Come with me," Ian said before he could answer. Without looking back, he strode up to the unassuming redbrick building, entering through a side door.

There were no windows in the lobby, just a reception desk with a very grumpy looking man slouched behind a computer. He barely looked up as we entered, and Ian didn't give him any notice, either, as he strode past. I had to jog to keep up with him.

The office where he finally stopped was definitely nicer than your average law enforcement office: leather chairs, big old-fashioned desk, and even a drink cart in the corner. Uncle Mike never would have gotten away with that at work, even if he had his own office instead of working in the bullpen with the other detectives.

"Wait here. I'll be back in a few minutes," he said, holding the door open for me.

I plunked down on one of the studded leather chairs with another yawn. When "a few minutes" turned into ten, I curled up and closed my eyes.

When I opened them, I had a stiff neck and the clock on the wall said it was almost six in the morning. The only light came from a little lamp on a side table. Ian was nowhere in sight.

"Wha's goin' on?" I yawned, joints popping as I stretched. My neck made an unpleasant grinding noise as I rolled my head from side to side in an attempt to work out the kinks.

Micha stood by the closed door, occasionally poking his head through the wood into the corridor to listen. "Ian went to make some phone calls. I asked him to let you sleep for a little while."

"Well, that was nice. Has he decided if he's going to arrest me yet?"

"I don't think he's going to arrest you, Evie," Micha replied. He took the seat next to me. For the first time since I'd known him, he looked...edgy. Micha, who never lost his cool.

"Then what is he planning to do with me?"

"Well, I assume he intends to introduce you to your father. And the rest of your family. It sounds like there's quite a few of them, and from what I've heard most of them work for the Night Shift."

I'd gathered something similar from the records at the Night Patrol office. Even though there wasn't an official connection, we still had access to some of their case files. While each city's department worked as an independent entity, there had been a push for more cooperation. Most of these pushes had been staunchly ignored by Jean, but then, he was Quebecois. They don't like to play nice with anyone who doesn't *parle francais* to their standards.

"He isn't here, is he?" I'd flown all the way down here in part to track down my biological father's family, but now that I was in the same city I was starting to regret it. On the list of bad decisions I'd made lately, it had to rank pretty high. Right under breaking into a museum.

"No. Not right now." His foot began to jiggle. Was he really fidgeting?

"Okay, what is it? What's wrong?"

"Nothing."

"Bullshit. You're nervous. And if something can make you nervous, then it's making me nervous."

He opened his mouth, then closed it, shaking his head. "No. Really. Don't worry about it."

"Micha, you of all people should know that saying 'don't worry about it' pretty much guarantees all I'm going to do is worry about it."

"It's nothing. There's just a lot of residual magic floating around here, and not all of it is good."

"Now that you mention it, I've got that eyes-on-the-back-of-my-neck feeling, too." I shivered, and some of the goosebumps on my nape seemed to go away. I pulled my sweater a little tighter around myself. If I was going to be surrounded by magic, then it was going to be a super wash cashmere blend, and not the residue of some illegal curse.

"It's also weird."

"What?"

"I'm not used to this many people being able to see me." Even in our office in Montreal, only two of the three officers could see him, and even then only if he wanted to be seen. Even my friend Adam, who was an empath, could only see him under certain circumstances. If Jean knew I brought my pet ghost to work every day, he didn't let on.

"I am not your pet ghost," Micha grumbled.

"Are we just supposed to wait here for Ian?" I changed the subject, trying to hide my grin as I unfolded stiffly from the leather chair and did a few quick stretches to get some of the kinks out.

Micha only shrugged. "I thought he was coming back, but he's been gone for a while."

I went to the door and peered out. The hallway was gray, bland, and empty, and smelled of old coffee.

Micha appeared at my shoulder. "Break room is that way," he said, thumbing in the correct direction. I followed his lead, hoping there would be bagels or something.

Instead, I found dried out, day old donuts. I ate one anyway; my last meal had been airplane pretzels. I watched the comings and goings of the office as I ate. The Night Shift definitely felt a lot more like a law enforcement office than I was used to. The Night Patrol office in Montreal was more like a collection of eccentric office workers who occasionally carried specialized firearms while indulging in some kind of live-action Call of Cthulhu LARP.

But then, I was just girl at the front desk. I didn't spend a lot of time downstairs, and I wasn't cleared for field work. What did I know?

Heavy footsteps on the stairs, and Ian appeared. He was followed by a man who cinched the LARP reference.

If Ian was well dressed, then I couldn't even come up with a word for the top hat, lace cuffs, and tail coat his companion was wearing. It was the height of fashion...around 1880.

"Evie, good to see you're awake. Come with me, please," Ian said, leading the way back to his office.

I followed, nibbling on another dry donut, mostly out of desperation than enjoyment. I suddenly missed the cafe down the street from our office: amazing hot chocolate that came in bowls the size of my head, flaky pastries filled with ham and cheese. Oh, and those little chocolate things...

My stomach growled audibly.

Okay, time for a new train of thought.

I followed Ian back to his office, where I took up residence in the same chair I'd spent most of the night in. By now, daylight was starting to peek through the gaps in the blinds over the only window. I hesitated to call it sunlight; it was too weak for that.

"So, this is the one you've been telling me about?" the cosplay contestant asked, flipping out the tail of his coat as he sat down, crossing his ankles and looking down his nose at me. I was torn between being offended, and laughing at him. I wasn't sure how much affectation one person could put on at one time, but somehow he was managing to pull it off. "Hm. She doesn't look like much."

"Look again. Evie, take off the sweater."

"Why? It's chilly in here."

"Just do it."

Sighing, I shrugged out of the cardigan. I was still wearing a long sleeved black tee shirt underneath, but goosebumps decided to trail their way down by back and arms anyway.

The strange man's eyes lit up. "Ah, I see what you mean!" He leaned forward, poking at the air around me and getting way too close for comfort.

I leaned as far back as my chair would allow. His face was inches from mine. "Hey, back off!" I turned to Ian. "Who the hell is this guy?"

"Evie, this is Special Detective Howl, our MUR— Magic User in Residence. He's eccentric, but you'll get used to it. You'll be spending a lot of time together."

I don't think the look I gave him conveyed the level of *you have got to be kidding me* I was feeling, but Howl was still *really* close.

Finally, he pulled back. "What do you mean?" he

asked suspiciously, eyeing Ian.

"Howl, you're the only magic user on staff who comes close to working with the same kind of magic Evie does. She needs training."

"So send her to Station Five with the other rookies. I don't take protégées," Howl snapped. The feeling was mutual. No way was I taking magic lessons from a BBC extra.

Ian looked pointedly at me. "There's also the small matter of the artifact you have in your bag. Howl is best equipped to examine it and determine if it is a threat."

I glanced over at Micha, one hand fisting the canvas of my messenger bag protectively.

"What artifact?" Howl asked, curiosity clearly getting the better of him.

Ian gestured for me to take it out. I looked again at Micha. I hadn't told anyone about our quest, not even my best friend back in Montreal, Adam. He was going to kill me when he found out the whole story.

The scarab was in a special pouch I'd made out of some stupidly expensive silk yarn—thread, really—and the thinnest DPNs I'd ever used. And it was double knit—two layers of fabric that had opposing patterns. One side was black and blue, the other blue and black. It kept the scarab from getting damaged during my hurried escape, and also kept it from showing up on those pesky x-ray machines at the airport. And from Howl's reaction, I was guessing that my "keep hidden" spells were also pretty damn good at covering any magical footprints as well. Hm. Good to know for the future.

I put the bag on Ian's desk. Very carefully, he removed the scarab. It fit neatly in his palm. On my left, Howl was completely rigid, eyes fixed on the amulet.

"And why on earth do you have something like *that* in your possession?" he asked, not tearing his gaze away. "And after going to such lengths to acquire it? Would I be correct in guessing your incorporeal friend has something to do with this?"

When I hesitated, Ian nodded. I took a deep breath. I'd never spoken out loud about my meeting with Hekate to anyone but Micha, and since he was in my head most of the time, he didn't really count.

"I..." I didn't know where to begin.

"I've been with Evie for centuries. Through a bunch of different lifetimes. Eight, actually," Micha said. "But before that, we knew each other as people. Back then, Evie was a novice at a temple dedicated to Hekate. She died protecting the most valuable object in the temple, which was a magical tapestry. It could be used for divining the future."

Howl's eyes narrowed. "I've heard of something like that, but if—*If*—those tapestries ever existed, they've all been destroyed or lost for centuries."

"Well, this one did exist. At least, it did then." I picked up the thread of the story now. "I saved it. Or Evadne did, anyway. And Micha helped. So when we died, Hekate said she would grant us—a boon, I guess you'd call it. We'd been about to get married, but couldn't, so she said she would have us reincarnated together so we could have the life we were supposed to."

"But Athena came looking for us. It turns out that Evie—Evadne—was promised as a baby to a temple of Athena in penance for what her mother, Arachne, had done. While she was in the temple of Hekate, Athena couldn't touch her, but Athena called in some underworld favors and tried to take Evie's soul after she died."

"Hekate couldn't fight her off, so she disguised us both, dipping our souls in the River Lethe. She camouflaged Micha's soul, so he would appear as a spirit—a guardian, instead of a ghost. Then she reincarnated me and tasked him with protecting me," I added.

"It's only been in the last few months Evie has started to remember. I still don't. But I've seen enough to know it is all true. Hekate and Anubis told us if we used that scarab with a special sarcophagus, then I'd be able to come back as a human again." He put a hand on my shoulder. I covered it with mine. He felt more solid to me know than ever, but his hands were still icy cold.

Howl arched one perfectly sculpted golden eyebrow. "Pray tell, why would a god and goddess from two different pantheons decide to help you?"

"Well, I don't think Anubis really wanted to, but Hekate talked him into it. They're kind of...dating? But I promised to do her a favor in return."

"And what is this favor?"

"Well, since I can see ghosts, and I have Hekate's blessing, I'm supposed to send any lost or newly deceased souls to her. It's a status thing, I guess. Her corner of the underworld doesn't get much use, lately."

The looks Howl and Ian were exchanging did not fill me with confidence. I could practically hear Howl thinking "What is *wrong* with this idiot?" Frankly, I couldn't blame him. I'd read enough mythology and fantasy to know you *never* make a deal with a deity, but I didn't know what other options I had. There was a chance this could be my last incarnation; my last chance to be with the person I loved. My soul was already damaged from a previous life. If Athena got her way and I met another violent end, I'd never be reincarnated again. If Micha and I were going to be together, then divine intervention seemed like the only way.

While Micha and I had been talking, Ian turned the scarab over in his hands. He passed it over to Howl. Howl held it gingerly, despite the gray kid leather gloves he was wearing, as if he expected it to explode at any moment.

"This is powerful magic," he breathed. "Ancient, very powerful. But not dark, I don't think. More...neutral. The magic is dormant, but still there. Stirring. It's waiting for direction." He set it back on the desk and pulled away quickly, wiping his hands off his pants.

Ian put the scarab back into the pouch. "I want to show this to some of our other magic users. This is not the type of magic that is worked lightly. I assume you know how this spell works?"

I nodded. Anubis had been kind enough to provide an instruction manual of sorts. I reached into my bag and pulled out my notebook. Inside were copies of the page, and my handwritten translation and pronunciation notes. I handed him the copies.

This time Ian raised the eyebrow. "You photocopied a priceless ancient magical spell?"

I shrugged. "I got it from a very grumpy god of death. I thought it might disappear if I left it unattended for too long. I figured a copy couldn't hurt."

Ian looked down at it, then shuffled through the notes. "And the original?"

"Stays with me." I meant for it to come out forceful, but it was more of a very stern squeak. I repeated myself, more firmly.

"For now," was all Ian replied.

***

Ian and Howl grilled me for over an hour on everything from the spell, the scarab and my past lives to Athena and her role in things (I'd been trying to keep that quiet, but apparently you can't get anything past Ian).

Finally, around nine o'clock, Ian told me I was "dismissed," but I needed to stay close while he and Howl hashed things out.

By then, my stomach was not even pretending it wasn't sentient anymore, so I decided to bypass the stale donuts and made for the front door.

One of these days, I'm going to get a smart phone. One day, when I'm not surrounded by ghosts who short out electronic devices at the drop of a hat.

In the meantime, since I was stuck with a cell phone that was more likely to survive the apocalypse than I was, I picked a direction and started walking, trusting my nose to take me in the direction of food.

My mom has a theory: Police departments are usually located within spitting distance of a donut shop. Fire departments, too, have their treat of choice—ice cream. There's usually an ice cream shop within a couple of blocks of every fire department, even in Toronto and Montreal.

I wondered what the fuel of choice for paranormal cops was, having only had experience with the Montreal office. Was it still donuts? If the fare in the breakroom was an example, I hoped not.

I was just contemplating the possibilities when I heard something on my left. In an abandoned lot, I could hear crying. I looked around; the street was deserted. The lot was blocked off by a crooked chain link fence that said NO TRESPASSING on a faded plastic sign. On the other side was waist-high brown grass and some abandoned lumber.

Since getting out of the hospital, I'd gotten used to seeing ghosts. Now that I wasn't actively ignoring them, it was a lot easier to tell the difference between a living person and a dead one. The crying...it was definitely from someone who wasn't on this plane anymore.

I glanced at Micha, but he was already gliding through the fence toward the sound. I pushed through a gap in the links and picked my way over rusty nails, broken glass, and other things that I really didn't want to look at very closely.

She was huddled against a pile of rotten boards. Maybe three or four years old. Micha knelt next to her, holding out a hand. "Hey, it's okay," he said gently.

"Mama!" the little girl wailed. Fat tears rolled down her dirty, red face. One of the ribbons in her pigtails had come untied and dangled limply, the end frayed and soiled.

I crouched down for a better look at her, but it was hard to pinpoint by her clothing how long she had been there. Her shirt was cotton and had a balloon on it. It could have been made at any point from 1980 through last week.

She was too scrunched up for me to see her shorts, not that they would have been much help. She was missing one pink sneaker.

"Mama! Where's mama?" She babbled on in a string of Spanish I couldn't understand a word of.

"Any idea how long she's been here?" I whispered

to Micha.

"A few years, I think," he replied, stroking her hair. "More than a year or two. Less than a decade." He shrugged.

"Does she have an anchor nearby?"

He shook his head. "Not one I can sense. She seems loosely tied to the whole area."

Well, that was a relief then—no anchor meant I didn't have to worry about looking for a body. I could take her description back to the Night Shift, and they could check to see if she matched any missing persons reports. I kind of doubted she'd died of natural causes, but if she wasn't missing, then there wasn't much we could do.

I reached for her hand. "What's your name?" I asked.

"Mama! Where's Mama?" she cried again, louder and more forcefully this time. Considering she was dead, she had one hell of a set of lungs.

I looked pleadingly at Micha. He sighed and scooped her up into his arms. He's way better with kids than I am. He also *likes* kids, which I'm sure helps.

He held her tight, bouncing her lightly on his hip while he whispered in her ear. Very slowly she started to calm down. Then, to my great surprise, he started speaking to her in Spanish.

The little girl replied through her hiccups. I just shook my head. "When did you learn Spanish? Wait, let me guess. You've been watching the Spanish language station in the middle of the night." Micha usually spent the time when I was asleep watching late night television. He could, as a result, quote more B movies than was really healthy and developed a fond affection for bad infomercials and black and white movies.

"Hush. I've been around for two thousand years. I've learned things," he said. "She says her mom went away. It sounds like there used to be an apartment building here, but it burned down."

"And she was one of the people in it?"

He nodded.

Well, in a way that was a relief. I wasn't opening an unsolved can of worms by talking to her. There was no sign of an apartment building now, so I decided it wasn't something I should be worrying about. A girl can only do so much, and between raising the dead, meeting my biological family, finding my real mother, breaking a curse, hunting down a psycho, and running from one goddess while working for another, my hands were plenty full.

I brushed my hair out of my face and took a deep breath. There was nothing we could really do for the poor kid, anyway, except send her on her way.

The doorway opened easily, more easily than I expected it to. Jean said magic didn't work well in Montreal because the city was an island; all of that rushing water disrupted the magic the same way magic interfered with cell phone signals and electronic devices.

For me, the doorway was just a block of white light that opened in the middle of the air. I could sense there was something behind it, but I had no idea what it was.

Micha said it was alternately beautiful and terrifying, and different for every person, but I hadn't been able to get him to elaborate. I knew he could see what the other ghosts saw when the door opened for them, but he never described his own vision of it to me. Even though I was dying of curiosity (okay, that was a really poor turn of phrase), I hadn't pressed. It seemed like something awfully personal to be sharing, anyway, even if he was in my head most of the time.

The last of the little girl's tears dripped down her cheeks. She sat absolutely still in Micha's arms, staring at the doorway. Then she was reaching, clambering down, and walking towards the door.

"Mama?"

Then she smiled, and ran through the door. It snapped shut automatically behind her.

I heaved a sigh of relief. I felt a little better knowing her mom was waiting for her on the other side, though it was a shame two lives had been lost.

"You're taking this in stride."

"Hm? Oh. I guess I'm just getting used to it, is all." The first ghost I helped to crossover had freaked me out, though it had been very touching to see him reunited with his true love, even if it was about seventy-five years late. Etienne waited outside her home every day for decades as she lived her life, waiting until the day she could join him.

It was hard to even fathom—waiting that long for someone, when they don't even know you're there. Watching as they grow older, marry someone else, have kids, grandkids...That kind of love is mindboggling.

Micha slipped his hand into mine. "Come on, we should get you something to eat," he said. "I have no idea what Howl and Ian are planning for you, but I don't want you passing out in the middle of it."

Two thousand years. Eight lifetimes.

How could I ever live up to that?

Chapter Three
Meet the Parents

After finally tracking down something to eat, Micha and I returned to the Night Shift building. I'd found a greasy cafe full of law-enforcement types not far from the vacant lot, and loaded up on hash browns, biscuits and gravy, bacon, orange juice, and tea. A full stomach reminded me I'd only had about four uncomfortable hours of sleep, and I was feeling drowsy before I was even halfway back to the office. We were still five minutes away when I noticed Micha getting edgy again.

"Don't tell me you can feel all of that excess magic all the way out here?" While I was already picking up on some of the many differences between the Night Patrol and the Night Shift, I was pretty sure they were equally paranoid about magical runoff and keeping anything questionable under lock and key. Jean had a vault in his office full of lead-lined boxes; according to Nick, a courier came once a year to pick up the boxes and transport them to a secure location in the Northwest

Territory. In a city like Chicago, which I could already tell had a much stronger magical vibe, there had to be a similar system in place, probably more stringent. Americans are, after all, paranoid when it comes to security and terrorism.

"It's not that. It's something else."

I yawned. "What now?"

"I don't know."

The back of my neck prickled, but I wasn't sure if it was because Micha was uneasy, or because my lizard brain picked up on something the rest of me wasn't aware of yet. I suddenly remembered the weird man with the burn in Boston. He'd really creeped me out, but I couldn't put my finger on the reason. I chalked it up to circumstance. I'd probably be suspicious of anyone I met while fleeing a crime scene.

"No, I don't think that's it. There was something off about him, though…" Micha's voice trailed off. We were both still contemplating it when we got back to the grungy red brick building. There was a bored looking guy with an enormous cup of coffee at the front desk now who glanced up when I came in.

"You're Evie? Ian is waiting for you in his office," he said.

"Thanks."

"I'm Steve, by the way. No matter what Howl tells you. It's Steve."

"Um, okay? It's ah, nice to meet you, Steve."

Micha and I exchanged a glance. He just shrugged. I hurried down the corridor before I could get pulled into another awkward conversation.

I knocked and Ian answered, calling me in. Howl was gone, and in his place were two enormous men that made Ian look a little less like a giant and more like just your average guy, and something that was either a very big dog or a small horse. The horse was wearing a service vest and harness.

The man on the left looked like he was related to a troll or maybe a giant; I didn't think anyone could make Ian look short, but this guy pulled it off. There was no way his shirt was anything but custom made. It would have used approximately the same amount of fabric as the sails on the Santa Maria.

He looked supremely uncomfortable in the comparatively small chair. His face was pale and had a greenish tinge to it under his red hair.

The man across from him had a slighter build; thinner, blond, and while still tall he was within the realm of reason, and not something from a fantasy novel. I shivered when I looked at him. His eyes were unearthly pale, and the tracks of black tattoos traced their way over his skin. A black line wrapped around his neck, peeking out above the collar of his shirt. I had to blink a few times before he came properly into focus. I saw two of him—just of him. The physical body in the chair, and the spirit occupying the body. They were identical. The soul clearly belonged to the body, but somehow they had become detached. It was as if his soul could float away at any moment.

The big man got slowly to his feet. I stared at him, eyes wide as his head nearly brushed the ceiling. Was there something in the water around here?

Ian spoke up. "Evie. I'd like to introduce you to someone."

I pulled my eyes off Andre the Giant and looked back at Ian, who was also standing now. He gestured to the mountain stooping under his light fixture.

"This is Connor Adder. Your father."

Connor raised a hand and shyly wiggled his fingers at me. Whatever greeting he said was lost in the rushing noise in my ears.

Connor Aiden Michael Adder, born 11/18/1973. Eyes, green. Height, 6'6".

The litany from Izzy's book, the one she had given me with her whole history, the whole story of how I had been conceived unexpectedly in an alley behind a bar after Izzy used a fake ID to get in, and then seduced a handsome police officer on a dare from her equally under aged friends, came back to me.

I wasn't great at Imperial conversion, but I was pretty sure that Andre—I mean, Connor—was more than 6'6".

"Evie."

Micha touched my hand lightly, and I jumped. "I— sorry. What?"

"Why don't we leave the two of you alone for a minute? There's a lot to talk about," Ian said. He, the blond man, and the dog were already moving toward the door. Micha looked at me in askance, but I reached for his hand and squeezed it instead. *Please don't leave me alone right now.*

"Hi. I'm Connor. Well, he said that already, didn't he? It's nice to meet you? I—I'm really sorry it didn't happen sooner. I didn't know you even existed—Well, that's a pretty lame excuse. I didn't—I had no idea." He was holding out one massive hand, waiting for me to shake it, but I was still in shock. He let it drop to his side, then sat back down, shifting awkwardly against the studded leather.

I circled the other chair, putting it between the two of us for a minute, trying to figure out what I was supposed to do. I hadn't even known the people who

raised me weren't my real parents until my eighteenth
birthday, when the contract Izzy had been forced to
sign, keeping my real parents, my adoption, and the fact
that I'd practically been ripped from my mother's
womb and placed into her own brother's arms before
the anesthesia had a chance to wear off, expired.

"Say something," Micha whispered.

I licked my lips. "I didn't know you existed, either.
I mean, I didn't know I was adopted. Not until Izzy told
me a couple of months ago. And then...some stuff
happened. And I didn't..."

Well, it was pretty clear where I'd gotten my
stunning social skills from.

"Well, sit down. I think we both had...delays. The
important thing is we're both here now." He gestured to
the chair. My fingernails dug into the leather hard
enough to leave marks. I willed myself to let go, and
then to sit down.

"So."

"So."

"Um, how is your mom?"

"Oh, she's—" It took me a minute to realize that
duh, he wasn't talking about my *mom*, Margaret
Cappelli, the woman who signed all of my permission
slips and put band aids on scraped knees and then acted
like it was a personal betrayal for me not to be
neurotypical, all while lying to my face.

He meant my *mother*, Izzy. The woman I'd always
thought of as my cool but kinda strange aunt, the one
who wasn't around much, but was always entertaining
when she was. The one that had picked up the pieces
when I got out of the psych ward and did her best to
help me put them back together.

My mother, who had been cursed by an evil

sorceress and turned into a spider.

"Ah...um...well...how much did Ian tell you?"

"Not a lot. I got a letter from Izzy a while back. She said you were in the hospital. I...I wanted to go, but I didn't know...I didn't think I'd be welcome. And I didn't want to throw anything else on you, when you weren't doing well. Izzy asked me not to contact you, under the circumstances. She just wanted me to know you existed. I didn't know what to do. I was in shock, I guess. I hadn't really thought about that night in years. Even back then, I didn't think we would see each other again."

"Izzy's missing."

That caught him off guard. "What?"

There was a sudden shift in his posture and his facial expression. Subtle, but I'd seen Uncle Mike do it a hundred times. "When was she last seen? Do they know what happened? Any suspects?"

"It's an ongoing investigation," I said automatically.

We stared at each other, and there was an instant of understanding.

"Cop," I said, pointing at him.

"Night Shift." he returned the gesture with a raised eyebrow.

"Night Patrol, actually, but same difference."

We exchanged small, hesitant smiles. Somehow, it made me feel good to know the cop gene was on both sides of the family. I still associated the badge with Mike; the one adult I'd been able to turn to as a kid without fear of judgment. That summer had been the first summer we didn't have our traditional birthday celebration. His was the twenty-third of June, mine the twenty-fourth. We would always do something special together, which usually involved me spending a week at his house. My summer felt all the emptier without it, but my birthday had been marked by one disaster after another. There hadn't been time for movie nights and laser tag.

We lapsed into another awkward silence. "So you're from Chicago."

"Born and raised. And you're from Toronto?"

"Born and raised. But I live in Montreal now."

"Why Montreal?"

I hesitated again, tugging on the sleeves of my sweater, pulling them self-consciously over my wrists. Almost a year since I cut into them with a butcher knife, but I still kept the scars covered.

"What...what did Izzy tell you about me?" I asked. "About why I was in the hospital?"

Connor looked away, his brow creasing. "She said you tried to kill yourself. That your uncle found you, and the doctors said you were going to be okay. But if something happened...she wanted me to know about you.

"I admit, I was angry at first. Angry, and shocked...I didn't know what to do. So I didn't do anything."

Shame laced his voice. He slumped over in his chair, covering his face with one hand.

"It's not an excuse. I swear, if I'd known about you, known anything, I would have been there from the start."

I balled my fists in the thick cables of my sweater. *Looks I can blame him for my indecisive nature, too.*

My brain went numb. I felt like I should be fighting this more. Shouldn't there be a level of denial? I didn't look a thing like giant sitting across from me. I had been *told* he was my father. Izzy's story, unbelievable as it was, somehow held more truth to it than the one

I'd been raised with.

Or maybe my relationship with my "parents" had just degraded so badly over the past year that I was looking for any excuse not to claim them as family.

The silence pressed down on us. I didn't know what to say. I felt like I was supposed to say something. Offer forgiveness, maybe? Tell him it wasn't his fault? Reassure him I'd been fine without him?

Was I fine? Would I have wound up at St. Mary's if I'd been raised by Izzy and Connor? If things had been different? Would I still have a cocktail of medications in my bag, and a standing appointment with a psychiatrist?

Micha laid a hand on my shoulder. Through the entire conversation, Connor hadn't commented on his presence. Hadn't questioned it. I could only assume he had as much magical talent as Mike—which is exactly none. I was grateful for that, at least. I wasn't ready for this conversation. Not the emotional hazards. I hadn't talked to my parents since I turned eighteen. Hadn't talked to Izzy, either, for entirely different reasons. I wasn't ready to do this with a stranger.

"This is really awkward," I mumbled.

He sighed. "You, too?"

"Yeah. Look, no offense or anything, but can we maybe skip the emotional greeting? I'm still processing and there's a lot on my plate right now."

It was like shutters closing over his expression. "I understand."

I'd said something wrong, and I knew it, but I wasn't sure what. Everyone always says you're supposed to be honest, but my experiences have taught me otherwise—honesty just makes other people uncomfortable. In reality, they just want to hear what they want to hear, and if you can't give it to them, can't live up to the expected script society has laid out, then you wind up on the outside of the conversation altogether.

But I didn't feel up to lying, either.

"Maybe we should just continue this...later." Like sometime next decade.

"Of course. Sure. We could just start with getting coffee or something."

I wasn't sure I wanted to take this conversation to a public place, but I nodded anyway. "Yeah, sounds great," I said weakly.

"Your people are looking for Izzy?"

I nodded. "Yeah."

He seemed to relax slightly at that, though I could imagine how hard it was for him to let go of that. "Good. But, um, let me know if you need help."

"Sure." Right. Like that would happen.

***

I'd been hoping to push all the awkward, gooey family drama until later, but I got outvoted.

We found Ian and the strange man with the tattoo in the foyer, apparently wrapping up an earlier conversation.

"Done already?" he asked when he saw us. I nodded.

"Well, in that case, there's nothing more you can do here for now, Evie. You may as well go home."

"...Home?" Was he forgetting I'd just traveled two thousand kilometers?

"Connor, can you take her? I still need to discuss a few things with Howl and Ian," said the other man. I

36

hadn't noticed earlier, but he had a cane, which he was leaning on heavily, despite only being in his thirties.

"Yeah. No problem. I'm sure Fynn and the others will want to meet her, too."

The tattooed man grinned wickedly. "Have you told Mom and Dad yet?"

"Um...no." Connor glanced at me. I was watching him with the blond—whom I was starting to figure out was his brother—like a tennis match. "They'll be thrilled, I swear, it just might take them some time to get over the shock. It only took them a couple of weeks to forgive Fynn when he brought home his son, and you seem much more well-adjusted than Thomas. This is only our first meeting, but you already speak English and you haven't tried to set me on fire yet."

"I'm sorry, what?"

"Fynn's son, Thomas. He's eight. He's kind of a long story, but the short version is his mom died and sent him to Fynn, who didn't know he existed. Thomas can set things on fire."

From the way he said it, I could only assume there were no matches involved in this. It made me realize I had forgotten to ask one very important question during our little meeting.

"So, what can you do?" I asked, peering up (and up and up) at Connor.

His face turned the same shade of red as his hair. His brother suddenly had a coughing fit that I'm pretty sure started out as a laugh.

"I... well, I don't do anything. Not like that. I'm a cop."

"Just a cop?"

"Just a cop."

"Fynn and I got the lion's share of the magic," the

blond said. "Fynn's my twin. You'll meet him tonight, I think."

"What's tonight?"

"Family dinner. There's a new member of the family, so we all have to get together. I'm sure everyone will be happy to meet you."

I opened my mouth to object, but no one was listening.

"Fynn should have a spare room she can sleep in, now that Simon is moving out."

"Yes, it'll be good to keep an eye on her."

I watched all of this with a rising sense of panic. Just how many people were we talking about here? Who was "everyone?" And there was no way I was sleeping in a stranger's house on my first night in a different country, whether I was tangentially related to them or not.

"Hey! Still here, guys!" I said, waving my hands. The three men all turned to look at me, as though they'd forgotten the subject of their discussion was still present. "I'll get a hotel room, okay? It's cool. You don't need to put me up anywhere."

"No, you're family. We take care of family—"

"No. I am not family. I might be your daughter and your...*whatever*—" I gestured to Ian and the tattooed man, whose name I still could not remember "—we might be related, but we are not family. You don't get to be family after five minutes of awkward pauses. I'm not looking for more family, I've got enough of it back in Toronto." I was shaking now. I could feel Micha beside me, his disapproval coming over our psychic link loud and clear. *Pull back. Don't be hasty*, he said.

But all of this was too much, too fast. If I'd been wondering where the anger and denial portion of my coping process was, I'd just found it. I turned back to Ian. "I came to Chicago for the sarcophagus, not a family reunion. Thanks for the introduction, but I'd rather focus on the spell and finding the Athenians. Izzy is my family. She may have lied to me, but she was there when no one else was, and I'm not going to let them hurt her. So either help me find her, or leave me the hell alone."

Ian tried to grab me as I walked away, but I danced out of reach and ran for the front door.

***

"Well, that could have gone better," Micha said, floating beside me as I half walked, half jogged down the street, the hood of my sweater up to keep off any unwanted gazes.

"I can't believe them. Talking about me like I wasn't even there. They're no different from the rest of my family," I said. I fumbled with my bag. The same notebook that had the translations in it also contained a list of local hotels and important places I'd pulled off the internet. I scanned the list and found a chain hotel near the airport that wasn't too expensive, then dialed information for a cab company.

"They meant well, Evie."

"Yeah, well, so did my parents when they took me away from Izzy. And so did Kelly when she tried to kill me. Just because they thought they were doing right, doesn't mean they *were* doing right."

"You're being awfully critical."

"And you're objecting way too much. If you're not going to be helpful, then just drop it."

"I'm trying to be helpful, but you're too busy being

stubborn."

I glared at him. A misty rain began to fall, and despite my thick sweater, I was shivering. I thought going south would be warmer, but apparently, I was wrong.

"You're not the only one who got thrown for a loop with this," he said, leaning in. He was close enough that if he'd had a body, our shoulders would have brushed. As it was, I could feel the cold radiating from him, and shivered again. "Give them a chance. They're trying. They're trying really hard to make you feel welcome."

There was a tight lump in my throat now. "I don't want them to make me feel welcome. I just want to do this and go home."

He raised an eyebrow. "I thought you wanted to meet your dad. Weren't you going to track him down, anyway?"

Yeah, that had been the plan. In a *Veronica Mars*, telephoto lens and tinted window convertible kind of way. Maybe I'd bump into him on the street, just for a closer look. I hadn't planned on family dinners and being related to half the people in the Night Shift, or pyrokinetic cousins.

In and out. That was all this was supposed to be. A pit-stop. Just enough to throw off anyone investigating the theft of the scarab if things went badly. Let things cool off before I tried crossing the border again.

And then there was the sarcophagus. According to my research, it had last been seen at an auction in Chicago in 1994, where it was purchased by a private collector. Anonymously, of course. After that, the trail went cold. I was hoping I would have better luck by pulling up local records than I would with my haphazard internet search in Montreal.

But all my plans had gone to shit. Now, I didn't even have the scarab. I wasn't even sure Ian would give it back. He'd said something out talking to other members of the Night Shift. If he was going to present my case and ask permission for me to cast the spell, I had a feeling I was never going to get the scarab back.

The damp seeped through the fabric of my sweater, and I regretted not bringing a heavier coat. I found my gloves and pulled them on, bouncing up and down on the balls of my feet to try to stay warm, hoping the cab would hurry the hell up.

I was craning my neck into the road, trying to catch a glimpse of yellow when I saw her—and realized I'd seen her before.

She was hard to miss, in an ankle length black cape, but I'd seen weirder. When you live in a big city—Toronto, Montreal, Chicago, New York, LA—you get used to seeing normal people do weird shit, and weird people do crazy shit. Honestly, seeing an extra from *The Lord of the Rings* wasn't even a blip on my radar anymore. I once saw a man on Rue Saint-Urbain wearing yellow tights and a chicken costume made out of newspaper and toilet paper tubes, dancing around a car covered in Astroturf and playing a ukulele.

So even if she wasn't *weird* per say, she was still memorable; which is why I recalled seeing her reflection in the window of a building three blocks earlier. And walking the opposite way up the street when I was coming back from breakfast.

Now, she stood on the other side of the street, stock still, watching me from under her hood. She was completely hidden. All I could see was the cloak and a pair of high-heeled boots with more buckles on them than a straight-jacket.

My hand went reflexively to my bag. My hood was up, which meant the enchantment making me semi-invisible should be working, but I'd never tested it in the rain, and the mist had definitely turned into rain.

As I watched, she raised a hand in a slow salute, just as the taxi careened around the corner. I stumbled out of the way just in time as it sent a wave of frigid, filthy water splashing over the sidewalk.

By the time I looked up again, she was gone.

Chapter Four
The Adder Family

The Canadian to American conversion rate *sucks*.

"I'm paying two hundred dollars a night for *this?*" I dropped my bag on the rock-hard bed. It was really about half that, American, but I could already feel the savings I'd built up over the summer draining away. At this rate, I would *have* to take the Adders up on their offered guest room by the end of the week.

The room reeked of disinfectant layered over the dull funk of stale cigarette smoke. There was a bulky television set on the scratched wardrobe, a wood-paneled mini fridge I decided after one look would not come into contact with anything I planned to eat, a microwave, and two paintings that looked like they had been made with a feather duster, in the same shades of maroon and teal as the bedspread, curtains, and honeycomb patterned carpet. Well, I *thought* the carpet matched. Beaten into submission by hundreds of passing feet and wheeled suitcases, and had lost any hope of ever recovering its color or nap.

The entire building oozed sadness and despair; this was the place where vacations came to die.

"Nope. Can't do it," I said suddenly. "I am not

staying in place like this."

It was the cheapest motel on my list though, except for the place with the coin operated beds that rented by the hour.

I peeled off my gloves and crouched on the carpet, trying very, very hard not to think about what was embedded in the fibers. I extended a single finger, just barely touching it.

I felt the fibers come alive, a sudden awareness. It went from being a filthy blend of nylon to something like a sea of half-sentient strands that shook themselves off, straightening up and remembering what they had been when they were new. Synthetic fibers are good at following orders, if nothing else. Like the waves made by a strong wind over a shallow puddle, the surface rippled and all the dirt and debris made its way to door, which I opened. There wasn't a broom, so I kicked the dirt out with the toe of my boot.

The room already looked brighter and cleaner. For the next step, I placed a trashcan under the corner of the bedspread, and repeated a similar process. The sheets were cotton and the bedspread was a blend, so it took a little longer. Cotton tends to be sluggish, but once it figures out what needs done, things move along a bit faster.

Since I was already adjusting the fibers, I decided to play with the horrible pattern. I couldn't change the colors, but I could change the design, by rearranging where the individual threads of teal and maroon were.

It took a while; longer than the actual cleaning. But when I was done the mattress was covered in a nice, clean plaid comforter.

I examined my work. "I can live with that," I decided, then gave the curtains the same treatment.

It wasn't the Hilton by a long shot, but at least I wouldn't feel the urge to spray everything with bleach before bed. Despite the smell, it was very clear nothing in the building had more than a passing familiarity with housekeeping.

I couldn't do anything with the bathroom. I decided ignorance was bliss and it might be time to learn how to shower with my eyes closed. Or maybe just forego bathing altogether.

"Why are you looking at me like that?" I asked Micha. He had already taken up residence on the bed and was flipping channels aimlessly.

"Like what?"

"You're giving me a funny look."

"No, I'm not. I'm just...I'm proud to see how you've progressed in the last few months. Five months ago you weren't even coping with being able to see me, and now you're using magic to redecorate hotel rooms. You've come a long way."

"It's a motel. With an *m*. Very big difference." I plunked down on the bed and rolled over to face him, propping my feet up on the headboard. In a way, I knew he was right. I'd made a lot of progress on...well, *everything*, since June. But it was still so overwhelming. There was still so much that needed doing.

That was why I needed the scarab and the sarcophagus. I needed to bring Micha fully into this plane. I needed him with me. He made me stronger.

He made a sound like a game show buzzer. "Nope, try again."

I frowned. "You know, I hate it when you do that."

"What? When I'm right or when I call you on your bullshit? Because I'm always right, and I will never stop calling out your shit."

"Both. But I meant, I hate it when you poke around in my head without me noticing."

"Well, I can't help it. Our psychic link isn't going anywhere for the foreseeable future. But the point I was trying to make, is you don't *need* me. You'd be fine on your own, you just don't realize it yet."

I raised an eyebrow. "Have you met me? Have you forgotten where I was when I first saw you? Did you forget part where I've got a cracked soul that's held together with psychic equivalent of chewing gum and tape?"

He turned on his side so that we were face to face. "I'm not what got you through all of that. You are. You, and Mike, and Izzy. You weren't ready to give up, you just needed a better reason to keep fighting."

"Exactly. And you gave it to me."

Micha shook his head. "I didn't. You might have been scraping rock bottom, but all I did was give you something to bounce off of. You're the one who climbed out."

I wasn't sure I believed him, but it wasn't worth arguing over. The fact remained that Micha would be more powerful if he were human. If we used Anubis' spell, then I—we—would stand a better chance against Athena, Kelly, and all the people who wanted me dead.

"You know, you might also stand a better chance with all of this if you tried talking to Ian about it."

"I'd rather not, thanks," I said, glaring at him. I rolled off the bed, grabbed my messenger bag, and began dumping things out on the little round table by the window, realizing too late it was slightly sticky.

My clothes were rolled and stuffed into plastic zipper bags, then scrunched down to get the air out. I had one extra pair of jeans, two shirts, and enough underwear and socks to last the week, and a cosmetic bag with a small stash of airport-friendly toiletries.

I had the little bag with my TSA-approved notions and a small ball of crochet cotton, a notebook, and my phone. Inside a knitted sleeve was my new laptop; it was about the size of a hardback novel, but not as thick, meant to withstand all kinds of damage. It was ugly and heavy and not very powerful, but it was good enough for checking email and Googling various paranormal phenomenon.

I was in the process of unwinding the cord when my phone rang.

"Hey, Adam."

"Hey. How's it going? Did you meet your dad yet?"

Fantastic. Not another one. "We...yeah..."

"And? How did it go?"

"Um...I think the jury is still out on that one."

"Was it that bad? Is he really awful?"

"No, it's nothing quite like that. It's just...really awkward, you know? And apparently, he has a huge family, and they all just want to sweep me up into it, and I'm like, really? I don't even know these people, and they're already trying to decide what to do with me." My phone beeped. Low battery.

"Evie, I think they are just as out of their depth on this as you are. I'm sure they are just trying to make you feel welcome."

"I just wish they would stop talking about me like I'm not even in the room." Now, if I were an outlet, where would I be?

"Just take a step back. You can't expect to fit in with them seamlessly right off the bat."

I made a noncommittal noise and crawled around on

the newly cleaned carpet, trying to find an outlet. "They wanted me to stay with them. And they want to have dinner tonight. Me, him, his brother, Ian, and a couple of other people I'm related to from the sounds of it. I don't even know him, and now I'm supposed to jump into the gene pool and get to know everyone else?"

"Who is 'him?'" Adam asked, his voice taking on an unusual tone.

"What do you mean? You know perfectly well who he is. Connor. My..."

"You can't even say it, can you?"

I sighed. "Okay, go ahead, Mr. Psych Major. Have at it." I jammed the cord into the wall socket with a little more force than was necessary, then climbed out from under the bedside table where it had been hidden.

"You have hardly talked about your parents—either set—all summer. I know you had a fight with your mom and dad a couple of months ago. But now you've got a second chance, and you can't even say the word 'dad.'"

"I have a dad. Connor Adder isn't my dad. I'm a biological mistake he didn't know existed until a year ago."

Adam let out a huge breath. "First of all, you are not a mistake. Don't let anyone tell you that you are. You may have been unexpected, but you're not a mistake." I may or may not have snorted at this, but he kept going. "Second, your relationship with your dad really isn't that great. It might help if you repair some of the damage there before trying to build new bridges. And just because Connor is technically your father, doesn't mean he's going to be just like your dad. Don't go in there hating him for crimes he didn't commit."

"He's known about me since December, and he

didn't do anything about it. He never tried to call me or email me or anything."

"You've known about him since June, and you didn't do anything about it, either."

"I flew to another country to meet him!"

"Evie, I know you. You were going to stalk him for a couple of days and then chicken out and fly home, if you even got as far as finding his address."

I spluttered an objection, even though I knew he was right. I was really not good with the confrontation thing. "Are you charging by the hour for this, Dr. Gold?"

"You can pay me in poutine when you get back. I look at it as extra credit. As long as I've got you for a friend, I'll be set on essay topics well into my doctorate. Really, you've giving me a leg up on my classmates. This is way above the level of a second year undergrad."

"I love you too," I snarked.

"One day, I'll use you as a case study. We'll do the talk show circuit together to pay off our student loans."

"Speak for yourself. I dropped out."

"Fine, it'll pay for your yarn habit."

I smiled. "Well, it's better than selling a kidney, I guess."

"Less risk of infection, too. Speaking of, your cat says hi."

Oh, no. I covered my face with my free hand. "What did Drac do now?"

Dracula was a sometimes stray that had adopted Izzy.

No, that was too strong a word. More accurately, he liked the food she put out for the neighborhood cats, and when he waltzed in and claimed the throw pillow on her couch, she was too afraid of the twenty-pound tuxedo cat to move him.

If he had a proper name or a home, I didn't know it and he didn't acknowledge it. I started calling him Dracula because of his markings (which included a lopsided black bow in the middle of his white bib) and his comical overbite.

While he still came and went as he pleased, he'd become more of a spoiled housecat since I moved in, so I asked Adam to keep an eye on him while I was away.

"He bit me. And he peed on my backpack."

I winced. "I'm really sorry. Is it bad?"

"He didn't get any of my books, but I'm going to have to recopy some of my notes. And the bite seems to be okay. Has he had all of his shots?"

"Um..." I chewed on a knuckle. I might be the only person on our street he allowed to rub his belly, but even I wasn't stupid enough to try stuffing Drac into a cat carrier. And I'd just love to see any vet try to give him an exam.

"Nevermind. It's fine. I'll keep an eye on it. But if you don't hear from me for a few days, check the ER."

"Okay. Well, let me know if you suddenly develop a taste for black leather cat suits and diamonds."

"I'm taking points for that reference. That was a terrible movie."

"Fine, fine. Look, I should go. Let me know if he misbehaves."

"I think it'll be more newsworthy if he behaves. He knows he's in trouble though. I haven't seen him since this morning. I know he's hiding somewhere, plotting my demise."

"It's not that bad. I think he likes you, actually. And you're safe as long as you feed him on time."

"That was not a love bite."

"If you still have all your fingers, then it was. He lets you rub his ears. Just stick with his head, don't fall for the cat belly trick, and make sure his dish stays full. You'll be fine."

Adam's agreement sounded doubtful, but when we hung up a few minutes later he agreed not to kick Dracula out to fend for himself until I got back.

I spent the next hour laying on the bed next to Micha. He'd found a musical from the '40s on the television and was watching it while I tried again to find some hint of where the sarcophagus was. I was hardly a top-level hacker, though, and I couldn't find anything after the Chicago auction.

"Now is one of those times when I really need one of those super-smart computer people they always have handy in movies," I sighed, closing the laptop as the male lead swung his partner around the cobbled walkway of what was obviously an indoor set made to look like a park.

"Sorry, I only destroy technology. I don't tame it," Micha replied without tearing his eyes from the screen.

I nudged his shoulder with mine. "What are you good for, then?"

"Oh, I'm sure we can come up with something," he said, leaning in until we were forehead to forehead.

For a brief moment, the bond between us flooded with affection. Micha laced his fingers through mine, his cold almost-flesh sending a chill up my arm and down my spine.

Just as he started to lean in for a kiss, the television let out a high-pitched shriek. I yelped and pulled back so suddenly I fell off the bed. Micha tried to reverse the power drain, but it was too late. The snowy image on the screen suddenly blinked out, along with the lights and the alarm clock. The good news was the noise stopped. The bad news was there was smoke coming from the back of the boxy set.

I glanced up at the damage. My feet were tangled in my laptop cord. It was a miracle I hadn't jerked it off the bed when I fell.

"Did you have to be so literal?" I asked, letting my head drop back down with a thud. "Ouch..."

"Sorry. I'm working on it."

***

By the time I went down to the front desk and managed to get someone to check the breaker, it was almost five o'clock. Miraculously, they determined that while the television was a loss, all the room really needed was two new light bulbs. The maintenance guy paused for half a second on the threshold, taking in the room's new decor, but just shook his head and didn't comment. When he came back half an hour later with the light bulbs though, he definitely paused to look at the bedspread, which had gone back to its original state. I just smiled, slinging my bag over my shoulder, and moved two doors down to the room management had "upgraded" me to: flat screen television, a fridge and microwave that weren't old enough to vote, and a bathroom with at least a passing acquaintance with bleach.

"Oh, thank god," I thought, inspecting the shower. I was in desperate need of one, but had been afraid of the one in my old room.

"Don't break this one while I shower," I told Micha sternly. He was already on the new bed (which had

52

gotten the same treatment as the old one, along with the carpet and curtains), laying on his stomach and idly flipping stations by flicking a finger in the direction of the remote in front of him, almost touching the buttons but not quite. He'd actually learned how to control the TV without a remote, but if he shorted something out, the remote was easier to replace.

Twenty minutes later, we were watching reruns of a superhero drama while I towel dried my hair, not really trusting the built-in blow drier while Micha was in the room.

My stomach rumbled audibly. This might have been because Micha kept switching to the Food Network during the commercial breaks, or it could have something to do with all the meals I'd skipped in the past twenty-four hours.

I thought I remembered seeing a fast food place not far from the motel, and tried to remember which direction it was in.

"You know, you wouldn't have to pay for your dinner if you took Connor up on his offer," Micha said reasonably, as the bad guy was left neatly packaged on the steps leading to the police precinct.

"That is so not the point."

"You're right. But you're not ready to talk about the *actual* point, so why don't you start by going to dinner and at least getting the introductions down?"

I sighed, flopping back on the mattress. "Do you have to be so damn reasonable all the time?"

"I am the voice of reason. In *your* head, anyway. Which is really kind of frightening."

I kicked him, but my foot went through his shoulder and sent the icy, pins-and-needles sensation shooting up my leg that tends to come with limbs which have fallen asleep unexpectedly.

He looked over his shoulder, stuck his tongue out, and ordered me to get dressed. "It's just now five. If you hurry, you can probably get back to the station house before Ian leaves for the night."

***

I gave Chicago's public transit system a try and found myself back in front of the Municipal Utility building forty-five minutes later. I'd put on a clean pair of jeans and a fresh tee shirt, but since pretty much all of my tee shirts are black, it didn't look like I'd done anything except get my hair wet. I braided it and pinned it up so it wouldn't be in my way, and kept the hood of my sweater up as the bus jolted and splashed through the damp streets. For the first time, I half wished I'd brought more in the way of cosmetics than moisturizer and tinted lip balm.

The old school limo I'd arrived in was parked in front of the building, idling. I climbed the steps and hesitated, but I didn't have time to think twice because Ian opened the door, a self-satisfied grin on his face. "I had a feeling you'd be back," he said.

I almost turned around and left right there, but Ian linked his arm through mine like he was escorting me to the prom or something, and lead me down to the car. Since the car was warm and dry inside, I didn't object. Too much.

"I don't usually attend family dinners, but I thought I would make an exception in this case," Ian said, tapping on the window. The car went into motion, bouncing down the rough drive and then turning onto the street. "I thought a familiar face might help."

Was I supposed to be grateful? He was so damn smug. Mr. Know-it-all. I remembered his words to Izzy: *It's my job to know*. His job to know everything. To keep track of any errant family members hanging on the fringes, I suppose. I was beginning to gather he was someone pretty important in the Night Shift, but I still had no idea what exactly he did other than dress like Rudolph Valentino's Irish cousin and poke his nose into other people's business.

"There will be several people there tonight, so try not to get overwhelmed," he continued. "First of all, there will be Connor, of course. He lives on the other side of town, but that little apartment isn't big enough for all of us. The house belongs to Fynn and Jack now, but it's been in the family for over a century."

"Who are Fynn and Jack?" I blurted, despite my resolution to be disinterested. I was only going for the food.

"Fynn is Connor's other younger brother, and Michael's twin." I had a hard time imagining there could possibly be two people like Michael. "No worries, they're very easy to tell apart, even if technically they're supposed to be identical. Michael was in a coma for several years, and it shows. But that's a very long story for a different night, and it's not mine to tell.

"Jack is Fynn's partner. They've two children, and a handful of strays they've picked up. Tara is nine and Thomas is eight."

"Thomas was the one that sets things on fire, right?"

Ian smiled, just a little. "Yes. He's doing much better with his control now, and his English is improving. I don't suppose you know any Russian?"

"Not a word."

"Well, like I said, his English has improved by leaps and bounds in the last year, and Jack speaks Russian fluently, and the other members of the household have picked up a bit here and there.

"As for that list of strays—Simon is another member of the Night Shift. He's a cousin, but I believe he's in the process of moving out. I'm not sure if he'll stay for dinner or not. Then he has a cousin, Devon. She's still in high school, but I think the two of you will find you have quite a lot in common."

Great. Why did it feel like I was being set up on a blind date?

"And I think that's it, for tonight, anyway. At some point you'll meet Connor's parents, but they live in Ohio now. And there are others who are in and out, but you'll meet them in time. We thought a smaller gathering would be best for tonight."

The list he had rattled off so effortlessly seemed like a large group of people, but when I thought about the Cappelli family gatherings, which usually involved a long table set for at least twenty and various children's tables at the periphery of the room like satellites, then it wasn't so bad.

I took a breath, half expecting an encouraging word from Micha—this was usually the part where he piped up. But I realized he was still hanging back, staying mostly invisible under Ian's watchful stare. We'd never been in a place where so many people could see him, when so many people could hear our conversations. We were so used to hiding them, hiding his entire existence, it felt almost like an invasion of privacy to know anyone we met could eavesdrop on our conversations now.

Would this be what it was like once he was human?

If we even made it that far? Awkward silences and pretending we didn't see each other out of embarrassment?

No, we would adjust eventually. Right?

The silence between Ian and I, however, was stretching, and I couldn't think of anything to say. He just sat there, looking out the window, like he wasn't bothered by it. I could hear my mom's voice echoing in the back of my head. *Don't be so antisocial. You're being rude, Evie. Why is it so impossible for you to carry on polite conversation? Shyness was cute when you were three. It is certainly less cute now.*

I was still arguing with that internal voice when the car pulled up to an old Victorian row house. It was clean, but not tidy. There were toys on the neatly mowed and raked lawn, which was turning brown. Two pairs of rain boots had been haphazardly discarded on the front porch. It was a house that clearly had very good care taken of it over the years, while at the same time offering more of a "lived in" atmosphere than "home decorating magazine."

Ian got out of the car and offered me his hand. If he hadn't, I might have stayed there forever, or knocked on the window and told the driver to take me back to the airport, or at least my motel.

The rain finally stopped. Inside the house, cheerful yellow light shone from every window. I could already hear voices. There was a car in the driveway and several more parked along the curb.

Ian gestured for me to lead the way—probably so I didn't bolt on him. I knocked tentatively on the door, but Ian reached around me and knocked harder.

There was the sound of scrambling and footsteps, and then a little girl opened the door. Her hair was in pigtails, and she had a cookie in one hand. She examined us through the screen door for a moment.

"Good evening, Tara," Ian said. "May we come in?"

Tara stared at me. I shifted uncomfortably, but then she flipped the latch on the screen door, allowing us to enter.

"I hope you feel better. Here, have a cookie," she said, holding out the cookie.

Bewildered, I took the cookie without thinking.

"Tara, you'll ruin your dinner. How did you even get the cookie jar down?" Asked a tall, dark haired man.

"Jack." Ian held out a hand in greeting, and the two men shook.

"Sorry about that. No Remy tonight?"

"Not tonight."

"Well, come on in. Dinner's almost ready, everyone's in the living room. Evie, it's nice to meet you. I'm Jack." He offered his hand to me.

I started to shake, but I was still holding the cookie. I switched hands quickly. "Sorry. I'm Evie." I flinched internally. "But you knew that."

Jack smiled warmly. "Don't worry about it. Can I get you something to drink? We don't keep alcohol in the house, but there's juice, milk, water...I think we have some sodas in the garage."

"Just water is fine," I said, my voice going small as we went into the living room, which seemed packed with people.

A dark haired young man about my age was sitting on the coffee table playing video games with a little boy about the same age as Tara. That made the boy Thomas, I supposed. The one who set fires. I couldn't remember the litany of names Ian rattled off in the car, but I thought his opponent was the one that started with an S? Maybe? Or was it Flynn? No, Fynn. Fynn was the twin. Fynn the twin. That made it easier to remember.

Tara curled herself into an arm chair to watch the video game tournament. Over on the couch a teenage girl lay on her stomach, feet in the air as she pretended to read a beat-up paperback. Even from across the room, it had the abused feeling of an unloved school assignment. My brain failed to come up with any suggestions of what her name might be. Ian said she was the cousin of a cousin, right?

The last chair was taken up by Connor, who looked even more awkward in the recliner than he had in Ian's office.

Squealing tires and a crash signaled the end of the round. "Damn, kid. When did you get that good?"

"Language, Simon," Jack said sharply. I peered around the corner and saw him laying out a large stack of plates and silverware. "Thomas, Tara, come set the table, please."

"Anything I can do to help?" Connor asked from his seat.

"Nope, we're almost ready. Devon, don't even think about it. Finish your homework," Jack added when the girl started to get up.

She sighed, flopping back down into a sitting position and putting her stockinged feet on the coffee table. She left the book open and unread in her lap, instead turning her attention to me.

"S'you're the foundling, then," she said, in a thick Irish brogue. "I'm Devon Murdoch."

"H-Hi. Evie Cappelli."

She raised an eyebrow. "You mean we've got one

now that isn't Irish? Well, that's a change."

"Hey!" said the little boy in the dining room.

"Sorry, little man."

There was a string of Russian from the other room, and then a reprimand came from the kitchen.

"Table's set!" Tara hollered.

We migrated into the dining room. I fell into step with the other cousin.

"Simon," he said, holding out a hand.

"Evie." We shook. He was wearing a tee shirt that looked like one of those "keep calm and carry on" things, but the message was in Japanese.

Everyone shuffled around like a game of musical chairs, taking their usual seats, which left me hanging back until it became clear which chair would be left empty.

"Here," Connor nodded, pulling out the chair next to his for me.

I sat down and our hosts carried in the meal—lasagna, salad, and peas and carrots. Sitting down to a family dinner without my family, and a facsimile of the food was like being in a parallel universe. It was oddly similar, and still completely foreign.

I could feel my hands starting to shake and kept them tight in my lap, only hesitantly picking up my fork when all the dishes had been passed around.

My stomach clenched, and I suddenly lost all the appetite I'd had just a few hours ago. I wished Micha was sitting next to me, but he'd gone "invisible." Only the most sensitive users of the Sight would be able to see him.

"So, Evie. Tell us about yourself," Fynn said.

As is typical for questions like this, my mouth was full.

I was briefly saved from answering when Michael limped into the room, followed by his enormous dog. The vague expression on his face made it appear he'd gotten lost in the upper reaches of the house and wandered into the dining room by accident.

No one commented on the new addition, but bowls and platters made another circuit around the table to the inane background chatter that always goes with large dinner gatherings.

I wasn't spared the spotlight for long, though. This time it was Jack that brought the conversation around.

"Connor tells us you're from Montreal, Evie. I've heard that's a beautiful city."

I nodded, unsure what I should add to that statement.

I was freezing—figuratively speaking—but I couldn't stop it. I couldn't even remember the last time I'd been expected to converse with so many people at the same time. I hadn't even shared space with a group this size outside of a subway car in months.

The link tingled; the psychic equivalent of Micha squeezing my hand.

In the awkward silence, the conversation turned to something Thomas and Tara were doing with their peas, under the encouragement of Simon.

Eventually the conversation started to flow around me, parting when it reached my part of the table and then continuing on the other side. I listened while Devon complained about a girl at school and Connor and Ian talked law enforcement with Fynn.

Jack seemed to weave himself in and out of the various threads, reassuring Devon, reminiscing about an old case involving a highly flammable truck full of coffee creamer, and gently closing a hand over

Thomas' when it looked like the kids were about to create catapults for the unwanted peas.

No one even seemed bothered that I was quiet, which was a change. I realized it was probably because of Michael, who was equally silent, contributing only a word or two.

Unlike the dinners I shared with my family—my other family—they neither ignored us nor pressured us for social interaction.

Something warm, heavy, and a little damp touched my leg. I peered under the table. Michael's dog rested his enormous head on my thigh. He looked up at my plaintively, begging for scraps.

"I'm pretty sure you shouldn't have lasagna," I informed him, but I smiled anyway and scratched his ears. From somewhere under the table came the *thump thump thump* of a happy tail.

"I see you've made friends with Cernunnos already," Connor smiled, reaching down to ruffle the dog's ears.

"I usually gravitate to whatever furry creature is in the room," I said, my first honest smile crossing my lips. "I've got a cat back home. Well, kind of. He sort of belongs to everyone on my street, but I'm the only one who can pet him and keep all of their limbs."

I started to relax a little. By the time Fynn told the kids to clear the table, I was telling Connor and Fynn about the Night Patrol.

"It's kind of weird seeing so many people. There are only four field agents in the office, plus me."

"You're not in the field?" Fynn asked curiously. "What do you do?"

"Well, our cover is this sort of resale-slash-thrift shop-y antique store thing," I explained eloquently. "I type reports, manage the shop, and check anything that comes in for spiritual or magical energy. Basically, I'm a combination receptionist and shop girl, but with hazard pay."

"Oh, so are you studying to be an arcanist?" Michael asked.

I wasn't entirely sure what that was, but I wasn't *studying* anything. "No. I just handle the front desk. If I find anything that feels off, I give it to Jean."

Two places down, Ian raised an eyebrow. "I'm surprised Jean Letrec hasn't taken more advantage of your abilities. Montreal hasn't had an artificer of any note in almost fifteen years."

Honestly, I wasn't even sure Jean knew I *had* abilities. They weren't exactly something I brought up in everyday conversation. And if I fixed the odd Channel dress so an extra fifty bucks could be tacked on to the sale price, or made sure a polyester leisure suit never saw the light of day again, I didn't think he noticed. As long as the shop turned a profit—which it had been doing regularly since I started working for him—he didn't really care what went on there.

"We're a small operation," he'd told me my first day, examining a beaded platform pump on display near the register. "Our government funding is almost nonexistent, and we use more specialized equipment than most police agencies have ever heard of. It's humiliating, really—our continued existence depends on our ability to sell shit like this for a profit." He always spoke in perfect, high-class French; the profanity shocked me a little.

That was the longest conversation we'd ever had.

"Really, it's fine. I'd rather not be in the field." I liked the quiet little shop. I got a lot of knitting done, I didn't have to risk my life, and no one bothered me. Okay, so it was a little boring, but I was making double what I had at the bookstore. For that kind of money, I could tolerate eight hours of boredom a day.

"But you've at least been through the basic certification, right? I mean, if you're handling artifacts and checking for anything that might have a spiritual attachment, then you must've gone through training." Simon peered around Connor's broad chest to address me.

I stared at him over the rim of my water glass. "My training involved ringing up sales and processing credit cards."

Silence that had nothing to do with my abysmal people skills washed over the table.

Ian was the one who finally broke it. "Excuse me, I need to make a call," he said, pushing back from the table.

"Pie. We have pie," Jack said suddenly, bouncing up and retreating to the kitchen.

"So let me get this straight," Connor said, draining his glass and turning toward me. "This Letrec guy, he's the one in charge of your division?"

"Yeah."

"And he's basically using you as a supernatural bomb detection squad, but he didn't show you how to defuse those bombs?"

"Um..." Geeze, when he put it like that, it sounded way more dangerous. "It's really not that bad. I mean, there was this ring with a ghost attached to it, but she went pretty quietly—" after she'd wrecked the shop and I had to tie her up with my best cashmere lace weight. I still hadn't finished that project because I hadn't been able to track down a matching dye lot to replace the skein. "And there was the time a witch tried to offload a cursed puzzle box, but Jean took care of that one."

After I hit the panic button.

"Sorry, what?"

Jack came back with a pie in each hand. I've never seen four people exchange a glance like that. Fynn pushed his plate away. "Kids, how about you take your pie into the living room, 'kay?"

Tara and Thomas didn't object, each taking a piece of chocolate pie and vanishing into the next room.

"You, too, Devon."

"But—"

"*Devon.*"

She sighed, collected her dessert plate, and stomped away.

Once the minors were out of the room, the adults gathered around the table. Through the window, I could see Ian pacing on the back porch, cell phone to his ear, and a look on his face that made me want to hide under the table. Every once in awhile, he would come closer to the house, and I'd hear a few words, sometimes in French, sometimes in English.

To my surprise, it was Michael who took the lead: "Look, it's going to take a while for the Night Shift to look into your story, and decide if the artifact you brought in is a threat. And somehow, I don't think you're going anywhere until it's cleared inspection." His eyes flicked briefly over my shoulder; the place where I could usually feel Micha when I was in a group. "That could take days, or weeks."

"But I don't *have* weeks!" I blurted.

"What do you mean?" Connor asked.

Dammit. "It's all in the translations I gave Ian. The scarab is like a key. It works with a sarcophagus, but no one has seen it since it was sold at auction in 1994. The last place it was seen was Chicago.

"The translations are part of a spell, an instruction manual for how to use it. The spell has to be started on a specific day to align with the Egyptian Calendar--November twelfth." The scarab was on loan from a private collection, and hadn't even made it to Boston until Halloween. Now, it was already November second. I only had ten days to find that stupid sarcophagus, or I'd lose my only chance at making Micha human.

"Don't worry about finding it. We already know where it is," Ian said. I jumped; I hadn't heard him come back into the house. "It's been in storage at Station House One for about twenty years."

I turned around in my chair to face him. "You mean you guys have had it this whole time?"

Ian shrugged. "An Ancient Egyptian relic rumored to raise the dead? Of course we have it."

"Not to derail anything here, but do I want to know what you mean by 'spell?' Or why you want to raise the dead?" Connor asked, raising his hand slightly, like a kid in school.

Fynn pulled a face. "Probably not."

"Right. In that case, how about I just clear the table and let you guys deal with the woo-woo stuff?" Connor pushed back his chair and started gathering plates. From the next room, I could hear the television, and it sounded like Thomas was taking challengers on the car racing game.

"Evie, don't worry about it," Micha said once Connor was gone. "I told you, it's fine. You don't have to do this."

"And I told you to stop being ridiculous," I shot

back before realizing I probably looked like a crazy person. To my surprise though, no one even blinked at my outburst.

"I shouldn't be your priority right now."

"I can't help Izzy right now. You know our best chance of helping her and stopping Kelly is if we work together, and we can't do that properly if you're Casper the Friendly Ghost."

Ian cut in. "This is all something I think we can discuss tomorrow. I've already got a couple of magic users going over the translations and the scarab. I'll have someone pull the sarcophagus out of storage in the morning. From what I've gleaned from those translations, however, it appears you'll be in the area for a while, since the spell won't reach completion until January first, so you've got a good six weeks you'll be cooling your heels in Chicago. Funnily enough, there is an accelerated training program that also takes six weeks."

"Accelerated...training?" I squeaked.

"Indeed. All of the basics. It's basically the police academy, combined with some specialized training for your specific talents, all boiled down to the absolute essentials. The rest will be on-the-job training."

"I think you have me confused with someone else. I am really, really not cop material. I'm much more the behind-the-desk type."

"I think you underestimate yourself," Ian said mildly, helping himself to a slice of pie and resuming his seat. "You did okay for yourself in Boston and Montreal. Your investigative skills could use some work, and you obviously need some self-defense training, but considering you were flying by the seat of your pants and had no training, no information, and no backup, you did pretty well."

"Yeah, but that was a one-off thing. It's not like I want to do this for a living." Truth be told, I didn't really have any idea what I wanted to do for a living, but I really didn't mind my current job. Low stress. When you're being treated for anxiety, having a low-stress job is a really good thing.

Ian raised an eyebrow, and then he, too, glanced at Micha. "So you weren't just planning on tracking down a felon, putting down a cult, rescuing a kidnapping victim, reversing a pretty powerful curse, and bringing someone back from the dead?"

I opened my mouth, but nothing came out. He'd actually missed the part where I was also working for a goddess.

All things considered...maybe supernatural boot camp wasn't such a bad idea.

Chapter Five
Fresh meat

My experience with college life was fleeting and ill-fated, and my single semester did not include things like dorm rooms, wild keg parties, or other stereotypical freshman things. My all-nighters usually involved more crying and pacing than studying or drinking.

So the experience of being on all fours, heaving my guts out into half-frozen mud while people cheered around me was new. And very unpleasant.

Unfortunately, it also wasn't the first time that week.

"Get up! Get up!" shouted the training officer. From the other end of the obstacle course, the three guys who had already finished the course cheered as if I'd set a new record. My stomach certainly felt like I had.

My muscles were jelly and I could hardly breathe. My brain fired random thoughts—bits and pieces that were more anger and frustration than anything coherent. Mostly, they were variations on how much I wanted to kill Ian and the rest of the Adders for signing me up for this.

"Get *up*, Cappelli! Get a move on! Are you going to drag your team down, or are you going to get your ass moving?"

I coughed again, wiping my mouth on the back of my glove, smearing cold mud over the lower part of my face. The last stragglers blew past me while I tried to decide which way was up.

There were only ten of us in the intensive Night Shift training program. Seven of those were former cops or ex-military. Of the remaining three, there was a telekinetic with something just short of super speed, and two guys the others referred to as versi, but I wasn't entirely sure what that meant. Most of them could see Micha, which lead to a slightly awkward moment during introductions when one of the former cops thought he was another student, and questioned why he was wearing a leather jacket and sandals to physical training.

And then there was me, the chronic couch potato who occasionally jogged a kilometer or two.

Eventually I staggered to my feet. The ground rolled under me slightly. I still had to climb a net made of tires, swing across a pit on a rope, and do the monkey bars before completing a ten-foot drop-and-roll and twenty-yard dash to the finish.

"Come on. You can do it," Micha said. But his face was creased with worry.

I shook my head. Numbness creeped from my fingertips up to my wrists and at least three of the blisters on my feet popped while I was climbing the wall at the beginning of the course. I was about two-thirds of the way through it, but this was my fifth time today. I was so bruised and stiff and sore I couldn't even stand up straight.

"Come on, Cappelli! Get your ass in gear!" Lieutenant Hamm shouted. He was already striding toward me. If I didn't start running, didn't start the next leg of the course, then I was going to be in major trouble, but I didn't think I could even pick up my law textbook at that point, let alone haul myself up the net.

The net seemed to get longer, taller, steeper the more I stared at it. My shoulders locked, curling in on themselves, and my lower lip began to tremble at the mere thought of walking toward it.

"Cappelli, if you don't get moving, you'll be running laps until breakfast tomorrow!"

I tore my eyes away and stared at the livid face of Lieutenant Hamm, then back at the net.

Very slowly, I shuffled forward, veered around the net and the platform it led to, and started walking in the direction of the locker room.

"And where the hell do you think you're going?" Hamm demanded.

"To shower." My voice tore on the words, pain and humiliation snapping until anger poured out.

"You'll get written up for this!"

"Go ahead!" I shouted back, not turning around. My stomach was empty, but I could feel the tell-tale twist that meant it wouldn't be defeated, even if I was.

I let the locker room door swing shut behind me and peeled off my Night Shift issued sweat suit, leaving a trail of clothing as I went back to the showers. I paused long enough to untie my boots and take them off. Peeling off my blood-stained socks was not much fun, and I was suddenly very glad I always used superwash yarn for my socks, since those were going to take a lot of scrubbing to get the blood stains out. Shrunken, felted socks would only add insult to injury.

And then I turned on the water and stood in the little tiled cubicle that only reached my shoulders, and cried.

I'm not sure how long I stayed there. Finally, I turned off the water and wrapped myself in a towel. I was shivering; the water had gone cold, but that wasn't what made me freeze.

One of the other girls in my class, Madeleine, was sitting on the bench, waiting for me. She held out a bottle of Gatorade almost the same shade of lavender as her hair and eyes. "Here, you need to rehydrate. Keeping your fluids up will help with the nausea."

I didn't move.

She sighed and set the bottle down on the bench. "Honestly, you should have seen me my first week. I had to be hooked up to an IV because I dehydrate so fast."

"That...sucks."

She tilted her head. "You know, if Simon hadn't told me, I never would have pegged you as an Adder."

I frowned, trying to place a face to the name and remembering the anime tee shirt from our family dinner. Why was Simon talking about me?

Nevermind. I decided it didn't make sense to stand there shaking like a leaf, so I went over to my locker and started putting on my own clothes.

"I'm Maddie, by the way. I don't think we got introduced earlier. I'm Simon's partner."

Hang on. "If you're his partner, why are you here?" I asked. It came out a little grumpier than I meant it. I winced, hiding inside my shirt which suddenly seemed to have arm holes in the wrong places.

"He got suspended. Long story. Anyway, they sent me through the accelerated training a few months ago, but I got pulled out early because of a case. Since I suddenly have down time, they decided to send me back to finish the course." She made a face. "I thought I was done with all of this, but it's really not so bad once you get the hang of it."

I made a noise that was definitely not agreement. "I'll take your word for it." With all of my limbs in the right holes, I tugged the shirt down, wincing as my shoulder objected.

"If you're stiff, I can help."

"Thanks, but I'm already doing yoga."

"Will you just sit down here for a minute?" she said, clearly growing impatient.

I pulled on my jeans, mostly because I was feeling contrary, and sat down beside her on the bench, staring at my bare feet.

"Here." She shoved the bottle of Gatorade into my hands. "Drink. You need the electrolytes."

Then she grabbed my stiff shoulder and planted her palm against my back.

"Hey, what—"

A tingling sensation went all through my arm and my upper back. When it stopped, the knot under my shoulder blade was almost gone, and I had most of my range of motion back.

"Better?"

"What was that?"

Maddie grinned. "That's my power. I'm electrokinetic. I can also charge your cell phone, if you ask nicely." She winked, and I finally smiled for what felt like the first time all week—or at least since I'd wound up in this hell they called training.

"Okay, that is pretty cool. And useful." I thought of Micha and the way my cell phone and laptop were always going dead. At least the unfortunate incident with the motel television wasn't a normal occurrence.

"Look, I know you aren't up for more of the

physical training today. It's hard. I get it. Not everyone can just plow through all the running and the climbing and shooting. You made it through three days, and that's a pretty decent accomplishment. And we don't want you to end up in the hospital, regardless of what Lieutenant Hamm might imply. And since I am technically your superior, and the assistant training instructor, I am authorized to give you alternative assignments."

"What kind of assignments?" I asked hesitantly.

Her grin only qualified as "feral." "When you did your intake paperwork, did you read paragraph 24, subsection E?"

***

"No. *Hell* no."

"It really isn't that bad." So said the girl with neck, wrist, and ankle tattoos.

"I can't even watch people get shots on television, and you want me to get a *tattoo*?"

"*I* don't want you to do anything. But you have the Sight, which means an anti-possession tattoo is mandatory."

"No way."

"Let me put it this way: Either sit down and get your ass inked, or you can go back to the training ground and run laps or do the obstacle course—or do push-ups until you start puking blood, or until Hamm decides you've paid for your insubordination."

I was almost tempted to walk out and try my hand at the tire net again, but Gatorade and the bottle of water Maddie made me drink on the drive over weren't making me feel *that* much better. I was up. I was walking. I was talking in coherent sentences, and the contents of my stomach were staying in place (for the time being). But there was no way I could make it through that course again. Just walking up the two little steps into tattoo parlor made my legs shake.

To make matters worse, Micha was laughing his head off.

"It's not funny, Micha," I hissed.

"No. It's hilarious. I have known you through nine different incarnations, Evie, and not a single one of them would ever even consider getting a tattoo."

...And there came the laughing again.

Maddie wasn't much better. Arms folded, eyebrow raised, her smirk not quite hidden, she waited for me to come to the conclusion she knew I would.

I threw my hands up in the air. "Fine! But if anyone is coming near me with a needle, then I *really* have to pee first."

***

"That wasn't so bad now, was it?"

"Considering you've got more piercings than a rock festival, and I really don't even want to think about how you got that lightning bolt tattoo around your neck, I'm not going to say what I really think," I said.

"Good girl." She ruffled my hair and led me back out her car. I flexed the fingers of my left hand, the skin around my wrist sore under the bandage. Maddie said I needed to pick something I believed in without reservation. Religious symbols worked the best, but anything would do, so long as I had belief.

It took me a while to come up with something. My last brush with religion had been half-hearted at best,

75

and ended when I was thirteen. You would think meeting a goddess would put me back on the path to redemption (at least in one form or another), but it didn't really take.

Finally, after fifteen minutes of Maddie hassling me to make a decision, I decided. The band of ink wrapped around my left wrist: two threads, in muted shades of green and purple, twined together. No beginning, no end.

Maddie didn't ask what it meant, maybe because she'd seen enough trainees get inked to figure it was personal. But Micha knew. He held my free hand while the red-headed tattoo artist worked.

"Just keep it dry, moisturize it regularly, and it'll heal up fine. You picked a very classy design," she said, dabbing at the area with a cotton swab. Even with rubber gloves and torn blue jeans, she looked like Jessica Rabbit.

"Good. I didn't really have a lot of time to think about it."

"That's intentional. Anti-possession tattoos have to be something you believe in completely. Something so much a part of you that it is second nature. You can't overthink them."

I followed Maddie out. The day hadn't decided if it wanted to be crisp or cold yet. I shivered a little, waiting for her to unlock the car, my gaze skimming over salons and tattoo parlors and quirky clothing stores with tie-dye and studded leather hanging in the windows. Most of them were converted row houses, not unlike the sort in Izzy's neighborhood.

My eyes traced the line of red brick down the street to a crowded intersection. For a moment, I thought I saw a half-burned face peering out at me, but then the doors clicked open and I climbed inside. Within seconds we were pulling away from the curb and rounding the corner, and the intersection was lost to view.

I pulled my sweater tighter and sank down into a seat that was way squishier than a 1970s Volkswagen Beetle had any right to. Even from halfway across the parking lot at the training ground, I'd been able to pick it out as Maddie's. Iridescent purple with silver pinstripes in a lightning bolt pattern and whitewall tires made it impossible to miss. It didn't have a radio or GPS, but it was still completely decked out and flashier than the average disco ball. It put Izzy's old Jeep to shame.

To be fair, most of the heaps I saw hanging off the back of tow trucks put the Jeep to shame.

Maddie, unsurprisingly, was a social butterfly. She chattered away as we drove back to Station House Five. Sometimes she asked questions, but mostly she was happy to just talk. Movies. Books. Cars. Whatever.

But she didn't ask about me. And she didn't ask about my family, either the old one or the new one.

And she said she liked my sweater.

That was a conversation I could live with.

We got back to the trainee dorm right around lunch time. The only good thing I could see about the whole mess was I'd been moved from my motel into a space I didn't have to pay for. The drawback was it was roughly the size of a toddler's shoebox, and didn't come with anything except a desk and a bed. I'd had to go buy bedding before I could even go to sleep my first night.

"We've got some time before the next session. Want to grab some lunch?"

"I can't. I really need to study for Law and Regulations if I'm going to make it through the test on Monday." Memorization was not my forte. It took almost a year for me to learn my cell phone number.

"Suit yourself. But make sure you eat something, okay?"

I promised, and she dropped me off at the door.

"Don't say it," I said to Micha as I dragged my heavy limbs up the front steps.

"Say what?" he asked innocently.

"You were going to say, 'it's not that bad.'"

He averted his gaze, suddenly taking an interest in the heavy clouds above. "I have no idea what you are talking about."

***

Station House Five was a reclaimed insane asylum. No, I'm not joking.

According to the engraving by the front door, it was built in 1876 and dedicated to Mrs. Henrietta Templeton by her devoted husband, Dr. Argus Templeton.

Outside, an effort had been made to tame the overgrown hedges, but the end result was they were over pruned in places, and in others had failed to relinquish their grip on the brick walls.

Inside, the building felt like a haunted college dormitory. It wasn't so bad in daylight, though there were still places where decades old graffiti showed through the relatively new coats of white and mint green paint. My first night, one of the other residents on my floor told me Station House Five was abandoned for nearly sixty years before being "donated" to the Night

Shift and turned into a training ground after some big disaster a few years ago. I was a little unclear on the details, but got the feeling it would turn up in one of my many classes.

The bulletin board in the entryway listed the usual things: a used laptop for sale, someone looking for a lost bike, someone else offering lessons in Spanish and tutoring services.

There were also some more unusual notices: specialized training for magic users would begin on November seventeenth. Students were reminded that anti-possession tattoos were mandatory for dorm residents (I'd thought that was a joke, until two hours ago), and the graveyard behind the hospital was off limits to anyone who wasn't certified, unless accompanied by an instructor (apparently, they had a problem with ghouls).

The smell of the cafeteria food lured me down the hall and I decided I could try studying in the bright dining hall instead of my cell-like room, which still had bars on the window and desperately needed a lamp, among other things. Did I mention the walls were padded?

I'd had a feeling I'd wind up in a padded room eventually, but this was not how I thought I would get there.

I went through the line, frowning at my tray. "I think I'm being haunted by Italian food," I said to no one in particular, looking at the pile of rigatoni on my plate, and a very tempting slice of garlic bread.

"No, I think that's just the signora in room twenty-seven," said a voice behind me. I jumped a little and moved out of the way to let one of the other students pass. He was tall and athletic, with dark curly hair buzzed close to his skull. He sported a cartoon character Band-Aid just above his temple and looked like he should be modeling for one of those clothing stores where they never actually wear clothes in the ads.

"Is she the one who keeps singing opera in the middle of the night?" I asked, cocking my head. I was lucky I had Micha—he was usually able to keep any unwanted visitors of the incorporeal kind out of my room, but they were still all over the place, and most of them had no idea they were dead. It was good I had finely honed the skill of being oblivious to everything that didn't directly affect me.

He nodded. "Yeah. She's convinced her lover is going to come for her after the curtain call."

"She does realize this is a dorm, right?"

"Nope. The assistant instructor for my hand-to-hand class had that room last year. He said she was committed in the 1800s because she kept trying to run away to join the theater. Total prima donna."

"So we get a concert every night." I sighed. I only had one pillow, and it wasn't enough to block out the noise.

Balancing his tray on one hand, he held out the other. "Duck Pizzuto."

"Duck?"

He made a face, touching a bruise on his dark forehead. "My hand-eye coordination isn't the best."

I wanted to ask, but shut my mouth very quickly and put my tray down safely at an empty table instead. "Evie. Evie Cappelli."

"Nice to meet you, bella," he grinned.

"What are you, a Florentine street vendor?" I asked in Italian. My grandparents immigrated from Florence in the 1950s, and our whole family still went back to visit every few years. The vendors in the famous leather markets call every woman beautiful, hoping to make a sale or take advantage of an impressionable tourist.

That got a laugh out of him, and he responded in kind. "That depends, bella. I can be whatever you want me to be."

A surge of irrational anger suddenly flared up. I was about to snap his head off (verbally, anyway), when I realized the anger was coming from the psychic link.

"She's taken, Abercrombie," Micha spat, his entire body rigid, like a hissing cat ready to spring. I'd never seen him so angry.

Duck didn't seem to notice, however. Apparently, my new friend was not gifted with the Sight.

"Um, it was nice to meet you. I need to go," I said quickly, snatching up my food and leaving a very confused boy behind as I practically ran up to my room.

Once we were alone, I whirled on Micha, "Have you lost your mind? What do you think you were doing? I was trying to talk to someone. Do you know how rare it is for me to meet someone new and not panic as soon as they say hello?" It was pointless question; of course he knew.

Micha was nearly incoherent with rage. "He was practically drooling all over you! And he used a ghost as a pickup line? Who does that?" On my desk, my laptop screen started to flicker, then the overhead lights.

"Hey! Dial it back, Casper!" I said, slamming the screen shut to try to preserve the battery. Then I reached for Micha's hands. The lights dimmed, and I wondered how many rooms he was pulling power from. A lot, I guessed. His fingers were almost warm to the touch, they were surging with so much energy. His grey-green eyes sparked.

"Micha!"

Suddenly, the shadows left his face. He stepped back, pulling his hand straight through mine.

The lights came back on. From next door, I heard the beep of something electronic resetting itself after a power failure.

Micha and I stared at each other across the tiny room, which was barely long enough for a twin bed.

"I'm sorry," he said at last, looking away.

"What happened?"

He didn't answer. I reached for him again, brushing my fingers against his cold, insubstantial ones.

"Micha?" It was barely a whisper. "What's happening? First the television, now this. What's going on? You've never done this before."

"I don't know," he said at last. "I don't know what's happening to me."

Chapter Six
Shocking Developments

Between Duck and Micha, I barely had time to scarf down my pasta and swap out the contents of my bag for the academic portion of the day: two hours of laws, regulations, and dealing with outside agencies (i.e. the people who couldn't see ghosts and were very liable to arrest Night Shift officers by mistake at a crime scene), and then three hours learning how to deal with all the stuff that went bump in the night.

I took so many notes in the law class I barely had time to process them; every word the instructor said went in through one ear, and out through my fingers. I flexed my hand and arm all the way to Paranormal Elements, which, of course, was held in the creepy, renovated basement.

Bare fluorescent bulbs flickered—either from all the ghosts or just from poor wiring, I wasn't sure—over long, lopsided tables and dented folding metal chairs. I laid out my notebook and pen, then got out my knitting while I waited for our instructor, Dr. Peters.

Paranormal Elements was the one part of training I wasn't failing miserably. For starters, I'd been reading fantasy novels since outgrowing picture books (not that my parents needed to know) so I had at least a passing familiarity with everything we'd talked about so far, even if Anne Rice and Stephenie Meyer had gotten it wrong, and for another, I had Micha, the font of all paranormal knowledge, inside my head.

Dr. Peters wasn't an idiot, though, and judging by her pale blue eyes, she definitely had the Sight. She took one look at me on the first day of class, glanced at Micha in the seat beside me, and said while he was welcome to sit in on regular lessons, she expected him to keep his answers to himself on test days.

At exactly three o'clock, Dr. Peters strode into the room. She always wore a snappy skirt suit and heels roughly the same height as the Empire State Building, blonde hair twisted up on top her head in a painful looking knot. She looked like she belonged in a board room, not some dingy basement teaching a bunch of college-age kids the basics of paranormal investigation.

She hardly waited a beat before rolling the chalkboard to the center of the room and starting her lesson.

"Good afternoon, everyone. I hope Law and Order didn't take too much out of you, because we have a lot to cover today."

The other students in the room chuckled at her use of the nickname for the Law and Regulation class. I *wished* L&R was as interesting as a good legal drama, but it was like a horrible combination of civics and the driest history course I'd ever taken. Our instructor, Dan May ("Dan, just Dan, please"), was a retired police captain and former Night Shift officer. He was a good guy and had some really interesting stories to share, but even he couldn't make lists of laws and their numerical codes anything other than a recipe for a quick post-lunch nap.

Dr. Peters continued: "We've covered a lot of very general information in the last two days. Today, we're going to get into some more detailed information about the types of things you might see in the field, and how that pertains to any abilities you might have." While she was addressing the class, a piece of chalk floated up and divided the board into three columns.

"How many of you have the Sight? To any degree?" she added, when one or two people hesitated.

Three quarters of the people in the room raised their hands, including me, but I noticed Madeleine, who generally looked about ready to die of boredom in all of our "academic" lessons, did not.

Dr. Peters nodded, then came to stand in front of me. She glanced at Micha, then back at me, like she was asking for permission.

I looked at him. He'd been slumped in the uncomfortable chair, brooding over the afternoon's events, but straightened when he became the focal point.

"Can anyone tell me the three types of hauntings?"

A few hands went in the air, but Dr. Parker was still looking at me. I tried to remember some of the terminology I'd come across in my books. "Um...residual?"

"Excellent. That's a good place to start." The chalk scrawled *Residual* at the top of the first column, underlined it, and began making bullet points down the left-hand side. "And the characteristics of a residual haunting?"

One by one, she pointed to students, taking down their answers. "Yes, that's right. The defining trait of a residual haunting is that it is something of a recording;

a spiritual copy of an event or moment of heightened emotion that has been imprinted on a place. Can anyone give me some examples?"

Oh, I know this one! I raised my hand—a rare enough thing in regular school, but almost unheard of since I'd started training. "The woman in gray or woman in white. It's usually a woman pacing a corridor or set location, a place where she was looking or waiting for something or someone."

"Exactly. We actually have two relatively famous 'woman in gray' legends here in Chicago, though technically one falls under the category of the vanishing hitchhiker, which would typically be an urban legend, not a ghost story. We'll get to that later, though. What else can you tell me about residual hauntings?"

The group was starting to grow more animated now, forgetting to raise their hands. "They're usually not malevolent, and they don't know they're dead. You usually can't interact with them," said a guy in the back.

The chalk scribbled the new information onto the board. "Yes. Very good. Okay, now that we've got the main points there, let's move on to the next type of haunting. Anyone?"

"Intelligent!" Someone called out, a little overeager.

Under Dr. Parker's direction, people began calling out the traits of an intelligent haunting. I started to feel like I was on some kind of paranormal trivia game show.

"Miss Cappelli, maybe you'd like to tell us a little bit more about intelligent hauntings," Dr. Parker said, gesturing for me to stand while the chalk continued to fill the space in the middle column.

"Me?"

"Well, you would seem to be the resident expert," she said, glancing over at Micha.

We shared one of our looks. He didn't say anything, but I felt a quick burst of reassurance from him; we still weren't used to people knowing he was there, but he was okay with it.

"Well, Micha's not really a ghost. I mean, he sort of is, but he's not haunting me. He's kind of a long story, actually."

"But he is anchored to you."

"Yeah. I mean, yes." I was clenching my knitting with both hands, and realized I'd dropped a few stitches when I stood up. I quickly put my project down on the table.

"Not to an object?"

"No. To me."

"So you have a connection, then."

I nodded.

"You knew him when he was alive?"

"Sort of."

Dr. Peters raised a perfectly sculpted eyebrow. "It must have been more than 'sort of.' It takes a very strong bond for a spirit to make a connection last after death—and to preserve the personality and intelligence of the person they once were."

How could I explain this? I really didn't want to tell the entire class our history, but Dr. Peters wasn't giving me a lot of options.

Micha stood up. "I knew Evie in another life. I had...outside help to be able to stay with her."

Dr. Peters tilted her head, clearly still expecting an explanation, but Micha stared her down and didn't say a word. Was it my imagination, or were the lights flickering a little more than usual?

Then she suddenly smiled. "Moving on. And the last class of haunting?"

"Poltergeist," answered a woman in the third row. A few years older than most of the other students, I thought she'd been a nurse or some sort of emergency responder before being recruited. She was staring directly at Micha. "It's German for 'noisy ghost.' They're usually semi-intelligent, but completely out of control. They're prone to hurting people. Scratching them. Slamming doors. Breaking stuff. Draining electricity."

"Very good, Ms. Decenzo." Dr. Peters checked her watch. "Let's take a ten-minute break, and when we get back we'll talk a bit more about hauntings, what causes them, and how to handle them."

***

When we got back to my room after class, I was nearly shaking with rage. "Who the hell does she think she is?" I shouted to the padded walls of my cell. I lashed out at one, slamming a fist into the rubber, and immediately regretted it. There was *definitely* concrete under there.

"Ow..." I squeaked, cradling my wrist.

Micha didn't say anything, just stood motionless in the doorway of my room. Even with the psychic link, he was unreadable. He was clamping down his emotions, and what I could pick up was mostly confusion with traces of...worry? Anxiety? Fear?

Finally, he came over and took my hand, resting his cold palm on the bruised side of my hand. He was better than an ice pack.

"You...you don't think they're right, do you? I

mean, you've been with me for centuries. You're fine. There's no way that you're...That's just ridiculous. Dr. Peters is full of it."

"That's just it, though," he whispered. "I've been with you for *centuries*. Most ghosts fade out after a while. They don't hang out for two millennia."

I shook my head. "No. It's going to be fine. You'll see. We'll just work on controlling your temper, or— or—"

But I had no idea how to un-poltergeist a ghost, if such a thing was even possible. "I'll check the library. There's got to be something there, right? But it'll be fine. I mean, as long as I'm okay, then you'll be okay." One of the reasons Micha was attached to me was because my soul was a scratch-and-dent model. Damaged by a string of unfortunate incarnations, and finally broken when one of those incarnations took her own life, my soul was held together with the metaphysical version of duct tape. Hekate said if I died violently, either by my own hand or that of anyone else, my soul and Micha's would go into the spiritual scrap heap for recycling. No more second chances.

But she'd never said what would happen if something happened to Micha.

"We're going to fix this," I insisted, squeezing his hand.

"I hope so."

***

I thought about skipping dinner and going straight to the library, but then remembered my evening meds needed to be taken with food, so I dragged myself down to the dining hall, grabbed a burrito to go and a bottle of soda, and ate as I trekked across the campus to the library. I absolutely did not get dinner to go because I was still embarrassed about the incident at lunch and afraid of seeing Duck again. That would just be ridiculous, and very much a high school thing to do. Not something young women with promising careers in law enforcement do.

"I thought you were just a shop girl," Micha teased, floating along beside me. His humor felt forced, but not as much as his smile.

Calling attention to it wouldn't help, so I played along. "Shut up. I'm getting field trained, remember? This time next year, I'll be like Buffy, only with a badge." Izzy had an addiction to '90s/early 00's supernatural television. In the six months I'd been living with her, I'd seen all of Buffy, Charmed, Angel, and a handful of other shows.

"Buffy worked fast food."

"Shut up."

I felt him smiling and relaxed a little knowing his mood had improved. I was way too unstable myself to be a guidepost for someone else. That was the position Micha filled.

The library was an outbuilding in the same style as the dorm, but smaller and slightly newer. It had been added on as a secondary ward at some point, but now all it housed on the first floor were rows and rows of books on law, paranormal activity, vampires, and all the monsters and bad guys I could look forward to hunting in the future. Maddie said it was the second largest library of its kind in the country. Considering the subject matter, I was surprised there was much competition.

Upstairs were artifacts and evidence that could be

checked out and examined by trainees for research purposes, but students need a note from an instructor, and the staircase was blocked off by a metal grate. I paused as I walked past, thinking it wasn't much different from the gate at the museum, but decided that road only lead to trouble and hustled into the reading room before I could change my mind.

The librarian was helpful enough, pointing me to a long row of books all about ghosts and hauntings. There were books and illuminated manuscripts from the middle ages locked in glass cabinets, and field notes from former Night Shift officers that had been photocopied and bound, sent out to the various departments for future reference. Some were old enough to be hand written. There wasn't a single commercially available book in the lot. Skimming titles, I started pulling volumes, filling my arms and claiming a table near the window.

You would think having two football fields of rare books would be enough for me to find *something* on the subject I was researching, but I wasn't that lucky. Though, if Dr. Peters asked us to write an essay on hauntings and the exorcism of malevolent spirits, I'd probably be able to write doctorate level thesis on the subject.

I closed the last book in my stack and stretched. Every vertebra in my lower back popped.

Micha looked up. Even though he couldn't move the books, he could turn the pages if I opened it for him. He had a stack of yellowed field notes open, but didn't seem to be having any luck, either.

"Anything?" he asked.

I shook my head, folded my arms and rested my head on them, using a volume on the summoning and control of spirits that was as thick as the width of my palm as a pillow. "I'm starting to think this has never been done before."

"Well, we did have the intervention of a goddess. And we've only been looking for a few hours."

"Two goddesses. And a god." Not that I really wanted to think about any of them. I had so much on my plate, I wasn't sure what to focus on. Help Micha, or help Izzy. Study, so I could keep my job and help Micha, or look into the Athenians and rescue my birth mother. And I really, really didn't want to think about the "bonding" I was supposed to be doing with my new family.

How could I even think about bonding with my new family, when my birth mother was being held captive in the form of a spider by a psychotic cult?

I shouldn't be here. I should be out looking for her—

But we're running out of time to save Micha, too. Izzy isn't on a deadline. At least, I don't think she is.

Ian had made it pretty clear that if I didn't go through training, then not only would I probably be out of a job when I got back to Montreal (if I wasn't out of one already), but the Night Shift would not assist me in any way. The bastard even hinted I wouldn't get the scarab back. It was already November fifth. I tried not to think about Ian and what he was doing with the scarab, because every time I did, I got a sick feeling in the pit of my stomach.

If he said no, and Micha went full poltergeist, then what? Would I lose him forever?

Micha reached out his hand, and I took it. "You won't lose me. After all we've been through, this is nothing. And Izzy will be fine. We've got a little time.

And the Night Shift. Ian said they were looking, right? You can't do everything yourself. You need help. You're doing everything you can right now, for both of us."

I nodded, even though I knew we were both just putting on a brave face for the other.

"I don't think I can do any more of this tonight," I said. My eyes were dry and blurry from looking at so many dusty pages. According to the clock on the wall, it was already after midnight. One good thing about Station House Five was there were no curfews, no closing times. The Night Shift kept odd hours, so nothing ever closed—the dining hall always had snacks and cold food available, and a vending machine for frozen dinners. The library was open all night. And since most of the rooms were padded, noise wasn't much of a problem.

I stacked up the rejected books and went to check out two I thought had at least some potential. I knew there was a coffee cart that usually showed up in the courtyard, and wondered if it followed the all-night rule, as well. I could use a caffeine boost.

"No, you could use eight hours of sleep," Micha corrected. "Or have you forgotten you have Lieutenant Hamm and his obstacle course in the morning?"

I groaned. Part of me *had* forgotten; or maybe it was just wishful thinking. "Why did you remind me? He's going to be on the warpath tomorrow."

"Which is why you should go get some sleep, instead of staying up all night reading. I'll be fine. You can put this off until tomorrow, after classes."

The librarian ignored my apparently one-sided conversation (or maybe she could see Micha and was just ignoring him; it was hard to tell sometimes), stamped my card, and sent me on my way.

The night was cold. Chicago might have been a little behind Canada, but winter was definitely on the way. I shivered and walked a little faster, trying to calculate mentally if it would be cheaper to buy a new winter coat, or to have Adam ship my old one.

"Evie." Micha's voice stopped me in my tracks. I followed his thoughts to a shadowed corner near the front gate, where a figure in a long cloak was standing.

"Arwen the Goth," I said, and I could tell by the way she straightened that she knew I'd seen her. She didn't move, however.

"Evie, don't!"

But I was tired and annoyed and pretty much fed up with people following me and trying to kill me. I always make stupid decisions when I'm sleep deprived. It makes me reckless. And more than a little irritable.

"Hey! Hey, you!" I shouted. For a minute, I thought she was going to run, but the minute she took a step, I reached out and *pulled.* Her fancy cape tangled around her ankles. She landed face first on the gravel driveway.

"Why are you following me? What is your problem?" I pushed through the wrought iron gate, heedless of the warnings Micha called after me.

The next thing I knew, my vision went black as something was pulled over my face. Hands latched onto my limbs, lifting me off the ground and carrying me away.

Chapter Seven
Party in the Cemetery

Much to my surprise, they didn't knock me out. Hands half dragged, half lifted me into a car before I could scream. I landed on my side. Someone pinned me to the upholstery. I tried to shout, but it was no good. More hands tied my wrists and ankles.

Micha!

There's four of them. One of them….I can't move! They've done something. I can't go for help! Panic flooded our link. *We're headed west. No, south!* he amended as the car made a sharp right-hand turn.

Dammit! We were getting further and further away from anyone who could help us. How could they be holding Micha captive, too? Who were these people?

"Your friend isn't going anywhere," said a woman. "Jin can control ghosts. He's being nice at the moment, but that ends if you try to escape." Her words were harsh, but there was a quaver in her voice.

"What do you want? Where are you taking me?"

"We just want to talk. Privately. Without your friends at the Night Shift." This voice was new, and seemed to come from the front seat. Male. Probably the driver. I thought I detected a hint of an accent, but couldn't place it.

"And you thought kidnapping me was the best way to do it?" Were they all lunatics?

"Don't worry, you'll be back by dawn."

"Sorry if I don't believe you."

The car slowed down, turning off and following a bumpy road at a much slower pace. Then it stopped, the hands came again, and I was hauled out of the vehicle. Someone untied my ankles so I could walk, and someone else prodded me forward. A third person took my elbow, guiding me over the uneven ground.

A few awkward paces forward. Two steps up, then a handful down into someplace cool and earthy.

They pushed me down on my knees. I landed hard and lost my balance, tipping sideways.

"Evie Cappelli, chosen of Hekate, you have been brought before your fellow Ferrymen to account for your actions."

I have two modes when I'm scared: frozen, and mouthy. Since the combination of sleep deprivation and adrenaline destroyed my mental filter, I went with mouthy.

"What are you talking about?" How the hell did they even know about Hekate? And how could I have pissed someone off when I'd only been in the country for five days?

I remembered the scarab.

Okay, nevermind.

Someone giggled.

"Shut up, Bri," another voice hissed.

The giggle turned into a full-fledged laugh. "S-sorry. Sorry! This so just so ridiculous, ya know?"

A long-suffering sigh, male. "Just take it off."

Someone tore the bag off my head. I realized

belatedly it was a cotton blend that would have been more than happy to fall apart if I'd asked, but I wasn't about to give away more than necessary. Better to save that ace for the right moment.

Now, the nylon rope tying my wrists, on the other hand...

The cool, earthy room was unmistakably a mausoleum, complete with two stone caskets and a wall made up of little glass memorial windows and brass plaques with names and dates.

There were live people in the room, too, but for a moment it felt much more crowded, thanks to the cadre of ghosts watching us curiously. They stood in the corners, or hovered near the ceiling. One just had his head and shoulders in the room, and looked like a prized stag mounted on the stone wall. He watched curiously, his hair slicked down and parted in the middle like a silent film star.

Goth Arwen was the giggler. She'd pulled her hood back, and for the first time I could see her pale, merry face. It was both younger and happier than I'd imagined. Her eyes sparkled over the gloved hand covering her mouth.

Next to her was a woman who looked like a very angry soccer mom. She'd covered her greying hair with red dye, but it was due for a touch-up. Her fluffy, faux-fur trimmed winter coat looked like it was trying to swallow her petite frame whole.

A few meters away, the man with the long-suffering sigh stood with two others. Asian, late middle age, and a little too stout to be healthy. A tweed blazer showed through his open pea coat, and he watched me through wire-rimmed bifocals. He looked more like a history professor than a kidnapper.

Next to him was a man so tall he would have fit in at an Adder family dinner. His head was shaved, but the cold didn't seem to faze him. Deeply tanned even in November, he had the longest lashes I'd ever seen. He reminded me of someone, but I couldn't place him.

The last member of the party was another middle-aged man, maybe a little older than Professor Tweed, but certainly more fit and better dressed. He looked like a shorter version of my boss, right down to the wingtips and silk tie. I wondered if the American's pencil mustache would grow to match Jean's walrus proportions with age and experience, or if mustaches got bigger the further north you went, like some kind of evolutionary protection from the cold.

"We apologize for the theatrics. It seemed necessary under the circumstances," said the professor. I took a guess and thought he must be the one Soccer Mom referred to as Jin, the one locking Micha in place.

"We really wouldn't have hurt you," Goth Arwen added, having recovered from her fit. "We just wanted to make sure you wouldn't cause trouble." Bri. That was what the others had called her.

"Speak for yourself," grumbled Soccer Mom.

"What my associate means is, we have all had...*encounters* with the Night Shift at some point, and generally prefer to keep their involvement to a minimum."

"Who are you people? And if you think kidnapping me is going to keep the Night Shift away, you've got another thing coming." Had they somehow missed the part where I was related to half the force?

I twitched my fingers. The ropes slipped off my wrists and I bounced to my feet, backing against the wall. Screw aces, I was getting the hell out. The others all moved when I did. Soccer Mom, Bri, and Jin all went back, but Mustache and Eyelashes both took up stances like they were ready to fight.

Micha stood close at my side, but as long as Jin was controlling his movements, neither of us could tell how much help he'd be. The other ghosts watched with interest, like this was some kind of sporting event that had just gotten good.

"We don't want to hurt you," Eyelashes said when no one else moved again. "We just want to talk."

"Really? Because a cup of coffee seems much more effective than a felony!"

"I told you this was overkill," Soccer Mom snarled.

"We weren't sure what they told you about us," Jin said calmly.

Mustache picked up the thread. "And when we found out Brianna had been seen, we knew we needed to act quickly, before you told someone." —Brianna pouted. She was maybe eighteen or so; it was hard to tell with the heavy makeup. Like me, she also had a white streak at the front of her hair, but hers was more prominent. When she started to object, he cut her off. "You were reckless."

Jin raised his hands, like he meant to come between the two of them. "Why don't we all just calm down. The point was for us to have a discussion. I told you this childish hazing would backfire."

"All of you, be quiet!" Mustache snapped. Then he seemed to shake himself, re-centering. He squared his shoulders, dropping the attack stance and strode toward me slowly, measuring. He glanced at Micha, but did not address him.

I tried to think of the best way to escape. I decided my first step would be to turn Mustache's tie into a noose; while he was distracted, I could run. Soccer Mom and Brianna would be easy enough to trip up in the long winter gear. That just left Jin and Eyelashes. How could I break the hold the older man had on Micha?

I was fully expecting Mustache to pull out a knife or a gun, or maybe some kind of magic whammy, but instead he just stood in front of me. We were exactly eye to eye.

And then he was holding out his hand. "Phillip Dare. It's a pleasure to meet you."

He said the last part stiffly.

"Yeah, I kind of doubt that," I said, wishing I could press myself further into the wall.

He dropped his hand when I didn't take it. "I'm very sorry, but you must understand our hesitation. You see, we knew you were here shortly after you arrived—Homer knew what you were from the moment you opened a gate into the afterlife. He is a priest of Anubis, one of his chosen avatars."

I glanced over his shoulder at Eyelashes, who nodded to me. He was standing straight, hands clasped in front of him. Suddenly, I could see the resemblance. Whether it was coincidental or not I had no idea, but he definitely looked like the Anubis I'd met the last time I saw Hekate.

Mustache continued: "As I mentioned, we have all had interactions with the Night Shift that were less than...amicable. It is not that we have done anything wrong, merely that this city has a bias against the darker side of magic."

"Most people have a problem with dark magic." The Night Patrol brought in a really screwed up witch back in August who enjoyed using bits and pieces of small animals to cast hexes on her coworkers. I still shuddered when I remembered the *way* she was brought in.

"Don't misunderstand me. Black magic is, of course, wrong. Harmful. But shadows must exist for there to be light. Death is a natural part of the cycle of life, and we are its guardians in Chicago; the Ferrymen. The ones who usher lost souls to the other side.

"The Night Shift...does not understand this. Chicago has had more than its fair share of evil necromancers and black practitioners in the past few years. They tend to suspect the worst of us, even when we are working to maintain the balance in this city."

"So you're all necromancers, then?"

Dare laughed. "No, no, no. Certainly not. Please, allow me to introduce you. Mrs. Harmony Reynolds here, she is a spirit medium. Very good with children. She was working with the little girl you so elegantly put to rest just a few days ago. And this is Brianna O'Connell. Brianna's father was a banshee; she can sense death when it approaches. Mr. Jin Park is also a spirit medium, but he has the added talent of being able to control spirits as well. Very helpful when dealing with less pleasant souls. And of course, I've already introduced Homer Basara."

"And what about you?" I challenged. "You haven't told me what you do."

He smiled. It was the kind of smile I remembered my principal giving my parents in third grade, right before he told them I was "causing trouble" with my "inability to share."

I had a brief flash of Mandy Jenkins' face as she'd torn my favorite stuffed rabbit out of my hands, threatening to cut the ears off with safety scissors, before the world snapped back into focus at the sound of Dare's voice.

"I'm a necromancer."

"Phillip, don't scare the poor girl," Jin admonished. "I think we've done enough of that already."

"You people are all insane," I inched toward the door.

"Not insane. Just not typical." Brianna grinned.

Jin pushed past Dare, entreating me. "Please, this was handled badly from the start. I'm sorry about all of this." He nodded to Micha. "Please. We have important matters to discuss, but perhaps now is not the ideal time."

"Evie, go!" Micha gave me a shove. I stumbled to the door, by the time I found my feet, the others were shouting. I heard Jin and Brianna, nearly drowned out by Dare.

I ran. In the distance headlights passed on the other side of the cemetery gate. Using them as a beacon, I made for the road.

The last time someone tried to attack me in a cemetery, Hekate sent her dog to protect me. There was no protection this time, though. Just me and my burning lungs and the pounding of my boots on the walkway as I tried to put as much distance between myself and them as possible.

I tripped and went sprawling. Pain shot through my limbs, but I scrambled to me feet, gasping. My name echoed in the night as the worst kidnappers on the planet called after me. I didn't stop. Didn't slow down. Didn't even look over my shoulder, until a meaty hand clamped down on it, raising me off my feet.

I screamed, expecting Basara, maybe, but instead I was drawn face to face with a squinting, dull eyed man with blackened skin.

The stench rolling off him made my stomach convulse. He held me by his face, as though sniffing me. Both eyes were milky white and oozing. Blistered, charred flesh covered his neck and climbed up one side of his face.

"Evie!" Micha shouted, but the man didn't notice him. I swung my legs, burying the toes of my boots in his thighs and stomach. He belched more of the awful stink in my face, until my eyes sparked with it, vision darkening.

He grunted, dropping me on the grass.

It wasn't the same man I'd seen in Boston. The burns were different, and this one was taller. But the smell was the same. They had the same grayish skin and both looked like they'd been bar-b-qued by someone who hadn't the faintest idea how to use a rotisserie.

I scrambled away. He reached for his belt, which held his shredded, filthy white–dress?—up.

"Evie, get away. Hurry!"

"I'm trying!" My voice came out shrill as he drew a sword. It was curved, and not made of steel. It caught the light from a streetlamp, glinting bronze, and suddenly I remembered where I'd seen him and the man from Boston before.

The temple of Hekate.

Micha raised his sword, jabbing the closest one in the side. His sword skimmed off of his armor, missing flesh by the width of a finger. His opponent brought his fists down on the back of his neck, sending Micha sprawling to the ground in a daze. Before he could roll out of the way, one of the other soldiers drove his spear into Micha's shoulder.

He howled in pain and I screamed, throwing myself over him. "Stop! Leave him alone!" I cried, torn between removing the weapon and allowing him to bleed with nothing to stop it.

The soldiers laughed, and the one with the spear retrieved his weapon, yanking it roughly from Micha's body. He choked on another scream. I tore off my shawl to press it to his wound, but one of the other men grabbed my arms and hauled me to my feet. "This one is coming with us," he said, holding my chin in his meaty hands and turning my head side to side. "Not the prettiest, but she'll do!" They roared with laughter again.

Micha managed to get himself into a kneeling position. Still holding his sword, he raised it—

And then one of the soldiers struck, his own blade slicing Micha's head from his body so quickly that I didn't even have time to scream.

The three Greek soldiers had killed my first incarnation, Evadne, only minutes later, at the will of Athena.

But that was thousands of years ago. What on earth were they doing in Chicago?

Necromancers, Micha and I thought at the same time. It had to be Dare and his friends, trying to bring me back.

"What do I do?" I asked, voice quavering.

"It doesn't have a soul, Evie. You can't kill it. It won't feel any pain. It's not alive, and it's not human anymore."

I backed up a few more steps, but the man—the thing—my brain hesitated to even contemplate the word *zombie*—came slowly closer. "That doesn't help me right now!"

"Run!"

I didn't stop until I was out of the graveyard and five streets away.

****

It was four in the morning before I finally got back to my dorm, collapsing on the thin mattress. In the dark and quiet, my panic and fear ebbed out of me with each heaving breath. Should I call Ian? Or the regular cops? No—I didn't want to get the Night Shift involved if I didn't have to. I didn't want to ask for help. They were already doing so much—

"It's not a crime to ask for help," Micha said from his corner of the room. He wasn't winded, of course, but if I didn't know better I'd say that he was off color. The fluorescent lights in the hall, visible through my partially open door, flickered slightly and seemed a little dimmer than usual.

"No. I can't. I don't want them involved." It wasn't just that I didn't want to ask for help; I was still wary of these new people. As eager as they seemed to bring me into the fold, I was still a little gun shy. Once bitten and all that, I suppose.

I rolled over on my back, staring at the ceiling. I intended to come up with a plan. To think things out. The last thing I needed was another crazy cult trying to hunt me down. Swarms of spiders were bad enough. Now I had to deal with zombies?

I closed my eyes for a second. The next thing I knew the alarm on my phone was buzzing and I had thirty minutes to dress, eat, and get down to the training ground.

By the time I got through the four hours of hell that

105

was the physical side of training (this time it included a hundred pushups and three laps around the training hall, in addition to everything else, as punishment for walking out the day before), I was barely coherent. Maddie practically had to scrape me off the floor with a shovel to get me into the cafeteria for lunch.

She plunked another bottle of purple Gatorade down in front of me. "Get some protein," she ordered. My face was already pillowed on my arms, but I gave her a thumbs up. She drifted away to wherever it was she ate her lunch.

It took a little prodding from Micha, but I finally convinced myself not to fall asleep (though I might have dozed a little; I'm not sure), and went to stand in line. With only ten minutes of my lunch break left, I stood in line for a sandwich and an enormous soda with as much caffeine as I could manage, then shuffled off to Law and Order, hoping the act of eating and drinking would keep me awake through the lecture, even if taking notes didn't.

For the rest of the week, I continued on like this— scraping through PT, trying not to sleep through lunch, dodging uncomfortable questions in Spooks 101, and staying up way to late researching ghosts, poltergeists, and generally trying to find anything that would help Micha if the Night Shift decided they didn't want to help the mentally unstable trainee and her mostly-dead semi-boyfriend.

And through all of it, I resolutely did not think about the Ferrymen, or whatever those psychos called themselves. I thought about at least telling Maddie about what had happened, and asking for her advice, but I didn't want to be a trouble maker. *Don't rock the boat*. That was the rule. Don't ask for too much. If there was one thing PT showed me, it was that showing weakness wouldn't get me anywhere. The more I struggled, the more extra laps Lieutenant Hamm gave me, the more he shouted and the more push-ups I had to do after everyone else hit the showers.

This is the same thing, I told myself. *If you can't handle this on your own, then how are you going to handle actual field work?*

I knew there was a flaw in that logic somewhere, and more than once Micha tried to point it out, but we were both pretty distracted. Since I already had a lot on my plate, I did what I always do when I'm overwhelmed—I ignored it in the hopes it would go away. That strategy worked pretty well, too. I actually forgot all about my zombie summoning stalkers until Friday, when I came out of the dorm to find Brianna waiting at the front gate.

It was just after Laws and Regulations. My perpetual state of sleep deprivation meant I was once again searching for the campus coffee cart, but it was never where anyone said it was. I was starting to think it was some kind of hazing thing; tell the new kid the coffee cart is in the courtyard, or over by the library, when there really isn't a coffee cart at all. Ha, ha, look at them run!

As if my thighs didn't already feel like Jell-o.

I stopped when I saw her, my hands clenching into fists. I wasn't sure if I wanted to go yell at her myself, or go see if I could track down security or something. At least there were no signs of the zombies.

"What do you think?" I asked Micha under my breath. He was so much better at reading people.

He tilted his head, then squinted like he was having trouble seeing her aura, or whatever it was he used to get a bead on someone. "She's not evil. Not really even that dark."

"Huh. You would think a kidnapper's aura would *have* to be dark."

"You may not want to tell her this, but her aura is actually kind of pinkish."

I snorted. "Okay. Let's go talk to the psycho, then." If Micha said she was okay, then it was good enough for me.

She waited until I was on the other side of the gate, examining her from the safe side of the iron bars.

"I think we got off to the wrong foot," she said, holding out a gloved hand. "I'm Brianna O'Connell, Ferryman of Northwest Chicago."

I didn't shake her hand. "Is that supposed to mean something to me?"

She smiled through black lipstick, baring glaringly white teeth. "It should, since you're one of us. One those chosen to usher lost souls into the afterlife."

I raised an eyebrow. "The only person you seemed to be ushering into the afterlife the last time I saw you was still alive."

Brianna blinked, then laughed. "Oh, silly. We weren't going to kill you. We didn't even want to hurt you or tie you up, but we didn't think you'd come with us otherwise."

"You're damn right I wouldn't." Why was I even having this conversation? I thought briefly of sending Micha to find Maddie, but then remembered Maddie couldn't actually see him, putting her on a very short list of people when it came to the Night Shift.

Her smile dropped. "Look, I'm really sorry about the other night. I came to apologize, and to try to make it up to you a little. I thought maybe we could get some coffee and talk. Like, actually talk. Just you and me. I know Philip can be kind of...forceful with his opinions. He tends to creep a lot of people out, but really, he's harmless. I think the creep factor is something that comes with the territory. Necromancers just can't avoid it."

"I really can't think of one good reason to go with you."

She glanced me up and down, at the sweater that was clearly not holding up to the famous Chicago wind, no matter how dense I told the fibers to make themselves. "Hot coffee. Central heating. No boring lectures or running laps, and I promise you'll learn more about the supernatural in Chicago from me in twenty minutes than you will from one of those blowhards in three hours."

"You had me at 'coffee.'"

***

The coffee shop she took me to was in a converted pub barely a hundred yards from Station House five, in an alley off the main street. It would have been nearly invisible if she hadn't shown me where it was.

I recognized a few faces from the dorm among the crowded tables—no one from the accelerated class, since they were supposed to be with Dr. Peters at the moment, but faces I'd seen in the dining hall or the common areas. It was enough to make me feel a little more at ease, though I did catch Brianna looking around a little nervously.

"Why don't you like the Night Shift?" I asked once we were seated, blowing on my cappuccino.

Brianna clutched her cup, warming her hands

against the thick ceramic. Her nails were painted a shade of green so dark it was almost black, overlaid with glitter. Her drink involved about twelve syrups, whipped cream, and was more sugar than coffee. I got a toothache just listening to her order.

"I told you, the Ferrymen help lost souls pass over. We do good. We help to keep the ghosts of Chicago from overwhelming the city."

Well, she had a point there. Chicago had more ghosts than Montreal by far. I knew of at least a dozen living in Station House Five, and spotted three drifting through the cafe while we waited for our drinks.

"We're all sorts, like we told you the other night. Mediums, necromancers, and some that are touched by the gods. My father, he was a banshee—full blood fairy. But my mother was human and I was raised here. I can sense when violent deaths are about to happen, and sometimes I can help people pass over. I prevent ghosts from happening.

"But every time someone uses death magic, guess who the Night Shift comes after? People like me, and Philip, and even Harmony. I mean, come on. The woman has four kids. She's not going to go around sacrificing babies just because she can see the dead. But the Night Shift isn't happy unless they have every magic user in the city at their beck and call. And Jin, the poor guy. He can control spirits. Mostly he uses his powers to clear areas with poltergeist activity, but those bastards have pulled him in for questioning at least twice since I've known him. He doesn't even *like* his powers. I think he'd rather go back to teaching high school math and just be normal."

I took a sip of my coffee and thought of Nick, one of the members of the Montreal team. He was a little odd, but he'd always been really nice to me. I knew he could control spirits, but I was a little fuzzy on the details. It involved bells, somehow. I wondered if he'd be coerced to join the Night Patrol, or if things just worked differently in Canada.

Well, there's a radical idea, Evie. Things might work differently in another country! Clearly, I had a lot to learn about more than just the Chicago branch.

Brianna glanced around again, like she was afraid someone would overhear her. She leaned in and whispered, "Look, we just wanted to warn you. That's all, really. The Night Shift isn't as great as they seem. And they don't care about the supernatural community they're supposed to be protecting nearly as much as they say they do. Something's been going on, and they're not doing anything about it."

"What do you mean?"

She shook her head, glancing a few tables over where three other trainees were swapping law notes and sharing an enormous French press full of gourmet coffee. "Only that one of us died last week, and they haven't done anything. They say it's up to the regular police, and they aren't going to find anything. The Night Shift might be liars, but at least they aren't idiots."

"What happened?" I was whispering now, too, leaning in until our faces were only a hand span or two apart over the little round table.

"Gloria Fisher. She was a medium, too. A friend of Harmony's. I guess they met at church or something. Anyway, Gloria did spiritual healing. Laying on of hands, that kind of thing. And of course, she could see ghosts. She was really good at helping families reconcile after someone died. I think she'd even been on TV once or twice a few years ago, but she mostly stayed out of the spotlight.

"Halloween night, she was walking home. She'd taken her grandkids trick-or-treating. They only lived six blocks away. So she's on her way home, and bang. Gunned down in the middle of the street.

"I saw it coming, but I only had a few minutes. I tried to call her." Brianna's eyes welled with tears. "I was on the phone with her when it happened. A man. He just came out of nowhere. I heard her ask what he was doing, and then he shot her. Right there."

I handed her a paper napkin. "I'm so sorry."

She sniffled, crying into the recycled paper for a few moments. When she finally dried her eyes, most of her heavy khol was gone, and what was left was smudged. "The CPD are investigating, since it's a homicide—plain old homicide, as far as they are concerned. Gunshot, two to the chest. Purse and jewelry gone.

"But I know it's something else. They even took her pendant." Brianna reached into the neck of her blouse and pulled out a long gold chain with a coin on it. "It's a drachma. All of us have one, to symbolize ferrying the dead over the River Styx. They have a protective enchantment on them. Nothing huge, but no one but another Ferryman should even be able to see it, let alone remove it. It wouldn't hold up against something major—like if a wizard really wanted you dead or something, but a garden variety mugger? He should have picked another target. Or missed the necklace when he was robbing her. But the Night Shift says that isn't evidence, and they're letting the police look into it since it's not a supernatural matter."

"Did you tell them you were on the phone with her

when it happened?" I asked. I couldn't believe the
Night Shift would ignore that.

"I did. But I couldn't tell them who did it, and there
was no evidence of magical interference, so they won't
get involved. Whoever's doing this, they're targeting
us. The dead know it. They've been restless for weeks."

She looked around nervously again. She was
starting to draw attention from some of the other
patrons who had the Sight. Now that I was looking at
her more closely, I could see the faint glimmer
surrounding her that meant she was part Fey. The
barista was also giving her the side-eye over the
espresso maker.

Brianna lowered her voice again. "Look, I know the
person who killed Gloria wasn't normal. I know a
vision and a phone call don't prove anything, but I can
feel it. And I know if this guy isn't caught, then he's
going to kill again. I'm prickly all over; death is near; it
just hasn't picked a target yet." She rubbed her arms. I
could feel goosebumps breaking out on mine, too.

"I still don't understand. Why are you telling me all
of this? You do realize I kind of work for the Night
Shift, right?" Sort of. In a way.

"I know. I thought maybe you'd be able to help. Or
at least, I wanted you to know what you're getting into.
I don't know who is being targeted or why. And even if
you don't want to drink the Kool-Aid or whatever,
you're still a Ferryman. You're still one of us." She
reached into her pocket, pulled out another gold coin on
a chain, and held it out to me. "We share a purpose,
even if our methods are different. Consider this a
formal invitation, of sorts. We wanted to give it to you
the other night, but, well, that didn't really work out."

I let her drop the necklace into my palm. The metal

had absorbed her body heat and was pleasantly warm against my skin.

I started to get a nasty feeling in the pit of my stomach, like when I'd stupidly taken Dr. Kelly up on her invitation to party with a hundred people who wanted to kill me and steal my powers.

Brianna started tugging at the edges of her cloak. "Look, I shouldn't even be here. People like me aren't really welcome in this area. So I've given you the message. Do with it what you want. But we could really use your help." She gave me one more pleading glance before pulling up her hood and standing.

"Brianna—"

But she was out the door, the eyes of at least four trainees or employees following her. I realized too late that I'd forgotten to ask her about the zombies.

Chapter Eight
Trust

I could have caught the second half of Dr. Peters'
class, but I didn't think I could sit through another
lecture. Instead I sat in my room with my laptop and
Micha, researching. I decided to start with the zombies,
but it brought up a lot of Cajun and African lore, not
much different from what I'd picked up from movies.
When I tried searching for *Greek mythology + zombies*
I got a little closer, but the vengeful spirits described in
various blog posts and Wikipedia articles didn't sound
like the men I'd seen.

"You're positive they're Greek in origin?" I asked.
For once, I couldn't remember what either of them had
been wearing. It had been so dark, and I was terrified. I
closed my eyes and pictured the second one reaching
for his sword. He'd been wearing filthy rags. They
clung to his charred form. Linen, maybe?

"That sword was a xiphos. They're basically a long
knife infantrymen would use if they lose their spears or
were fighting too close to use it."

I raised an eyebrow. "How do you know that?"

"I…well, it's in your memories. You remember
being Evadne, in ancient Greece. She would know."

I raised an eyebrow, not quite believing him. When I glanced up, his brow was furrowed, arms folded across his chest as he stared at a spot on the linoleum floor. My laptop abruptly lost its connection to the internet. "Are you okay? You're quieter than usual."

He shrugged, pacing the length of my room and didn't answer.

"Micha, I know you aren't okay. Every time you get on this side of the room, you knock out my Wi-Fi signal."

"Sorry."

I closed the laptop and put it back on my desk, scooting over a little closer to the wall to leave a thin strip of mattress open.

At first, he didn't take the invitation, standing stubbornly in the middle of the room.

"Micha, come on. Moody and standoffish is my shtick." I patted the fleece blanket serving as my bedspread.

Reluctantly, he sat down beside me, stretching his long legs out. He was dressed the same way I always saw him: jeans, classic rock tee shirt (today it was AC/DC, probably because I'd been listening to "Highway to Hell" before breakfast to try to wake myself up), faded jeans, and sandals. He could, to an extent, change his appearance (like the tee shirts), but I wasn't sure how much would carry over if we were able to make him human. Would he still have the auburn hair and grey-green eyes?

He didn't look at me, just stared at the wall. He was there, just this side of visible. I could feel him, but he wasn't really solid enough to touch.

It's hard to describe what it's like having a person that you know is there, but also really isn't. It's a bit like touching a soap bubble. I knew he was there. I could feel him against my skin, but if I tried to touch him, it destroyed the illusion. He could make himself semi-solid—to me, anyway—but that required a lot of energy (hence the blinking lights and the busted motel television) or for me to be half asleep. If I was in the right mindset, then we could almost share a plane.

"I'm sorry," I said, and for a minute, I thought I had actually caught him off guard. He could read my mind, my emotions; he was a part of me. He had to be really out of it if I was surprising him.

"What—No, you don't have anything to be sorry for. Didn't we go over this?"

I cut him off. "I'm sorry I'm not better at this. I know something is wrong, and you're worried. I'm worried, too. But I'm not very good at being there for you. For anyone. I mean, no one has ever really needed me to be there for them, so I'm not really even sure what it entails—"

"You're rambling."

"You're smiling."

"You're cute when you ramble." He leaned down to kiss my nose. A light, cold touch. "You don't have to do anything. I just want you to worry about you."

I shifted uncomfortably. "See, that's what I've been doing for almost a year now. And I think I'm pretty okay right now. But now you need help, and I think you've been focused on me for so long you don't even know how to worry about yourself anymore."

Micha gave me a lopsided grin. "You've been listening to Adam." Adam, the empath who was majoring in psychology.

"Hey, I've been seeing a shrink at least once a week for the past year. Some of that psychobabble was bound to rub off." And the fact that I was frequently reminded of my own inability to ask for help in session might have had a little something to do with it, too. I wasn't great with my own problems, but I was a pro at diagnosing them in others.

We sat there for a minute, nose to nose, forehead to forehead.

"Micha—"

"There you are!"

My bedroom door banged open. I let out a yelp and jumped about three feet in air, bumping my head on the padded wall in the process.

"Oh, sorry. Did I scare you?" Maddie asked. "Sorry. I thought I'd come look for you when you didn't show up in Peters' class. You looked half dead after those drills this morning."

"Mostly dead. And how did you even find my room?" I couldn't recall telling Maddie which floor I was on.

She shrugged. "I asked around. Apparently, all I have to do to find you is ask where the ghost girl is."

I stared at her. "'The ghost girl'?"

"Yeah. I mean, I can't see him, but most people around here can, and I guess that's pretty unusual behavior for a ghost."

"I... okay." I glanced over at Micha, who snorted and shrugged a shoulder.

"That's not surprising considering the number of people with the Sight in this building. Yesterday while you were in the shower someone asked me for directions to the firing range," he said.

"I would think the loud bangs would give it away," I deadpanned.

Maddie blinked her violet eyes at me. "Oh, you're

talking to him now, aren't you? Sorry, I don't have the Sight. My powers kind of mess that up."

"Don't worry about it. And I'm fine, by the way. No check in necessary. I just had something I needed to take care of."

"You know, you really shouldn't be skipping classes, especially if you're on the accelerated track. I missed a couple my first go around, and I really regretted it later."

"Seriously, it's nothing," I lied. I thought for half a second about telling Maddie about Brianna and her friend Gloria, and the zombies. Madeleine had been a member of the Night Shift, active duty and everything. Maybe she would know of a way to help the Ferrymen. Or stop them. I hadn't decided which. But she'd also been demoted or suspended or something, so maybe she wasn't the best person to ask. On the third hand, though, it wasn't like I could just ask Ian or one of the other many Night Shift officers I was apparently related to. Being related was one thing. I wasn't about to start asking for favors. Not when I wasn't even ready to call them family yet.

Since I was running out of hands, I decided to just brush it off. "It's fine, don't worry about me."

"I have to, Bambi. I can't help it."

"Did you just call me Bambi?"

"Yes. Because you always look like a deer caught in the headlights."

I groaned. Great. Not only was I "ghost girl" but now I had a stripper name, too.

"Can't you just use my real name?"

"Do you prefer Cappelli or Adder?" Maddie's grin was vicious.

"You know what? Never mind."

Maddie pushed her way a little further into my room, looking around at the bare walls and the thin blanket on my bed, then glanced at the half-open bottom drawer of my little dresser that was being re-purposed for dirty laundry, since I had neither a laundry basket nor hamper, nor even the clothes to fill a single drawer.

"You know, you're going to be here five more weeks. You can decorate a little."

"Yeah, I know..."

Maddie raised an eyebrow.

"Do you have any idea what the exchange rate is right now?" I asked pointedly. "And I was only planning on being here for a week, not two months!"

The lavender haired trainee opened her mouth, then closed it again. "Okay there are so many things wrong with this, I don't even know where to start."

I sighed. "Do you want something, or are you just here to criticize my decorating and study habits?"

"Well, now that the first two are out of the way, I thought maybe we could grab some dinner and then work on our L&R homework. Dan is planning a quiz for Monday."

"Haven't you already taken his class?"

"I did. Last year. And I dozed through most of it. And I'm not having any more luck staying awake this time, either."

***

The next day was Saturday. It was so glorious not to get up for PT, I could have slept through all of it if not for the caterwauling prima donna in room twenty-seven.

"I really hope this isn't a regular weekend thing for her," I grumbled.

"We could always try to help her move on again," Micha suggested.

"We tried that, remember? She actually likes it here." She'd started a Wagner solo in the hall in the middle of L&R and wouldn't leave until Dr. Peters and one of the TAs took her in hand. She was more than happy to have the residents of Station House Five as her captive audience, even if no one in the building liked opera.

Since she wasn't going anywhere, I put in my headphones and reached for my laptop. First order of business: email. Connor and I had exchanged a couple of messages that could be counted in syllables; those awkward messages of people who know they should communicate, but don't know how. Story of my life, and apparently a trait I came by honestly. Izzy was the same way—only she didn't bother with the *should* part. If she didn't want to talk to you, she flat out didn't.

I rubbed my eyes and clicked on the next message. It was so weird; I kept reframing my life, my entire personality, based on who my "new" parents were. I had always looked at myself like a distorted reflection of my mom and dad, trying to trace my features and my personality back. I had my mother's stubbornness, my father's eyes. Except no, I didn't. My eyes came from my mother. The stubbornness...well, I may have gotten a double dose on that one.

I had another invitation to a family dinner I'd been ignoring. I weighed the options once again, pitting what I *should* do with what I *needed* to do. I didn't have to ask Micha for his input. I'd traveled thousands of kilometers to meet these people. I might as well do it.

The next email was from Adam. He hadn't seen Drac for a few days, but that was pretty normal. The cat was just this side of feral, so if he went missing for a day or two it wasn't the end of the world.

He included a selfie of himself and his boyfriend, Isaiah. *Took Isaiah to his first Alouettes game. Can you believe he's never seen a live hockey match?*

I smiled. I could, actually. Isaiah showed up in Montreal in August, because apparently that's where Cappellis go when we get exiled from Toronto. A second cousin and a few years older, he'd grown up Stateside and basically been disowned when he came out to his parents. No one heard anything from him for two years, until he broke up with his boyfriend, moved to Montreal on a whim, and met Adam in a New Age shop. I guess the Adders weren't the only relatives I had coming out of the woodwork lately.

I replied back to Adam, and confirmed with Connor that I would be at Sunday dinner at Fynn and Jack's. Apparently, so would the rest of their family. I wasn't entirely sure what the "rest of" meant, but I could feel myself regretting it as soon as I hit send.

With that done, I gathered up my meager possessions into a plastic bag and prepared to go down to the laundry facility. I'd bought a package of underwear, one of socks, and another shirt when I realized I'd be staying a while, but I still barely had enough to get me through the week. My PT clothes were all Night Shift issue, and had the funk that came from being worn too many days in a row.

I was just stuffing the last of it into a torn plastic bag from the corner store when someone knocked on my door. Figuring it was Maddie, come to pester me about studying or socializing or something, I opened it.

Much to my surprise, instead of an albino with a lavender dye job, I found a short, freckled, red haired man who barely came up to my nose.

"You're Evie?"

"...Yes?"

He held out an envelope of thick cream stationery. "Ian told me to give this to you."

I took the envelope. By the time I'd examined the wax seal with the Night Shift logo embedded in it, the little man was gone.

"That was weird," Micha said when I shut the door.

"No kidding." I slit the envelope with the closed point of my thread snips. Inside was a notecard of the same heavy stationary, and two lines written in old fashioned script that look like it came from a fountain pen. *Chicago National Trust*, followed by a series of numbers.

"What the hell is this?" I muttered.

Micha was looking over my shoulder. "It looks like an account number and a pin."

"Why would he send me an account number?"

"I don't know. But I think you'd better add *go to the bank* to your to do list."

***

The bank was one of those big city anachronisms. Outside, steel and glass provided a backdrop for black granite steps and a pair of carved lions. Inside, it was all marble floors, with brass gates (backed with what I assumed was bulletproof glass) separating the tellers from the general public. The ceilings had to be three or four stories high, and the whole place looked like it was the height of Jazz-age style, perfectly maintained or replicated.

I waited in line until a woman in a violet suit and glasses with neon purple frames waved me forward.

"Hi, I need to check the balance on this account please?" I said, passing the card through the gate.

She tapped on her keyboard and blinked when the information came up. "You're Genevra Lucretia Maria Sophia Cappelli?" I flinched at the use of my full name, but handed her my passport.

"Do you have an additional form of identification?"

I sighed, and found my Ontario driver's license.

"One moment please."

And then she slid the little door shut, cutting me off.

I leaned on the counter and tapped my foot impatiently.

"Do you want me to follow her?" Micha asked, craning his neck to watch as she vanished into a back room.

Tempting as the thought was, I didn't get a chance to answer.

"Excuse me, Miss Cappelli?"

A bearded man in an expensive pinstriped suit held out his hand. "Stanton Lewis. I'm the branch manager. I'm so pleased you came in today. If you'll just follow me, we have some paperwork for you to fill out, and then we can release your trust."

"Release my...trust?" To say I was flabbergasted was like saying Canada got a little chilly in the winter.

"Yes. I'm sure you'll find everything is in order. The account has been monitored regularly, and now that you're eighteen, you can take possession of it."

"I...have a trust fund?"

***

Yes. Yes, I did have a trust fund. Half an hour later, I exited the bank with a thick folder full of paperwork, more cash stashed in my bag than I'd ever made in my working life (even before factoring in the exchange rate), and a shiny new bank card that felt like magic and made all my worries disappear.

I looked again at the receipt showing my current balance, after the withdrawal. There were more zeros there than I'd ever seen in one place.

Giddy, overwhelmed, and suddenly terrified of being mugged, I managed to find my phone in my oversized bag and hit the number Maddie programmed in the day I got my tattoo.

She picked up on the third ring. "Hey, Bambi."

Breathless with excitement, I said, "Maddie, I need your help."

Instantly she was on alert. "What happened? Where are you? Are you okay?"

"No, no. I mean, Yes. I mean, I'm fine. Everything is fine. Everything is fucking fantastic." I started laughing and it took me a minute to calm down.

"Evie?"

"I'm still here. I'm good. I just need your help with something."

"Name it."

"I need to go shopping."

***

Unsurprisingly, Maddie knew all the best places to shop in Chicago—everything from high end boutiques to hole in the wall thrift stores.

"You're sure you don't want something nicer? That

125

dress would look really good on you," she wheedled, pointing to the purple and blue plaid ensemble one of the mannequins was wearing.

"And when would I wear it?" I asked. Jeans and a tee shirt were really more my speed.

"Whenever you wanted to," Maddie replied without missing a beat. "Maybe Sunday dinner?"

"How did you know about that?"

Maddie shrugged. "Simon invited me."

"Simon was your partner, right?"

"Technically, he still is. He's just suspended and I got bumped back to training until he's reinstated."

I held up the matching bag, considering it. And the three-hundred-dollar price tag. I tried to do the conversion in my head, gave up in disgust, and put it down again.

Maddie rolled her eyes and grabbed the bag. "You need to splurge."

"I splurged. I bought those boots." They were knee high, and the most expensive piece of apparel I'd ever bought.

"Sweetie, shoes are a *necessity*. Handbags are a *luxury*." She wiggled her eyebrows and led the way to the checkout. I laughed and started to follow.

"The purple would look good on you," Micha said, casting a look at the mannequin.

I bought the dress, too.

***

I'm not really sure how we fit everything into Maddie's car. Clothes. Shoes. She'd even talked me into some makeup and a few pieces of jewelry that wouldn't turn my skin green. None of it was really excessive; I thought I'd shown a lot of restraint (well, except for the dress. And the bag. And the boots), but I could definitely replace most of my drab, black, worn out wardrobe when I got home. My new wardrobe was still mostly black, but a lot classier. There was a lot more purple, too, which I attributed to Maddie's influence.

There were also things for my room—proper bedding. Pillows. A lamp. A laundry basket and detergent. Maddie finally drew the line at the bookstore ("I am not helping you carry five bags of books up to the third floor!"). If she thought I was bad in the bookstore, then I was glad I hadn't yet Googled the location of the nearest yarn or craft store, in the interest of avoiding temptation. I had a feeling there was a sweater's worth of cashmere in my future.

With all that—and more—loaded into Maddie's Volkswagen, I was surprised it had enough pep to keep going, especially since it was probably older than Maddie and I put together.

"This is the last stop, I promise," I said as the car bounced down the rutted drive, stopping in front of Station House Two. "And I'll only be a minute. Hopefully."

"No worries. I'm going to say hi to a few people. I'll meet you back here when you're done, okay?"

I nodded and got out of the care, thankful for my new winter coat. I made a mental note that when I did find that yarn shop, I needed to get something that matched so I could make a hat and scarf. Maybe some gloves. *Cashmere. Or maybe quiviut...*

I waved at Steve, who barely glanced up from his newspaper. On the front page, there was a huge headline about a serial killer. DOUBLE TAP STRIKES

AGAIN, it read in bold Gothic print. Below, *Killer takes second victim in seven days.*

"I always have the best timing, don't I?" I muttered through gritted teeth, veering right toward Ian's office.

Micha rolled his eyes. "Oh, come on. It's not like you can predict when a serial killer is going to show up."

"Yeah. But it just figures I happen to be in Chicago when one decides to show up."

"To be fair, he was probably already here. Just not killing anyone. At least, no one anybody noticed was dead."

"Okay, I'm taking away your laptop privileges if you're going to watch true crime shows all night."

"I do not watch true crime shows all night."

"And I don't care how you feel about Garcia and Morgan, you aren't watching *Criminal Minds* in the middle of the night, either. Do you know how screwed up my dreams were last night? I have enough nightmares already."

"Yeah...sorry about that. I'll try to keep it down next time."

I rolled my eyes. "No more crime shows when I'm trying to sleep."

"Sorry."

He actually looked sheepish for a minute. I bumped his shoulder lightly with mine. Micha's penchant for both true and fictional whodunits was, in a twisted sort of way, him showing support for my new profession. I think he was trying to encourage me, but mostly I tried not to think about why cops wore bullet proof vests, and longed for the days when I could hide behind the counter in the shop, playing on the internet and knitting while all the spooky stuff happened in other places, to other people.

I stopped outside Ian's door and knocked.

"Come in."

"I just wanted to say thank you," I said, producing the envelope from my pocket. "I really wasn't expecting it. It is mine, right?" I thought about trying to return everything we'd bought, and had a momentary panic before Ian gave a rare smile.

"No, it's all yours. I apologize for not getting it to you sooner."

"Can I ask...where, I mean...how...?"

"The trust was set up for you when you were born. As I told you before, you are an Adder, whether you take the name or not. We take care of our own."

I raised an eyebrow. "Like cops." *Or the mob.*

"Very much so." His smile softened a little. "I've been in the position before where I was alone and had no one to stand with me. I swore none of my family members would suffer the same treatment."

"Well, thanks. I mean, really. I don't even know what to say." It was scary how much Ian had done for me since he'd found me beside the railroad tracks in Montreal. A few seconds later, and I'd have been a front-page story and another statistic on mental health gone wrong.

It was nice, on the one hand, to be taken care of. To have someone looking out for me. But it was terrifying to think of what I owed him now. It was a debt I hoped he would never call in.

"I also wanted to ask..." God, this was awkward. "I mean, not to be rude or anything. But I wanted to know if you'd made a decision about the scarab yet."

"Well, it's not really up to me. I've presented the case to the administration, but it's going to take time for them to make a decision."

"But—" I caught myself just in time, swallowing a protest. "It's just, the ceremony has to be performed by Wednesday night, or we'll lose our chance." If I told him Micha was starting to show signs of becoming a poltergeist, would it make them more or less willing to help us?

Don't risk it, Micha thought, and Ian's desk lamp flickered.

He glanced at it briefly, but seemed to dismiss it. He checked his watch and started straightening the folders on his desk. "Hopefully, I'll know something by Monday or Tuesday. In the meantime, just concentrate on your training. The Night Shift will be more willing to help if you show you're an asset to the force."

"But I work for the Montreal Division."

"Doesn't matter. You're still part of the club, so to speak."

Another of those rare smiles, but this one was all business; a pleasant spin on what was otherwise a dismissal. I decided not to press my luck, even though I'd fully intended to ask about the Ferrymen and Brianna's friend.

"We'll see you on Sunday, then," Ian said. It wasn't a question. I nodded. "Excellent. Now, if you'll excuse me, I have some work to do. I'm the...liaison to the Elf King, and we've got a bit of a situation. I'm afraid that takes precedence right now."

I shouldn't have been surprised by his mention of the Elf King, since I'd already reviewed Dr. Peters' syllabus for the course and read most of the textbook in my search for answers, but I couldn't help the little start I gave anyway. How long would it be before things like necromancers and banshees and elves stopped surprising me?

"Never, I hope," Micha said with a smile as we left the office a few minutes later. "I like your sense of wonder."

"It's not so much wonder as terror and shock, I think."

He grinned. "Yeah, but admit it. You think all of this is really cool. Like ending up in a book."

"Or a television show?" I asked with arched eyebrow.

"Or that." His smile was infectious.

"I just wish it would stop trying to kill me. Or the people around me." My smile slipped as I thought of Izzy again. I *knew* I was doing all I could—my training would help me find her, and to bring Kelly in. The Night Shift and the Night Patrol were both looking for her, and I knew they probably sent feelers out to other agencies as well. Eventually, someone would hear something, and we'd be able to save her. But after four months of radio silence, it didn't feel promising.

Micha reached for my hand and gave it a light squeeze. "We'll find her." I nodded.

Maddie wasn't done yet when I went back out to the entryway, so I waited by the front desk. Steve was done with his newspaper, discarding it at the corner of the desk. When I reached for it hesitantly, he nodded, gesturing for me to take it, and turned back to the game of solitaire on his computer.

I meant to look for the comic strips, but found the front page instead and the photo that had been hidden while he was reading stared up at me from his cluttered desk.

Brianna.

I snatched up the paper and began to read. Brianna

O'Connell, age twenty, was murdered on her way home from work. She was taking a shortcut through Mount Olive Cemetery when she was shot twice in the chest. Police matched the gun to the same one used in the murder of Gloria Fisher on October 31. Her purse and all of her jewelry were taken. CPD were warning citizens to be wary at night, as there appeared to a violent mugger on the loose, and were downplaying the possibility of a serial killer.

"You need three for it to be a serial," Micha murmured in my ear, reading over my shoulder.

"Steven, can I borrow this?" I asked.

"Knock yourself out," he said, more interested in his game than anything I could say.

"Thanks."

***

When we got back to Station House Five, Maddie rounded up four strapping recruits to help carry everything up to my room (I'd been generous to Maddie, as well, since for the first time in my life I had more than enough cash to go around, but she had an apartment off campus). After everything had been taken upstairs, I pulled a bill out of the wad in my purse and handed it over to them. "Drinks on me tonight, guys. Thanks for your help."

Duck, who'd been among those enlisted for the heavy lifting grinned as he held up the crisp hundred-dollar bill. "You sure do tip well," he said, inspecting it through the fluorescent lights.

"I'm having a good day."

"You want to join us?" he asked.

Overhead, I heard the lights begin to hum

dangerously. "Sorry, I need to get this stuff unpacked," I said, trying to reach behind me to pinch Micha.

"You sure?"

"Next time." Two days ago, I would have said I could really, really use a drink. But after a full day of shopping and people and socializing—not to mention the shocking news about Brianna—I needed some space to sort things out.

Once I was alone with Micha again, I surveyed the damage. Bags and boxes filled the tiny room, tumbling over each other in piles that blocked off my dresser and the desk. Suddenly I was exhausted and longing for that drink—but not the company of rowdy trainees.

"I feel like an old woman," I muttered, stepping over the box containing a new desk lamp to collapse on my bed.

"You're an old soul. And there's nothing wrong with keeping your own company. You've been doing really well lately at reaching out."

I mumbled something into my pillow that might have been agreement.

"Are you going to unpack tonight? Because incorporeal hands don't do very well with packing tape or twist ties."

"Just be thankful I didn't go to Ikea."

"There's no room in here for new furniture."

"Exactly."

Slowly, I started excavating my purchases from the layers of packaging, going over everything. It reminded me of the day, only a week earlier, when he "helped" me pack for my trip to Boston.

"What do you think will happen? If they say yes, I mean?"

Micha looked up from the shoes he was examining

on my dresser. "If the Night Shift decides to help us? If Anubis' spell works?"

It was a game we'd been avoiding: The What If game. What if Micha were human? What if we could have a normal life? What then?

"It's just...The day the ceremony has to be performed is this week. And we haven't even talked about it. We've been avoiding it."

"I didn't want you to worry about it."

"Micha, I just robbed one of the top museums in North America to get one of the pieces we need for this spell. I think it deserves a little discussion."

He leaned back against the desk so we were face to face. "Honestly, I don't know what there is to say. I don't know what will happen. I don't know if it will even work. Or how. For all I know I could wind up being reborn as a kid, or with no memory of anything that's happened in the past year, or ever."

"Stop. Just stop." I dropped the clothes I'd been folding back on the mattress.

He shrugged. "You said you wanted to talk about it. I'm just saying...there are a lot of unknowns."

"I know. I just..." I was scared. The closer we got to the magic date, the more nervous I got. Whatever spell Anubis used so I could understand the ancient papyrus with the instructions on it was wearing off. My protection from Hekate was wearing off, too. There were now only a few silver strands left in my hair. The other day on my way to class, I'd seen a line of spiders crawling up the outside of one of the buildings. Sure, maybe they were normal spiders doing something that normal spiders did. It wasn't like I'd been studying them over the summer—I'd been too busy with ancient languages and picking locks, and digging into the Night

Patrol computer system to try to find more information on Kelly and Traverse.

But it could also be the Legion, looking for me. Trying to find some way around Hekate's spell.

"You've been holding back. Ever since that night. Don't lie, you know I can tell when you do. I know you're keeping something from me," I said, cutting him off when he started to object. He looked away. "Micha, we've been through this once before. You have to tell me everything. You promised you wouldn't keep secrets."

"I'm not keeping anything from you. I just...haven't really shared everything."

I gave him a withering look. "And this is different, how?"

He held out a hand. I went to him, stood in his embrace. He brushed a stray lock of silver from my forehead. "You already know how I feel about getting involved with deities."

"Bad idea. All around. There's countless myths to back it up. But I don't think we have another choice here."

"I know. And that's why I didn't say anything. You entered into a contract with Hekate. You can't back out now, not if you want to stand up to Athena, too. So you have to hold up your end of things. I just can't help but think there's more to this. There's no such thing as an altruistic god."

My poor, lapsed Catholic heart started palpitating. If Micha hadn't been holding me, I probably would have crossed myself out of habit. "I think I know a few million people who would disagree with you."

"My point is, she wants something in return."

"She's getting something in return."

"I think she wants more than just souls."

"Like what?"

"I have no idea. And that's what scares me. Humans, I can read. I can tell when they're lying. Goddesses? Not so much. It's like talking to a wall. One that can come down on you at any time."

"So you think we should back out? I could tell Ian tomorrow to just drop the whole thing." But if I did, then what would happen to Micha? What would happen if he lost control? In all our research, we'd found countless ways to banish poltergeists and other ghosts. How to keep unwanted souls away, how to summon and control them. But nothing could tell me how to take a poltergeist and return it to its original form—back into the spirit of the person it once was.

Hekate said our souls were tied together. Saving me saved him, too. But that meant the opposite was also true. I might have gotten a second chance, but it wasn't enough to save us both.

"No." He brushed his lips over my forehead. "It's too late. If they say yes, then we have to see it through."

"*If* they say yes."

Chapter Nine
The Game is Afoot

As much as I looked forward to an evening with a movie and just Micha for company, there was one other stop I had to make.

After unpacking, I donned my sweater and new winter coat and went back to the cemetery.

It was a little harder to find the second time, but I finally did. I recognized the angel statue near the gate, since I nearly ran into it in my manic escape. It reminded me a bit of the war memorial in Outremont.

"Well, this isn't creepy at all," I muttered, pulling out a flashlight and swinging the beam over the walkway. Far off in the distance was the looming shadow of the mausoleum.

As I'd hoped, they were already there when I arrived. Harmony, distraught in her voluminous purple coat, dabbed at her eyes on a damp tissue. I interrupted her mid-tirade.

The three men all looked up when I entered. Jin and the tall man, Basara, both seemed surprised I'd come, but Dare was impassive as ever.

"What are you doing here?" demanded Harmony, her tone as accusatory as if I'd killed Brianna myself.

"I came to find out what happened to Brianna. I just saw her yesterday. Now the paper says she's dead."

"The paper doesn't lie," Dare said sarcastically. He raised a glass to me, then knocked it back. They were using one of the stone caskets as a bar, lining several glasses and a bottle of liquor along the top. I'd apparently caught them as they were toasting their fallen comrade.

"What happened?"

"Why do you want to know?" The soccer mom snapped. Her face was red and blotchy with grief. "So you can turn around and give the information to your friends at the Night Shift? So they can bring the rest of us in for questioning? They've already gone after Phillip. Hauled him in this afternoon for questioning. They think just because we work with death, we're interested in making more dead bodies, but it doesn't work that way!"

She choked back a sob. Basara detached himself from the cluster by the booze, handing her a handkerchief and wrapping one long arm around her shoulders. She barely came up to his underarm, but she leaned on him, sobbing into the dark wool of his coat.

"Yes. If you want to know, I do want to take back information to the Night Shift. I want to help them find out who killed Brianna. I might disagree with you people, but I don't think she deserved to die. I think at heart, Brianna was a good person." If not for the circumstances of our meeting, we might have been friends. Given time, I might even have gotten over that. She was a friendly, gregarious sort of person, despite the black lipstick.

"I'm sorry you guys feel wronged by the Night Shift. I can't change what they've done in the past. But

I do think they want to help. If you don't want them to see you as potential killers, you need to give them something else to work with. Why would someone be picking off the members of your little club if you're not doing anything wrong?"

Dare bared his teeth at me. "You think just because you've sat through a few of their classes you know what's going on here?"

"No, I don't. That's why I came here, so you could tell me."

He actually seemed taken aback by the retort. His mouth snapped shut so fast I heard his teeth click.

"Poor Brianna," Jin moaned from his corner. He'd been quiet so far, but now that I looked at him, it was pretty clear he was already three sheets to the wind. "Poor, poor girl. So young to die. It's a shame we couldn't have been there with her. We could have made her passing so much easier."

A thought struck me, and I wondered why I hadn't thought of it before. "Wait, none of you have seen her ghost? But all of you can see ghosts."

Basara nodded. "Yes. Our particular gifts all mean we have the Sight. But neither Brianna nor Gloria left behind a ghost. They must have moved on immediately after death."

"That's weird. I mean, I know I'm new at this, but I've seen enough ghosts to know victims of traumatic death don't just move on. They'll hang out for at least a few days until they figure out what is going on."

Basara shrugged. "It's unusual, but perhaps they moved on more quickly because they were Ferrymen."

That made sense, I supposed. "Brianna did say death was coming. She didn't know who was going to die at the time, but she knew someone would." Maybe she prepared herself, somehow. She'd said she was part Banshee. Maybe the rules were different for the Fey.

I felt a prickle of unease. With a start, I realized it was coming from my link Micha. Every part of him had gone tight and rigid, but I couldn't tell why.

There were no electric lights to flicker, except an old, bare bulb in the center of the ceiling that didn't seem to work, anyway. At least, the Ferrymen seemed to prefer candlelight for their gatherings. But there was a definite feeling of stray electricity in the air that preceded one of Micha's fits.

The others were starting to notice it, too. One by one, each pair of eyes swung in his direction.

"Micha," I hissed.

The feeling was building; it was like he was a bomb about to go off, and I had no idea what triggered it. "Micha!"

I grabbed his shoulder. My hand met his leather jacket and what felt like a solid body underneath, but it was so cold my fingers went numb almost immediately.

"Micha!"

"Jin, do something!" Harmony's bloodshot eyes went wide with fear.

But Jin just stood there stupidly, with the bottle in one hand and a plastic cup in the other. Slowly, I watched the liquid inside float upwards, through the neck of the bottle, then out into the open air.

The psychic link buzzed with what I can only equate to static. The link forged by Hekate herself was suddenly picking up interference like a cheap stereo.

I shook him, screaming. The bare bulb suddenly flared to life, two or three times brighter than it should have been before the glass burst, raining shards on us. At the same time, the candle flames leaped, burning ten or twelve centimeters high, then higher still.

Then it was like Micha himself cut out. My hands went straight through him and his image began to waver, flickering in and out.

I couldn't reach him physically, so I turned inward, toward our link. As soon as I reached for it, the interference was suddenly overrun with a single emotion: Terror.

The sensation hit me so fast, it was like diving into a pool of frozen water. For a moment, I couldn't move, couldn't think. When it closed over me, Micha's terror turned into my panic. Something pulled me down, dragging me into the depths of darkness and fear so complete I would never get out again. There was only one course: I had to run.

Where didn't seem to matter. The darkness in my head merged with the shadows of the cemetery. I bolted out of the mausoleum, leaping over low markers like hurdles until I reached the gate, then swung around one of the wrought-iron posts and chose a direction at random. Disjointed imagery flashed before me. I passed a clothing store, gate rolled down for the night, and through the window there was a woman screaming. Someone was chasing me, I didn't know who. Lots of someones. But I couldn't see them. They were there. I knew it. But then I took another corner and they were gone. The feeling of pursuit remained, driving me faster, further.

A light changed. I couldn't remember which color meant stop or go, but it didn't matter. There were lights everywhere, and none of them made any sense. I kept running. A horn blared. I narrowly missed a very intimate meeting with a city bus and the pavement, but stumbled onto the sidewalk just in time.

Another left, and then a right. My lungs burned. I couldn't feel my fingers. My heart lodged itself somewhere north of where it was supposed to be, and threatened to come up with my dinner.

More lights, but these were just spots in front of my eyes. I tried to blink them away but I couldn't. Pain shot through my ankles and knees with every step. Just when I thought my lungs and legs would give out completely, the link snapped like a broken rubber band.

I collapsed in a heap. I couldn't tell if the lights were stars or neon or just bright spots on my own retinas. My entire body was on fire. Needles of pain drove themselves into every inch of me.

I don't know how long I was insensible, but when the lights finally faded and the pain eased, I opened my eyes and found myself lying next to the sidewalk, half covered by someone's hedges.

I'd made it into a residential area. A quiet street with white picket fences in front of postage-stamp lawns. An owl hooted and I jumped. On silent wings it glided into the sky, leaving me alone in the street.

"Micha?"

I...I'm here.

His presence sent a wave of relief through me. My tense limbs released the last remnants of adrenaline. When I turned to look at him, though, all I saw was a faint outline against the darkness. Micha had never looked so ghostly before, not to me. When I reached for his hand, my fingers passed through him without the slightest resistance, without even a cool breeze or noticeable dip in temperature.

"What happened back there?"

He faded into shadow, but I still felt his presence in my mind as strong as ever, just very...tired. Micha was *never* tired.

I don't know. It was like when the Ferrymen took us, but worse. I couldn't control anything, and the more I tried to fight it, the worse it got. Then you ran, and when you reached the end of my tether, it pulled me out of range of whatever—whomever was causing it.

"You don't think it was Jin, do you?" I frowned up at the sky. The mild-mannered teacher hadn't seemed together enough to pull off something like that. He was half a shot away from curling up in a corner and crying.

"I don't know. He's the only person I've ever met who could do something like that. Well, I suppose Nick probably could, but his methodology is different. Nick requires ceremony to exert control over spirits, and this...this was something different. This was a fight. Every time I stepped things up, so did he. Or she, I guess. It was like...like a test, almost. As soon as I passed one level there was another one waiting for me."

The rumble of an old gasoline engine and a bright set of headlights announced Maddie's arrival. I propped myself up on my elbows as her car pulled up to the curb.

"What are you doing here?" I asked over the roar of the Bug.

"Following you. What are you doing here?"

"What do you mean, you're following me?"

If the hedges hadn't already been dormant for the winter, the look Maddie gave me would have finished them off. "Ian told me that if I ever wanted to be reinstated, I needed to make sure you didn't get yourself killed. Now get your ass in the car. Why are you under the bushes, anyway?"

Grumbling, I crawled back out to the sidewalk. The ground was still moving a little, but with the help of a nearby tree I managed to stand. "Have you been spying on me the whole time I've been here?"

"Spying is a very strong word. More like I've been keeping a very watchful eye on you. Now get in the car. Unless you want to walk back to the station."

I wanted to walk back, just to spite her, but my knees were still shaking and I had no idea where I was. We had a brief stare down. Maddie raised an eyebrow. Swearing in French and Italian, I jerked open the door of the Bug and climbed inside.

Maddie shifted the car into gear, pulling back onto the road. "I'll give you some credit. You did not make tailing you easy there. I actually lost you there for a bit when you cut through the country club. Run like that in PT, and Hamm'll probably leave you alone for the rest of training."

"How did you even find me?"

"Electrical signals. Everybody has a unique one. We've spent enough time together that I can find yours, if you're close enough."

I couldn't decide if that was cool or creepy. I wished I had a similar method of tracking down Izzy.

"So, you want to tell me why you're running through the streets like a crazy person?" Maddie asked after a block or two of silence.

There was a tear in the sleeve of my new coat, probably thanks to my fall and those damn bushes.

I ran a hand over the damage. After a moment, the nylon wove itself back together.

Part of me still didn't want to say anything. I didn't want to cause trouble. I just wanted to put everything behind me. But through the fog of his exhaustion—which was pulling on me, too, by that time—I felt Micha's prodding. *Tell her.*

Carefully, I laid out what had happened, from the time the Ferrymen took me, to what had happened with Brianna, and then the events of that night.

"At first, I thought it must be Jin, because he can control spirits, but he was so out of it I don't think it could have been. I don't know what the others can do, though. I mean, I know that Harmony is a medium, and Dare said he was a necromancer—"

"He's a *what?*"

"A necromancer. But I'm not really sure what that means—"

We'd been cruising in the left-hand lane, going south on 94, but suddenly Maddie jerked the wheel to the right, cutting across two lanes of traffic to take the next exit.

"What are you doing?" I shouted over the blaring horn of a minivan. I held on to the "oh shit" bar on the dash like my life depended on it—it sure as hell felt like it did.

"If we're dealing with a necromancer, then we need to get Ian involved, *right now*. Necromancers are nothing to mess around with. We've had two in the last five years, and trust me, they fuck shit up *bad*. If he's set his sights on you or your little friend, then there is some serious trouble headed your way."

***

We arrived at the old Municipal Utility building in record time, due in part to Maddie driving like a particularly unhinged kamikaze pilot. Gravel crunched under the old Beetle's tires as it ground to a stop. Her head was on a swivel as she led me into the building, as if she expected Phillip Dare or his zombies to leap out at any moment.

Despite the late hour, the station was the busiest I'd ever seen it. Steve was still at the front desk. I wondered if he ever went home. I dodged a pair of Special Detectives heading out the door, discussing the best way to deal with demonic possession, but I didn't get a chance to hear their thoughts on it because the hem of Maddie's flared skirt was already disappearing down the hall.

Ian was still in his office. Did *anyone* at Station House Two ever go home? Or did they just sleep under their desks or something?

"Oh, good, you're still here," Maddie sighed with relief as she pushed open his door with only a cursory knock.

Ian rubbed his eyes. It was a relief, somehow, to know the man did actually get tired and wasn't some kind of robot. "Yes, well, we've got a bit of a situation. The Elf King is livid. One of his courtier's children has been murdered, and it appears to have been done by human hands. Though how a human managed to kill a banshee, I have no idea."

Banshee? "You mean Brianna."

Ian and Maddie both looked at me. "Brianna O'Connell. She was half banshee, half human. She was killed last night."

"Yes, she was." Ian raised an eyebrow, waiting for me to elaborate.

"She came to me yesterday. Said that a friend of hers, a medium, was killed last week. She said she went to the Night Shift for help, but they sent her to the regular police because of how Gloria was killed. She said there was no way a normal mugger could have murdered her because of some protective charm she was wearing." I suddenly remembered I had one, too, and reached into my purse for the drachma, passing it over to Ian.

"How did you come by this?" he asked, turning it over in his hands and examining it carefully.

I told him about the Ferrymen and their offer, wincing when I got to the part where they abducted me. Somehow, Ian didn't seem surprised by this news.

"Did you accept?"

"No." I looked away under the weight of his gaze.

"But you didn't turn them down, either."

I shook my head.

Maddie jumped in impatiently. "Tell him about tonight."

Ian was already half out of his chair, the coin clutched in one large hand. At Maddie's words he sat down again. "There's more?"

I sighed, once again retelling the events of the evening. By the time I got to the part about Micha, Maddie and I had taken the seats facing Ian, ready for a long night.

He made me go over everything in excruciating detail two or three times until at last, he turned to Maddie. "I need you to take Evie to Station One. Have Michael check her and Micha over. I need to stay here and get the task force together." He was on his feet, pulling on his jacket and halfway to the door before he finished speaking.

"There's one more thing," I said. Ian paused, as if he couldn't believe there was actually *more* to the story. I told him about the zombie in the graveyard.

Ian covered his face with one hand. "And you didn't mention this sooner? Why didn't you say something in the first place?"

I swallowed hard, drawing back into the high collar of my coat. "I didn't know…I wasn't sure…I mean…" I couldn't get the words out. Suddenly, everything I'd been telling myself for the past few days seemed incredibly stupid.

"It wasn't Dare."

"What?" Ian looked at Micha, his pale shadow just visible beside me.

The few words exhausted him, but I knew what he was trying to say.

"It wasn't Dare who made the zombie. At least, I don't think so." I told him about the one in Boston. "At first, I wasn't sure what it was. I kind of forgot about it, until the second one showed up. But Dare wasn't in Boston. He couldn't have sent that one after me."

"Evie, you've been working for a goddess, were in possession of an incredibly rare and powerful artifact, and have a very unusual skillset. It's possible he's been watching you for a while.

"And Evie? Until further notice, you are on lockdown. You are not to leave the training grounds without an escort until this is resolved." His eyes flicked to Maddie again. "Take her straight there when you're done. No detours, no stops. Coordinate with Captain Hedge. We're going to need to increase security."

My eyes flicked from Ian to Maddie and back again. "I don't understand. Why would they want to hurt me, or Micha? They wanted us to join them." Unless Dare was acting on his own, trying to scare me so I'd run to the Ferrymen for help. Or maybe the others were in on it. I could see Basra or Harmony helping him, but Jin and Brianna didn't seem duplicitous or secretive.

Ian already had one hand on the doorknob, but he

paused just long enough to answer. "I'm not entirely certain yet." He held up the drachma with his free hand. "But I think this might give us a good place to start."

***

The clock tower crowning Station House Five said it was after one in the morning when Maddie and I finally pulled into the parking lot. I was barely coherent; Maddie had to nudge me awake to get me out of the car.

"I think you'll be fine," Michael said at the close of his examination, which mostly involved him staring at me very intently, frowning, and asking odd questions while I sank deeper into exhaustion. "Whatever they did, it drained Micha badly—and by extension, you." I'd been given a prescription for at least twelve hours of rest and lots of fluids, which I was more than happy to take—In that order. Maddie provided one of her ever-present bottles of purple Gatorade, but it sat mostly untouched in the cup holder for the entire ride back.

The exam, which included a short interrogation for Micha, took the last of his strength. In the eleven months I'd known him, there'd never been a time when I *wasn't* aware of his presence. Sure, I ignored him plenty, especially at the beginning, but as I crawled into bed that night, still fully clothed, I thought it was the closest I'd come to being completely alone in months.

Wakefulness returned slowly the next morning. I kept my eyes closed, drifting in the space halfway between sleep and reality.

That in-between was where Micha and I could meet. There was warmth, and comfort. His arm around my waist, his face nestled in my hair. He lay against my

149

back with his fingers laced through mine.

There were no words; speaking spoils that state. For a few minutes, we flowed into each other. No boundaries, no division.

Just before the light from my tiny window fell on my face, bringing me fully awake, I felt his thumb trace the line of my jaw, and a feather-light kiss on the cheek before the physical sensation of him was gone.

I rolled over with a sigh, grudgingly acknowledging the day.

"Better?" I yawned, reaching over my head in a stretch, then pulling the covers up over my face. Whatever time it was, I could still use a few more hours of sleep.

"Better," Micha replied, his voice stronger. I pulled back the comforter enough to peer at him. He definitely still qualified as "ghostly" in the light, but at least now he was more than a blurry outline. In a show of irony, he'd traded out the AC/DC tee shirt for The Grateful Dead. I snorted and pulled the blankets up again.

"You know it's after three, right?"

"After three what?" Anyone other than Micha probably would have just heard incoherent mumbling.

"Three in the afternoon. And you've got an L&R quiz to study for, and dinner tonight."

The next phrase out of my mouth would have been *perfectly* clear even to someone who didn't know English. For good measure, I also used French and Italian.

"Good, now?"

"Alright, alright. I'm up."

Within an hour, I was showered, medicated, and dressed in something that wasn't horribly embarrassing if seen in public. I decided to multitask by taking my

notes down to the cafeteria and spent the next two hours
and far too many cups of coffee studying while I ate
some combination of a very late lunch and an even later
breakfast.

Other students came and went. Micha went into
something like hibernation, saving his strength while I
concentrated on other things. I sat there with my
headphones and my notes, ignoring my surroundings
until someone sat down across from me.

Duck had a tray full of grab-and-go snacks—mini
boxes of cereal, granola bars, candy, and a few pieces
of fruit, as well as a fresh bag of microwave popcorn.

"Is that all for you?" I asked, slightly incredulous as
an apple rolled off Mount Junkfood, stopping at the
spine of my book.

Duck grinned. "I can share, if you like."

Inside, I felt Micha stir, the hairs on my arms
standing on end.

Chill out. Go back to sleep. He's just a classmate, I
told him. What was his problem with Duck, anyway?

Grumbling, Micha backed down, though I suspected
it was more because he was still weak than because of
anything I said.

"I saw you over here studying, and I was hoping
you could help me study for Law. I'm having a horrible
time with the last chapter we went over on Friday."

"And you want *me* to help you study? We aren't
even in the same class."

"Well, yeah. But you seem like the studious type.
And you're in the accelerated course, so you've already
covered that chapter, anyway."

"You do realize that just because I'm quiet, it
doesn't mean I'm some kind of genius, right?"

He grinned. "I know. And you realize that just

because I'm wearing a jersey, I'm not a dumb jock, right?"

"I don't know. I mean, the Blue Jackets? Who in their right mind roots for the Blue Jackets?"

"Poor saps who grew up in Columbus, that's who." He offered me a fruit roll up as a peace offering. "So. Chapter eight?"

I cleared a space for him and his plethora of snacks, and we started comparing notes. Duck's note taking style was haphazard; where I wrote down nearly everything our instructor said, he hit the main points and relied on memory for the rest.

"How do you remember all of this stuff?" He asked, flipping through pages of my densely-packed handwriting.

"I don't. That's why I write it all down."

He shook his head, skimming through my list of investigative techniques not permitted in court. I wondered briefly why I was even taking L&R, since it was undoubtedly different from the laws I would actually be dealing with in Canada, in the off chance I ever arrested someone.

Movement outside caught my attention. Through the broad windows lining one wall of the cafeteria, I spotted two men and a woman, Night Shift badges prominently displayed, talking and pointing as they walked the grounds. I immediately recognized the woman; a tall, curvy red-head, she'd been the one to give me my tattoo. After a brief discussion with the two men, she would stop every few meters, draw something on a sheet of paper, and press it to the side of the building, chanting something. There was a brief flash of light, and they moved on to the next area.

"What are they doing?" I wondered aloud.

"You haven't seen them?" Duck's mouth hung open.

"Seen what?"

"Early this morning a bunch of Night Shift officers showed up. They've been beefing up the wards all day, and there are actual guards at all the gates. You need a pass to get into the parking lot now, and they were installing a special lock on the front door. I had to get one of them to let me in when I came back from the gym. I guess once they're done, we all have to go down to the auditorium, and they're going to re-tune the wards to recognize each of us individually."

He leaned in, lowering his voice to a conspiratorial whisper. "There's all kinds of rumors going around. Someone on my floor said he heard they were worried about terrorists, but they blame everything on terrorists these days, so I don't think it's true. And Charlotte, she's in my PT group, she said she heard from her roommate that these ninja assassins tried to kill one of the trainees, and they're all freaking out because apparently, this trainee is some kind of foreign royalty in disguise or something."

I nearly choked on my fruit roll up. Ninja assassins? Foreign royalty? Was he serious? "You don't really believe foreign royalty would train with the Night Shift, do you?"

"Nah, but it's fun to speculate. I almost think this is part of our training. Like, whoever figures out what really happened first, they get bonus points on their final exam or something."

"Well, I'm pretty sure whatever happened, it didn't involve ninja assassins." I tried to picture the Ferrymen as ninjas, and failed. They were so haphazard. They were more on par with a very disorganized book club, and about as athletic. Though I wouldn't want to go three rounds with Basara, that was sure. Well over two meters tall, he was the only one who appeared even remotely threatening.

"Hey, you wanna help me?"

"I thought that was what I was doing?" I replied offhandedly, flipping through the text book and trying to find the regulation number for someone who resisted arrest. I was pretty sure Duck had it confused with the one for assault.

"No, I mean figure out what really happened?"

Should I tell him, and cut the suspense? I was about to, but when I looked up, Duck looked so eager, like a dog waiting for his human to throw a ball. *Come on, let's go get 'em!* his eyes said.

"You know, I've got a lot on my plate right now. But you have fun," I replied. The idea of a mystery was so intriguing to him, I just couldn't take that away. Micha sighed with disappointment.

Chapter Ten
Bad Connections

Michael answered the door that evening when Maddie and I arrived, with Cernunnos not far behind. Unintentionally (at least on my part—the jury was out on Maddie), we had dressed like dark and light versions of the same thing. Maddie, in her typical rockabilly style, wore a lavender twinset the same shade of purple as her hair, and a swishy purple and white plaid skirt with a full crinoline underneath, and lavender heels that added a good five inches to her height.

With my dark gray sweater and my own plaid dress—royal purple and blue shot through with black and gray—and my new boots, we looked like some kind of bizarre before and after photo shoot, though I wasn't sure who was the before and who was the after.

"Evie, Madeleine. Good. Come in." He limped out of the way, holding the door open for us.

The scene in the living room was much like it had been the first time; Simon and Thomas playing videogames, but this time Tara and Devon were playing, too. The younger children manned the controllers while their mentors called out tips and encouragement.

"No, he's on the left! Hurry, hurry!" Devon urged Tara. On the other side of the couch, Thomas sat on Simon's lap. Simon held the controller with him, instructing him in the best method for achieving bonus points.

"You must be Evie," said a new voice. Occupying an armchair was a very pregnant woman with strawberry blond hair. "I'm your aunt, Shannon. It's so good to meet you. Connor and Fynn have been telling me all about you."

Unsure what to say, I just smiled awkwardly and waved. "It's nice to meet you?" *Damn*, meeting family is awkward.

Shannon introduced her husband, Oliver, but there wasn't much time for chit-chat. "Evie, could you come with me, please?" Michael asked, nodding in the direction of the kitchen door.

"Um, sure." I followed him through the kitchen, where Jack was pouring drinks for Shannon and Oliver and Fynn was getting the dishes down from the top shelf so the kids could set the table.

"The pizzas just went in the oven. I think there's about twenty minutes before we eat," Jack said.

Michael nodded. He opened a door I would have thought was a pantry, but turned out to be a very dark set of basement steps. He flipped a light switch and made an *after you* gesture.

I hesitated, but when I glanced at Jack and Fynn, they were already going back to join the others and didn't notice.

"It's okay, I just need a private word, and those are hard to come by in this house," Michael said, picking up on my uneasiness. "I have a work room down here. It will only take a few minutes. Consider it a follow up exam."

I put a hand on the railing and descended slowly into the bowels of the house. The basement had what I would call a "normal" level of creep factor; that eerie sense all unfamiliar (and some familiar) basements have that's the product of disuse, darkness and damp. Metal shelves storing seasonal clothes and outgrown toys lined the walls, and a washer and dryer in the corner with a full laundry basket waited under the chute.

But then Michael came down, and pulled up a trap door in the floor, and the creep factor went up a few notches.

A staircase descended into darkness. Michael and Cernunnos went down without pausing. I peered over the edge of the opening until a light came on. Still, I didn't move.

Michael appeared again, looking up at me from the floor below. "You can come on down. It's perfectly safe."

"I'll take your word for it," I muttered, slowly descending into the sub-basement.

Except, I realized as I reached the bottom, it *wasn't* a sub-basement. The ceiling on one side slanted, and two dormer windows looking out on packed earth, glass broken and the holes filled in with plywood. The wood floor creaked as I went to join Michael at the table across the room. A row of bare incandescent bulbs ran down the peak at the center of the ceiling, and in the darkened corners of the room piles of lumber, a toolbox, and work lights on tripod stands waited for someone to plug them in and go to work.

"What is this place?" I asked. Old photos still hung on the walls; Victorian portraits curled and darkened with age and water damage. A slightly musty smell came from the space under a round window, this one intact, where a carved settee sat, the velvet gone moldy.

"This is the original Adder house. A lot of buildings in Chicago sank over the years, and the people just kept building on top of them. The original house is from sometime in the 1870s, but the one upstairs is from the 1920s. Fynn's been working on fixing things up down here, making it a little more structurally sound. It's in remarkably good shape, all things considered."

"You have a house *under* your house. This is crazy."

A small smile twitched the corners of his mouth. "You can control fabric with your mind and have a ghost following you around, but the architectural quirks of our city are what you find 'crazy'?"

"We only build our houses once in Canada. Mostly." I knew there were a few places were old foundations had been reused, and I knew of more in Florence, but usually they were just that—foundations. Not entire buildings hidden underground.

Michael gestured to the second chair at his work table. There were papers laid out in stacks, and things that looked like they might be charms of some kind, but I was hardly an expert. He pushed them to one side and rested his arms on the table. "I wanted to talk to you a little more about the incident on Friday n ."

I shrugged. "Okay. What do you want to know?"

He glanced to my right, and I realized with some surprise that he was actually waiting for Micha to make an appearance. Equally taken aback, my spirit companion bloomed into existence next to me.

"Feeling better today?"

Micha nodded. "More myself."

"That's good. No more fits, no more setting off the electricity unexpectedly?"

"No."

Michael's eyes flicked over to me. "Evie. You don't look so sure."

I looked at Micha. He didn't even have to shake his head; I knew he didn't want me to say anything. I turned away. "There have been other incidents. Not since last night, but recently."

Michael waited silently for me to continue. In the poor light of the bulbs overhead, his eyes took on a truly eerie appearance, and I thought again of the way his soul didn't really seem to be attached to his body.

The dog put his head on my lap. Automatically, I started scratching the coarse fur behind his ears. I was pretty he was an Irish Wolf Hound.

"I'm worried about him," I confessed at last, and then the whole thing came spilling out. "He's always been...different. Not like regular ghosts. He's more..."

"Aware. Adaptable." Micha tugged at the hem of his tee shirt. "I've met a lot of ghosts. Talked to them. I mean, who else am I going to talk to, when no one else can see me?" He gave a hollow laugh. "But most of them...they're kind of stuck in the time they died, or at the time when they felt the strongest. I've never been like that. I *like* seeing things change, seeing time move forward. I've always been so proud when I see Evie— in any of her incarnations—grow and change and learn. But I've never been as objective as the other guardian spirits I've met. I could never pull off being so detached. At first, I thought that was my failing, the reason why things always went wrong for Evie, so I would try to pull back, but it never worked. I'm just...I'm not made like that, I guess. And now, knowing what we do about Hekate, I suppose it makes sense."

"Tell me about Hekate. About what she did. Ian told me a little, but I'd like to get your perspective."

"The first incarnation we know of, Evie was the daughter of Arachne. When Athena punished Arachne, she started to take her anger out on the entire family. Arachne's husband promised their daughter, Evie, to Athena's service in payment. But her nurse took her and ran, afraid of what she'd seen. The nurse died on the road, and Evie was taken in by a temple of Hekate."

I picked up the story. "Because I was under the protection of another goddess, Athena couldn't find me, not until I was an adult. Back then, Micha was human. We…we were supposed to get married. But then Athena found me. She sent a greedy king to invade the island where we lived, and both our previous incarnations were killed. In the process however, we did a favor for Hekate by protecting one of her prized artifacts. So when we died, she promised we would be reincarnated together."

"But Hades made a deal with Athena. They were going to punish Evie and I for siding with Hekate. Hades took my soul, dipped it in the river Lethe to erase my memories, and then was going to send me back to earth to wander for eternity. It would have worked, too, if Hekate hadn't found my soul and sort of…converted it, I guess. She disguised me as a guardian spirit, instead of a ghost, and linked my soul to hers. I don't actually remember any of this, but Evie does. And it lines up with what Hekate told us back in July."

Michael nodded thoughtfully. "So the two of you are connected, then?"

"I can't go more than maybe half a kilometer away

from her, usually. And we can sense each other. She knows what I'm feeling, and I know what she's thinking."

"It's a very one-sided connection." I frowned. That had always bothered me.

"I think it's just stronger on my end because I don't have anything to distract from it," Micha said.

Michael asked a few more questions. He was particularly concerned with the link between us, and what Micha could do.

"And what about this heist the two of you pulled? How did that work?"

We recounted the story for him, just like with Ian. Once again, he was very interested in what Micha did to the electronics.

"Did anything like this ever happen in the past? I mean, before Evie?"

Micha looked thoughtful for a moment, then shook his head. "No, I don't think so. But mostly it seems to be electronics that go wrong, and there weren't many of those in her previous incarnations. Up until Jenny—that was the last one, back in the 1930s—there wasn't any electricity at all, and even then there wasn't a whole lot for me to interfere with. They lived in a pretty remote area."

"They?"

"Jenny and her husband."

One of the bulbs overhead began to flicker. Micha clenched a fist, then shoved it into the pocket of his leather jacket. The lighting returned to normal.

Michael's face turned pensive. "Well, that's very...interesting. Thank you for telling me."

"There's something wrong, isn't there?" I leaned forward in my seat. "I know something is wrong. Can we fix it?”

“I don’t know. From everything you’ve told me, and what I see by looking at the two of you, I think one of the Ferrymen was trying to either drain Micha, or control him. He’s a very old spirit, which makes him quite powerful. Most ghosts are lucky to last a few hundred years, but one that goes all the way back to Ancient Greece? That’s quite the feat. You’d be a boon to anyone who works with spiritual or death magic.

“But they obviously weren’t expecting you to be linked so tightly to a living person. They wound up pulling on Evie, too, which they weren’t expecting. And it gave you just enough leeway to fight back instead of bowing to their will.

“But, I think the link may be damaged, now. In fact, from what you’ve told me and what I’ve learned from Ian, I think the link has been damaged from the moment you first saw him, Evie. You said you’ve been practicing your tricks with electricity over the summer, correct?” We both nodded. “I think that might have made things worse. The stronger you grow, Micha, the more distant you become from Evie. To put it simply, you’re finally outgrowing the place Hekate made for you, but without those constraints you’ve become unstable.”

“So what do we do?” I asked.

Michael didn’t say anything at first, but then he sighed. “Hope Ian can convince the advisory board to let you use the sarcophagus.”

***

Hours later, back in my dorm room, I searched through my bag for my evening round of medications and found the bottle of sleeping pills Dr. Archambault prescribed ages ago. I almost never took them, because they gave me really screwy dreams, but between the long nights I'd been pulling all week, stress, and then sleeping for most of the day, I knew there was no way I'd put in the necessary eight hours without them. I was reaching that point of exhaustion where I would not be able to function the next day if I didn't get at least a few hours of rest, disturbed or otherwise.

One pill was enough to knock me out. I'm sure my sleep deficit was a big help in that respect. And just as I'd feared, I was immediately thrown into a disjointed nightmare.

It was another of *those* dreams—the dreams I'd had off and on since June, ever since I'd re-absorbed the chipped-off bit of my soul that was Evadne, my first incarnation. The glimpses at another lifetime I didn't quite remember, like a flicker out of the corner of my eye that vanished when I tried to look at it full on.

Sometimes, I watched the scene, a spectator as events unfolded like a movie in front of me. Other times, I was on the receiving end of the action. The jarring shift was even more disorienting when my alarm rang at six o'clock, shocking me from sleep so suddenly I tried to sit up and roll over at the same time. I fell off the edge of my narrow bed and had an impromptu meeting with the concrete floor. I don't know what idiot decided the walls should be padded and not the floor, but he should try falling out of bed and see how well he likes it.

"Are you okay?" Micha asked, tilting his head to look at me.

I mumbled something Italian that did not translate well.

Micha only laughed. "I'm not sure that's anatomically possible."

"Shut up, or I might be tempted to try."

"I'd really like to know where you'd find a goat in the middle of Chicago."

"Shut up."

I tried to pin down some of the details of the dream. Who was I running from? What was the threat? *And why was I a man?*

"You can be reincarnated into any form," Micha said, sitting cross-legged on the narrow bed. "Men, women—once you were even a rat."

My head shot up. "A rat. Are you joking?"

He just grinned. "Nope. You were a very cute rat." He mimicked whiskers and a twitching nose with his fingers. "Of course, the whole plague thing was a little bit of a turn off, but you were still very cute."

"I didn't realize animals got guardian spirits."

"Well, they don't, but *someone* had to keep an eye on you..."

I narrowed my eyes at him. "You're joking, aren't you? You're making this whole thing up."

"We'll just have to wait and see how many of your old memories come back, won't we?"

I threw a pillow at him, but like the Cheshire cat he faded away to just a grin, leaving me to get dressed.

Two cups of coffee later, I was eating a granola bar in the PT building, still grumpy, but dressed, medicated, and waiting with the other trainees for Lieutenant Hamm to arrive. Maddie didn't look much more awake than I felt. It was clearly Monday, and just as clear that very few of us were looking forward to another four hours of torture at the hands of the good Lieutenant.

I was wearing my Night Shift issue sweats (recently laundered) and wishing I had a sweater—more for comfort than anything else. My nightmare left me feeling off-kilter; I remembered very little of it, except the fear. I was running for my life through a forest. It was fall. It had all the feeling of a New England horror movie; something witches or demons or something. I couldn't nail down anything specific about it, though, just that I'd been horribly afraid, and if the person—or people—I was running from caught me, I was dead.

There wasn't time to contemplate it, though. Hamm finally arrived, striding in like he owned the place. I guess, in a way, he did, since he was the more senior of the two PT instructors. He was also the same height as me and had a tendency for "small man syndrome." He reminded me of a very bad tempered dachshund a neighbor had when I was growing up. It nearly took off two of my fingers and my dad's nose.

But, considering I was Hamm's least favorite trainee, maybe that was just my own personal bias talking.

He clapped his hands twice to get everyone's attention, even though we were all waiting on him. "Good news, everybody. You've all been cleared for firearms training, so we'll be starting this morning. Two hours on the range, then it will be back up here for the course. Best shot will get to hit the showers ten minutes early."

I think it goes without saying that I was not the best shot.

To be fair, the first hour and a half of the session was spent on safety and regulations and learning the various ways we could accidentally kill ourselves or someone else.

The range was in the basement. Another creepy basement with flickering fluorescent lights. At least these flickering lights had nothing to do with Micha.

We were each provided with safety gear, a Glock, a full magazine, and told to stand on one side of a long counter divided into cubicles, I guess so we didn't distract each other. Hamm went through our instructions one more time, then told us to open fire.

"Well, you might be able to hit the broadside of a barn, as long as it stays very, very still," Maddie said when the round was over. She pushed the button on the side of my stall that pulled the target paper forward. There was a small perforation on one corner of the page, but otherwise it could have been fresh from the box sitting behind me.

"Raimes! What the hell is this? You didn't even hit the target! And there's still ten rounds left in your magazine!"

I peered around the corner to see who Hamm was dressing down, since for once it wasn't me. He was down on the far end of the range with a small, lithe kid who was usually one of the first people to finish the obstacle course. He could lift more, run further and faster than anyone else, and must have been raised in the circus or something, based on the level of flexibility he demonstrated during our warm ups and cool downs.

Apparently, however, he was even worse with firearms than I was. "I'm a werelion! I have teeth! I don't need a gun—"

Hamm stepped quickly to the side. "Put that down! Don't go waving it around!"

I leaned over to Maddie. "Did he just say werelion?" I whispered, though I'm pretty sure no one could hear me over the argument Hamm and Raimes were having, anyway.

"Don't worry about it," Maddie said. She gestured to the woman standing next to me to come closer so she could correct our stance for the next round of shooting.

Hamm finally got Raimes in line again, and ordered us back into position. The three former cops joined Maddie and Hamm in examining the line, so us amateurs effectively had our own personal coaches. "You jump every time you pull the trigger. You know it's not going to hurt you as long as you point it in the right direction, right?"

I winced. "I don't like loud noises." I had to shout to be heard over the reports of the other pistols. "And isn't the point of shooting someone to hurt them?"

"Well..."

I turned back to the target, took a deep breath, and fired off two more shots. One of them even made it into the black outline of a generic bad guy.

I had a serious headache by the time we were done. My shoulders hurt from holding up the Glock, which was heavier than I'd expected. Of course, the pushups and pull ups and the hundred other exercises I had to do every day didn't really help with the tension, either.

And I still had all of that to go through, too.

With a sigh, I turned in my sidearm and followed everyone back upstairs to the gymnasium. On the landing, I paused to watch a line of spiders climb up the wall. I watched them suspiciously, fingering the stray strands of white at my forehead. Just that morning when I'd been getting ready, three more strands came out on my hairbrush, leaving me with just two or three. The small part of my brain that contained my vanity was tempted to just pluck them out, but I'd gotten used to the silver over the past few months, and I wasn't about to put an end to Hekate's protection before I had to.

I would have stayed there supervising the spiders all day if I hadn't been interrupted by the buzz of my phone. The name on the screen made me sigh. I debated answering through the first four rings.

"Are you coming?" Maddie asked, trailing behind the others on her way upstairs.

"I—yeah. Just a minute. I need to take this."

I watched her go upstairs before answering.

"Hi, Uncle Mike."

"Hey, Ginny-bug. How are you?"

The greeting was the same one he always used, but hesitation laced his words. Not long ago, I would have said my uncle was my favorite relative. I suppose it was still the case, since he was the only one I was still speaking to. But things had been tense since I found out the truth about my parents, and that he'd known all along. How could I trust people who kept those kinds of secrets?

"I'm fine. You?" *Just keep it light. Easy. And above everything,* short. I hated being mad at him. He was, after all, the one who found me and got me to the hospital last year when I tried to kill myself. Guilt turned my anger sour, taking away the righteous feeling that made ignoring calls from my "mother" so easy.

"Okay. I just wanted to check in, make sure you got back to Montreal safe since we hadn't heard from you."

Oh, shit. I covered my face with my free hand. *Merde.* I'd mentioned the trip to Mike the last time he called, just kind of off-handedly, but back then I'd thought I'd only be gone a couple of days.

"Well, I'm still in Chicago."

"Why?"

"I'm doing some training for work."

"What kind of training?" he demanded, incredulous, and I remembered belatedly that he still thought I was a clerk at a used clothing store.

Double *merde*. I was really cocking this one up. "I... well..."

He grumbled. "How long are you going to be there?"

"I'm not sure yet. Through the New Year at least."

"Two months? What the hell are you doing there for two months?" he spluttered.

This is why I need to stop taking calls from my family. "Look, I need to let you go. Our next session is starting."

"Tell me where you're staying. What's the hotel?"

"It's not a hotel." Dammit, why did I say that?

"Where are you staying?" I could hear him shuffling for pen and paper, his detective's instincts taking over. *Saint ciboire de tabernak.* It was either tell him, and give away my new secret identity as Night Shift Officer-in-training, or *not* tell him and watch him bring down the wrath of the Cappelli clan and probably the Toronto and Montreal police departments, the whole RCMP, and possibly the FBI.

"Listen, I'll call you later. I need to go," I said finally. Maybe Ian would know what to do.

Except Ian had a heaping pile of shit on his plate right now, thanks to the Ferrymen, a serial killer, and an Elf King. And the crap Micha and I had already saddled him with.

"Evie! What is going on? Where are you?"

I sighed, mentally flipping a coin. "Chicago. I'm at a training facility on the west side."

"Which one?" The agitated edge in his voice twisted me up inside until I finally gave in.

"Station House Five. Route 64." I hung up before he could ask anything else.

***

My conversation with Mike left me feeling uneasy. I only picked at my lunch, poking my salad with no enthusiasm as I contemplated the situation with my family. Part of the reason I couldn't process Connor and the Adders was the situation with the family I was raised with. The family I had trusted and loved and depended on, who had been there through the first day of school and every major birthday, who had taught me everything I knew about the world and formed my ideas about it, had shoved me into a box so small, the only way out I'd been able to find was a butcher knife and an open vein. For years I had struggled and asked for help, but it was never forthcoming.

The problem was always *me*. *I* was the one who was too sensitive. *I* was the one who was over thinking things. *I* was too shy, too quiet, too anti-social. But no matter how hard I tried, no one ever looked for a deeper reason. No one ever thought "Hey, something might actually be wrong here." Even after I was released from the hospital, things didn't change. There was something wrong with my brain, sure. But none of them seemed to understand that it wasn't *my* fault; I couldn't control it. I needed help to keep those thoughts and emotions in line, and I'd had to go five hundred kilometers to find someone willing to give it to me.

And then, I found out about the lie.

I wasn't sure how I felt about any of them anymore. Yes, they were my family. Yes, there was still some amount of love buried (deep, deep) inside, but when it came down to it, I didn't want to talk to them. I didn't want to be around them. I'd had too many years of being treated like an inferior, like something in me was broken and needed fixed. I *wasn't* broken; I didn't *need* fixing. I just needed someone to read the god damn instruction manual and be willing to work with my quirks.

I felt a bit like Izzy's old Jeep. Most of the time, it ran. Bits and pieces of it had been replaced and repaired over the years, but it still started most mornings—if you knew the trick: turn the key, hold it for a few seconds, then pump the gas twice. Pump too early, and nothing would happen. Too late, and the engine made a screeching noise. Too much gas, and the engine flooded and it would take an extra ten minutes to get on the road.

It had taken time to learn those tricks. Izzy could tell me all day long how her car liked to be treated, but only practice and patience could teach me how it worked.

Back in Toronto, I didn't have anyone patient enough to learn the tricks that kept me running except Mike, and our relationship had gone straight into a ditch. I'd been written off for the scrap yard a long time ago.

That was the realization that finally sent me over the edge last Christmas. I was home for the holidays. Two weeks alone while my parents were on a cruise— Dad's gift to Mom.

Christmas Day was spent at my grandparents' house. I hardly said a word. No one spoke to me. When I tried to join in the conversation, no one noticed. They just talked over me. Eventually, I wound up in the kitchen, washing dishes by myself and listening to laughter and talk floating in from the living and dining rooms. It wasn't until I'd finished putting away the silverware and went back out to the living room that I discovered everyone else had opened their presents, and no one had come to get me.

I never opened my presents. Grandma tried to insist I should, but I didn't want to with everyone looking at me. I told them I'd open them at home, when I celebrated Christmas with my mom and dad on New Years.

But that never happened. I spent five days alone in the house, trying to talk myself out of the dark place I'd fallen into, but I couldn't. The darkness closed in around me, suffocating, until the last sparks of light I'd had left went out.

I spent New Years in the hospital. My mom brought my gifts, thinking they would cheer me up. The first and only thing I opened was the souvenir my parents brought me from their trip. A bath kit—shower gel, loufa, the works.

It was the type of thing you gave an acquaintance. Someone you are obligated to give something to, but don't know what. The kicker? The scent was lavender. I'm allergic to lavender. When I was eight, a babysitter decided to do a "spa night" while my parents were out. She wound up calling them in a panic when I suddenly broke out in hives. You would think a mother, a nurse would remember that about her own daughter, but I guess when the kid isn't really hers, she can't be bothered.

If my own mother—or at least, the woman who called herself that, the one who raised me, who bandaged my scraped knees and was there for parent-teacher night—couldn't be bothered, what about the people who had forgotten I was even in the house?

I left the gifts in the common room of my ward, with a note that anyone who wanted it could take one.

Dr. Fisher and I had several very long sessions about that one.

Talking to Mike dredged up all of this. Though Micha tried to offer comfort, I could feel myself spiraling. When classes were over, I went back to my room and locked the door. I sat on my bed with my knees up to my chest, and waited. I didn't know for what. To see if anyone noticed, I suppose. To see if I was still invisible. For the earth to open up and swallow me whole, or for the world to pass on around me.

I put my head down on my knees, drawing myself in as tightly as I could. Outside, the first snow of the season started to come down in fat, picturesque flakes.

My new comforter draped itself over my shoulders. When I peeked up, Micha sat beside me, close enough I could feel his semi-solid presence, but with the thick blanket between us it was more comfort than cold.

"It's over, Evie. That's the past, and it's gone. I know it hurts, but you need to move forward."

I wiped nascent tears from the corners of my eyes. "I don't know how. I thought I did for a while, but I don't anymore. I don't know how to fix it. I don't even know if I want to."

"You have to. Your family loves you, they just aren't very good at showing it. They don't understand. You've always been quiet, and they see that as you keeping them at arm's length."

Pain turned to anger in a flash. "They should have tried harder. They are supposed to be my family, but they never *tried*. If they could see I was struggling, then they should have *tried*."

"You're very good at not asking for help."

I have a hollow laugh. My tears started to flow more freely now, and I couldn't stop them. "I can't believe you're taking their side in this, after all this time."

"I'm not taking their side." His temper was flaring now, too. The overhead lights began to flicker, and the temperature began to drop. "How could you ever think I would take their side? Everything I have ever done has been for you!"

I'd never seen Micha angry before. And certainly never at me. The room got so cold I could see my breath in a white cloud. One of the fluorescent tubes made a loud *pop* and went dark. The pens and notebooks on my desk began to slowly lift a few inches into the air. I drew back into my blanket like a frightened turtle.

As suddenly as it started, everything stopped. Micha looked away. The lights went back to normal. My study materials dropped back onto the desk. But the goosebumps dotting my skin from head to toe didn't budge.

"I'm sorry," Micha said quietly.

I blinked, and he was no longer next to me, but across the room. He stared at the floor. Then he was kneeling in front of me. There was no movement; he just *was*, from one blink to the next, like a poorly cut stop-motion film.

He looked up at me. I was still wrapped up so only the top of my head peeped out from above my cocoon. "Evie, I need you to listen to me very carefully. I need to know you're going to be okay if something happens to me, if Anubis' spell doesn't work."

"What do you mean?"

"Things are...uncertain right now. There's something wrong with me. You know it, I know it. The Night Shift knows it. If they say no, if this doesn't work, I don't know what the result will be."

My voice shook. "What are you saying?"

"I'm saying that if it doesn't work, I don't know if I'll come back, as a ghost or anything else."

"But if you don't come back, then what will happen to me?"

"I don't know. I think—I hope—that you'll live your life. You'll be fine."

"Two days ago, you were worried that if you became a poltergeist, it would destroy my soul along with yours."

"That's another possibility." He said it so gently, so calmly, it was like he'd just said "It might rain later. Or maybe snow."

"And now you think if this sarcophagus thing chews you up like a paper shredder, then I'm going to be just fine?" My voice hit an uneven pitch.

"I don't know. I hope the spell will be enough to disconnect us, if it doesn't work. And if it does, if you are still here, still alive, then I want to know you will be okay. Promise me, Evie, that you're going to be okay without me. Because if you can't, then I can't go through with this. I need to know you'll be alright."

I covered my face and didn't answer. God, everything was falling apart. There were days I couldn't even get out of bed without encouragement (or coercion, depending on which side of the blanket you were on), and now he wanted me to promise I'd live my life and be happy if he died—*again.*

Emotions crashed over me so fast, so strong, I couldn't even process one before the next hit. Hurt, anger, confusion, loss, fear—they tumbled over me, one after another. I fought to remember my affirmations, all of the things Dr. Fisher and Dr. Archambault had been telling me for nearly a year.

I took a few deep breaths and wiped my face again. Micha watched me expectantly.

"I don't know." It was the most honest answer I could give.

Chapter Eleven
Casting Spells

The opera concert started early, right after dinner.

I only went to the cafeteria because Micha insisted I eat something, even though I wasn't hungry. I got a plastic-wrapped salad and a yogurt to take back to my room; I wasn't in the mood for Duck or Maddie or anyone else. I'd been spending so much time around other people lately that it was really draining my reserves.

I was almost to the staircase when an Italian soprano capable of shattering glass echoed through the corridor.

I groaned when she hit a particularly high note. There was no way I was going to be able to relax with *that* for background noise.

The hand holding my yogurt clenched into a fist that threatened to split the foil top. I counted to five, but her singing only got louder, more intense. The air in the hallway sizzled with spiritual energy.

Any appetite I might have had fled when it saw my temper flare. I threw the crumpled yogurt cup—which was now leaking—into the trash, then made a quick pivot, retracing my steps past the dining hall. I kept going, trying to remember the room number Duck mentioned when we first met.

I pounded on the door of number twenty-seven. And then I pounded again. And a third time.

Finally, a black guy with rough curls sticking straight up from his head in a ten-centimeter crown and massive DJ headphones answered the door.

"I want to talk to your ghost," I said.

I was tired and angry and hurting, and I knew my expression promised death to anyone who crossed me. I didn't even come up to his shoulder, but he paled visibly and stepped out of my way.

Huh. The trainees on the first floor got suites, apparently. I found myself in a tiny living space, just big enough for a threadbare couch and a television set on a rickety Ikea stand. It was also very clearly a men's dorm; dirty clothes, pizza boxes, and food packets from the cafeteria littered the floor and covered the furniture. There were three doors coming off the room. The music was coming from the far left.

I knocked, but there was no answer. I pushed the door open without trying again.

"Will you shut the hell up?" I snapped in Italian.

The singing stopped abruptly. The vocalist was a petite woman with dark hair and big brown eyes, dressed in an elaborate bustled dress of blue silk. She stared at me with doe-like eyes.

"*Puoi vedermi?*"

"*Si.* And a whole lot of other people can see and hear you, too."

This sent her into raptures. She practically danced around the room. "It has been so long since anyone has appreciated my singing. You have no idea what kind of hell it is, to be hidden away here—"

I sighed. "Well, it's going to be a while longer before anyone appreciates your singing. It's actually pretty disruptive. People are trying to work. And sleep. And no one likes opera anymore."

She gasped in horror, one hand flying to her breast. "Not like *opera?* But it is the purest form of music! The stories, the emotions! They sweep the listener away—"

"Your listeners are all wearing ear plugs," I interrupted.

"Evie..."

I ignored Micha. The crestfallen singer examined an empty potato chip bag at her feet. Clearly, the resident of this room was no tidier than his suite-mates. "Look, I'm sorry, but please, *stop*. You're driving everyone here crazy."

She looked up at me with tears in her eyes. "But if I do not sing, then how will my Paulo find me?" she begged.

I stared at her, at her dress that had been out of fashion for almost a century and a half. "If he hasn't come by now, then he's not coming."

Micha put a hand on my shoulder. I pulled away. The singer's face crumpled. For a moment I thought she would start to cry, but then she looked up again, steely hatred in her eyes.

"No. You are wrong. He will come. He promised. After the curtain call."

"Lady, you're in an old mad house. One that hasn't even been a mad house for almost a hundred years. You're squatting in someone's dorm room and keeping people up at night with your caterwauling. So stay here, or leave. Go looking for Paulo for all I care. Just shut the hell up, got it?"

I slammed the bedroom door behind me. Headphones was waiting in the living room, a perplexed look on his face. He'd pulled one speaker away from his ear.

"What did you do? No one's been able to get her to shut up."

"I told her the truth. She doesn't belong here." I let the suite door bang shut behind me.

"Evie, I don't think that was a good idea," Micha said, following behind me.

"I'm really not in the mood to talk about it, one way or another. I don't care if it was the right thing to do. She's quiet, that's all I care about. And I would appreciate it if you would do the same and just leave me alone tonight."

Sometime later, after my neglected salad wilted on my desk and I'd watched way too many episodes of a television show on my laptop, I thought solitude was not as satisfying as I'd hoped.

***

"...do I want to know what happened?" Maddie asked hesitantly.

It was the next morning, and we were between rounds on the firing range. Surprisingly, I'd just put six rounds through the head of the paper silhouette hanging at the other end of the range. I'd been aiming for the chest, but at the moment it hardly seemed to matter.

"I'd rather not talk about it."

Behind me, Micha leaned against the cinder block wall, pouting and staring at the back of my head. I ignored him.

180

"Does this have something to do with your ghost?"

I slammed a new clip into my gun and set it down on the counter, waiting for the cue to start the next round. I clenched my fists against the scarred wood. I'd gained such a reputation the previous week as "the girl with the ghost" that it was pretty obvious to anyone who could see Micha that there was something going on between us. The fact that our relationship was no longer private only made me angrier.

"No."

Everything in my life was suddenly spinning out of control. Izzy, Micha, the Ferrymen—It was all going crazy. And to top it off, I was down to just one strand of silver; Hekate's protection wouldn't last the week. As it faded, so did Anubis's gift. In a fit of paranoia, I'd stayed up half the night reviewing my notes. The hieroglyphics were just pictures now; I couldn't remember most of their translations. In desperation, I turned to my own translations and pronunciation notes, which I'd written down as soon as I realized his gift of language wasn't permanent.

Maddie raised an eyebrow, but didn't question it. Instead, she put another box of ammunition on the counter next to me. "Well, whoever this is, just remember murder is still illegal in the state of Illinois."

"Don't worry. He's already dead."

***

A text message waited after PT. It was from Ian: *Spell has been approved. Tomorrow night, dusk. Station House One.*

My stomach did a strange little back-flip. I sent back a quick *thanks*, and went to change.

I took so long in the shower, the locker room was empty when I finally got out. Wrapped up in one of my fluffy new towels, I padded back out to the changing area, digging through my bag for my blow drier.

"I don't want to talk about it, Micha," I said. His thoughts bored into me, digging though the tough outer shell I'd worked so hard to cultivate. To an outsider, it might look like some kind of emotional fortress, holding everyone at bay. But I knew it was about as strong as an eggshell. It wouldn't take much to bring the whole thing crumbling down, and Micha was the person best suited for the task.

"We have to talk, Evie. I told you, I can't go into that thing if there is something unresolved between us."

"I thought it was just if I couldn't promise to be happy if you didn't come out again."

I turned the blow drier on its highest setting, bending over and flipping my hair forward so I wouldn't have to see or hear him. Unfortunately, his voice was also in my head, so it wasn't such an effective strategy.

"Evie, please. I love you. You know that. I just need to know you will be okay. I don't want...I don't want you to lose everything you've worked so hard to make in the past few months just because I'm gone."

I flipped off the drier and slammed it down on the bench. "And if you're gone, then what do I have left? How am I supposed to do any of this without you? Do you think for a minute any of them—" I gestured vaguely to the door of the locker room, intimating the world outside "—would give me the time of day if Ian weren't telling them to?"

"Evie—"

I shook my head. "You know what? Nevermind."

This was probably his way out; he must have been looking for a chance for something like this for centuries; a chance to dump the damaged soul he'd been saddled with and move on to someone better. Something better.

"Evie. Stop it. You know that isn't true."

I went back to drying my hair, doing my best not to look at him.

Micha took my wrists, gently tracing my scars with his thumbs. I turned off the drier.

He leaned in close, until our faces almost touched. "In case you've forgotten, I didn't know we were linked until we met Hekate. I didn't know, because I never tried to leave. Because no matter what, I want to be with you. It doesn't matter how bad things get, you and I were meant for each other. You know it's true. And if things are hard, even if you're depressed and angry and stubborn as hell, I'm not going anywhere.

"I know it's difficult and you don't want to talk about it. But I need to look out for you. I need to know you will be okay.

"Even if everything goes perfectly, and in two months I'm human again and everything is fine, you can't make me your reason for living. You can't center your whole world around me. I told you once that if walking away and never seeing you again was what it would take to make you whole again, then I would do it. I meant it. I don't want to be the reason you can't move forward with your life."

I couldn't say anything. I was too busy sniffling, trying not to sob. Micha released one wrist to reach up and brush away my tears. He leaned over, kissing each salty cheek.

"You have friends now, Evie. You have family who

loves you and family who wants to know you. I know it's hard. But you can do it. But until you figure out what *you* want, what your reason for being on this earth is, you're not going to get better.

"I want to take that journey with you. But in case I can't, promise me you will do it alone. Please."

I was crying openly by then. I buried my face in his shoulder, inhaling the scent of leather and ozone that always accompanied him.

I couldn't speak, couldn't form the words. Instead I nodded, trusting our link to relay the message.

Yes. I promise.

It felt like my insides were being torn out to even think it. A betrayal to Micha, to me. I closed one hand around my tattoo, only recently released from the protective covering. The colors seemed bright against my skin. Purple for me, green for Micha. Wound together, with no beginning and no end.

Thundering feet outside made me look up. I shivered, suddenly cold. I was still only wearing a towel, long hair damp and dripping in places down my back.

The sound came again, this time with shouting and slamming doors. Quickly, I pulled on my clothes and ran out into the hall, boots unlaced with my duffel open and my coat draped over my shoulders.

"What's going on?" I asked, catching up to one of the guys from my class, Raimes.

"There's someone trying to get in through the front gate. Someone said it's some kind of monster," he said, pulling on his coat and following the others outside.

Lieutenant Hamm was trying to direct traffic in the yard. "Everyone! Back inside!" he shouted, but no one was listening. Everyone stared at the front gate, where the guards on duty had their pistols trained on a large, lumbering form.

A zombie.

This one didn't look familiar. He didn't have a sword, his filthy grey rags hanging down to his knees. He didn't seem to mind the cold.

The guards fired another volley. I watched in horrified fascination through jostling shoulders. Finally, they seemed to hit the sweet spot in its skull, and the zombie fell. The crowd surged forward for a closer look, but by now more instructors had left their classroom, along with the teaching assistants.

"Everyone! Back inside!" Dr. Peters' voice was icier than the layer of snow on the ground. She held out her hands, and a gentle telekinetic push drove everyone back two steps.

That was enough. Reluctantly, the group filed back into the dorm. I was shaking with cold—or maybe something else as I stood still, staring at the corpse through the iron bars of the front gate. My mouth was dry and my stomach, which had been longing for lunch, gave an uncomfortable lurch.

"Evie!" Duck's face appeared out of the crowd. I looked up at him, my eyes frozen wide.

He took one look at me, his smile dropping. "Come on. You should get inside. You must be freezing," He said, flipping my hood up over my damp hair playfully. When I didn't say anything, he wrapped an arm around my shoulders and steered me back into the foyer.

For once, Micha didn't complain.

***

I could hardly concentrate the next day. The perfect

little grouping in firearms training the day before proved to be a fluke; my shots were all over the place, and I couldn't have hit the broadside of a barn if it had been three meters from my face.

At lunch, I went back to my room, obsessively double and triple checking I the materials for the spell, or all of the pages were in order, or I still remembered how to pronounce some of the trickier words, even with my translation sheet and pronunciation guide.

The afternoon could not have dragged on longer. I tried to concentrate on my work—I really did—but it was a losing battle. After skipping more than my fair share of meals in the past few days, I took a sandwich from the fridge in the cafeteria and sat in the entryway, waiting for my ride and nibbling on turkey and avocado more from obligation than any real desire or hunger.

Finally, Ian's long black car pulled up in front of the building. His driver hopped out, opening the door for me, and I climbed into the empty vehicle.

I fidgeted with the black and white stone Hekate had given me for the entire drive. It looked like onyx or maybe ebony, but there were white veins shot through so it looked like a rib cage. The stone contained the last fragments of Micha's former physical self, compressed down into something not much bigger than the buttons running down the front of my coat.

We held hands on the drive, silently praying everything would turn out as we hoped. At last, the car pulled up to an old-fashioned bank, all brick and stone and oozing Gilded Age wealth. The nine-pointed star of the Night Shift was etched into the glass doors like a frosted sun.

Fynn waited in the lobby.

"How are you?" he asked. I couldn't tell if he was

concerned about my mental state leading up to a major magical working, or if he was just being polite. I just nodded, burying one hand in my coat pocket and squeezing Micha's tightly with the other.

He led me down several flights of concrete stairs into a dark, cold basement. The deeper we went, the more my skin prickled with ambient magic; the wards were the strongest I'd ever come across, much stronger than the ones Jean had around our office in the Old Port.

Fynn took us to a room scarred with smoke. A protective circle was permanently embedded in the floor. Black streaks shot out from it, soot stains on the concrete. The remnants of magic gone wrong.

Some of the streaks were an ominous rust color.

Ian, Howl, and Michael were already waiting, along with a few faces I didn't recognize, but assumed were some of the magic users and other members of the Night Shift Ian had had to get clearance from.

He introduced the newcomers, but I was shaking like a leaf and couldn't focus on the names. I checked the time on my phone. The papyrus had specified dusk as the proper time to begin the spell, "when Amun no longer watches overhead."

"We've only got a few minutes," Howl said, checking his own watch, which hung from a chain on his waistcoat. I only caught a glimpse of the face, but it appeared to be covered in celestial bodies, instead of numbers. He still looked like he'd wandered out of a Victorian novel, but there was a little less lace on his person this time.

"Evie?" Ian nodded in my direction. I reached into my bag, pulling out my supplies and turning toward the sarcophagus. Someone had been kind enough to provide a book stand. Micha took my notes and arranged them on the wooden frame while I took out the ingredients.

The sarcophagus was already open. Inside, I could see mounds of dark earth—one of the ingredients the spell proscribed. Well, in the original spell, it had specified clay from the banks of the Nile, presumably since that was what Egyptian artisans would use to create *shabti*, clay figures that would serve their masters in the afterlife.

Since Micha wasn't tied to Egypt, however, the Night Shift had substituted something a bit more local.

"It's from Lake Michigan. If there'd been more time, I would have tried to get some from the St. Laurence, but you wouldn't believe how tricky Customs can be on things like that," Ian said, coming to stand behind me.

I nodded. "I think it will do." *It has to.*

I pulled the next ingredient from my bag, but my hands shook. I handed the re-used pasta sauce jar to Ian. He twisted off the lid. Muttering the blessings as instructed, I sprinkled more dirt into the open box. This time, it was consecrated ground—earth from Mount Royal Cemetery.

Task complete, I placed the stone in the center of the sarcophagus. I started to feel like I was planting Micha like a sunflower, and choked on a hysterical laugh.

Ian and Fynn lifted the lid, sliding it back into position. It gave a final sounding *snap* as it locked in place. Ian reached into his breast pocket, producing the scarab he'd confiscated on my arrival.

"You're sure about this?" he asked, balancing it in his palm.

I looked at Micha. We both nodded.

Ian handed over the scarab, and he and Fynn stepped out of the circle, leaving Micha and I alone with a very elaborate coffin.

We exchanged a look. The text hadn't specified when he should enter the sarcophagus, but I thought it might be around line fifteen, when I got to the part about summoning the spirit of the deceased.

The sun wasn't visible in the basement room, but Howl started a count down with the aid of his watch. I stood in front of my notes and tried to calm down enough to speak clearly. Micha held tightly to my right hand.

Howl gave the signal. Slowly, I started the incantation, careful to enunciate each word correctly. Egyptian magic was all about the *words*; one misstep, and the whole thing could go horribly wrong.

The words were a guttural staccato, an utter change from the flowing pace of French or Italian. I resisted the urge to make the syllables flow more smoothly, to create bridges of sound between each word that would make them roll off the tongue more easily.

The tingle of power I'd felt when we first entered the building began to build, changing pitch. Around me, Ian and the others spaced themselves out, still remaining outside the circle, outside the spell, but watching, waiting. Guarding. Against what, I wasn't sure.

The painted carvings on the outside of the sarcophagus began to glow, the etched lines bordering the edge of each panel filling with power.

Line fifteen—roughly translated, it read "I call forth the one I desire, that they may reside in this holy place of creation, to be born anew."

Before I could even blink, Micha's hand was torn from mine. Like a vacuum cleaner gone wild, the sarcophagus sucked him inside.

I hesitated just a fraction of an instant before I pulled myself together and moved on to the next part. I couldn't stop myself from shaking, though.

The light show was more dramatic, now. A sudden breeze lifted my long hair, flinging it around my shoulders. The temperature dropped at least ten degrees, and the illuminated carvings were getting brighter.

I continued chanting. There were still ten lines left, but my knees were getting weak, and my head felt fuzzy. What was happening?

Eight lines, then five. I squinted against the brightness. Inside the circle felt like a small tornado. The wind tore at my coat. Long strands of black hair whipped my face. It took both hands to hold my notes down on the stand.

Nothing outside the circle was visible. I was trapped inside a four-meter wide ring, and the only way out was to finish the spell.

I had to shout to hear my own voice. *Just a little more!* There were only a few lines left.

"Take this offering, that flesh may be made new—"

When I was practicing, I'd always thought the offering referred to the earth and bone inside the sarcophagus.

I was horribly wrong.

At first, I didn't know what caused the searing pain in my arms. It tore down the inside of my forearms so suddenly I screamed. Outside the circle, the shadowed forms of Ian, Fynn, and the others reacted, but couldn't break through the circle. Blood dripped down my fingers, but instead of splattering onto the ground, the sarcophagus pulled it inside, like Micha.

I'd reached the end of the incantation, but the miniature tornado was still going full force, maybe even growing stronger. My vision began to spot as more and more blood was pulled from my body. My breath came in short, panicked gasps. I needed to stop the bleeding, but what would happen if I cut it off? What would happen to the spell and the huge amount of magic I'd built up? How could I have misunderstood the incantation so badly?

My right knee buckled. I landed hard, knocking over the book stand. My eyes threatened to close, but I was afraid to let them. I had to find a way to make it stop, but the sarcophagus was pulling power and blood too quickly. My last thought before I blacked out was simple: *We are so fucked.*

***

The first thing I became aware of when I woke up was an intense case of *déjà vu.*

I lay on an uncomfortable bed reeking of antiseptic. Something beeped over my head, and there were bright fluorescent lights burning through my eyelids.

I twitched my fingers slightly, and pain shot from my fingernails all the way up to my elbows, making me groan.

"Evie?"

The familiar, masculine voice made me want to cry. *Oh, god. Not again.*

When I finally managed to crack one eye open, Uncle Mike was leaning over me, scruffy and disheveled. His winter coat was draped over the back of his chair, and he was in just jeans and a cabled sweater. I recognized it as one my grandmother gave him a few years ago for Christmas.

My mouth was so dry that my tongue couldn't form words. Mike reached down and gently took my hand in his, stroking my forehead with the other.

"How do you feel, Ginny-bug?" he asked.

Before I could answer, the door of my room opened and Ian came in with two paper cups of coffee.

"Oh, good. You're awake," he said, offering one of the cups to Mike. When he didn't take it, Ian left it on the bedside table, pulling up a second chair for himself and settling back into it. "You see? I told you she would be just fine." Then, to me, he added, "Your uncle and I have been having a very good talk while you were out."

My mouth worked, but my throat felt like it had been sealed shut. Mike let go of me long enough to grab the giant cup of water sitting next to his coffee and offer me the straw. After taking a few sips, I was able to clear my throat and speak.

"What are you doing here? What time is it?" How long had I been out? It was a good twenty-four hours before I came around last time, but somehow that didn't seem to be the case here.

"I got worried after our last phone call. What were you thinking?" I could feel him building up to a full-blown Cappelli Tirade, but Ian cut him off.

"Maddie found him lurking at Station House Five. When the guard wouldn't let him in, he started raising Cain until Captain Hedge was called. Unfortunately, that was about the same time we were pulling into the ER. You lost quite a bit of blood, but the doctors don't think there will be any lasting effects. Though I do have to make sure you see a Night Shift psychologist before we can put you on active duty."

I looked down at my bandaged wrists and sighed. "I was never *on* active duty. Why can't I just go back to working the front desk?"

"Because anyone with the Sight *has* to be certified, for their own safety. And you would be surprised at just how risky your job is, particularly if you're handling cursed or haunted objects."

I glanced over at Mike, wondering what he thought about all of this. He only shook his head. "Mr. Mulhaney has explained...what you do. I'm still not sure I believe this. It's ridiculous."

"I know it sounds crazy, but it's not. Really." I wasn't sure how I could explain it in a way he would understand. My family weren't exactly believers in the occult or supernatural as it existed outside of Mass.

Mike's face twisted slightly. I'd seen that look before; the one that meant he needed to say something he didn't really want to.

"It explains a surprising amount. When you're in my line of work...you see things. Stuff that can't always be explained by madmen with guns or serial killers or domestic disputes gone wrong." He looked like he wanted to say more, but wasn't willing to give Ian any more credit than he needed to. Still, I caught Ian smiling before he hid it behind his coffee cup.

"Detective Cappelli and I still have a great deal to discuss," he said instead. "We should leave you to get some rest. The doctor said while your wounds are relatively deep, they're very clean, so you'll be able to go home in the morning. Well, later in the morning." He pulled out his pocket watch to check the time. "It is a little after two now. Once you've finished this round of IVs and gotten some sleep, you'll be allowed to leave. Maddie has already volunteered to pick you up at eight. She's very worried about you, as are your other friends. But for now, I think some sleep is in order."

Mike looked like he was about to object, but finally ceded to Ian's more imposing nature. He kissed me on the forehead, squeezing my shoulder. I gave him a light hug, wincing slightly. "Get some sleep, Ginny-bug. I'll see you tomorrow. We need to have a long talk."

"Yeah. I've heard I'm overdue for quite a few of those," I sighed.

The two of them left, turning out the lights behind them. I lay on my back and watched the last dregs of O-negative drip into one tube, while on the other side a combination of fluids and antibiotics drained into my system.

It was so quiet. I could still hear the sounds of the hospital around me—the squeak of rubber soles on linoleum, the gimpy wheel of a cart as it moved down the hall. The clack of keyboards at the nurses' station just outside.

There weren't any ghosts in my room. No former patients, no lost souls. Either the hospital was too new to be saturated in death, or there wasn't anyone clinging to this ward. Or Ian had warded the hell out of my room. Literally.

This was a different quiet. The quiet of being alone in my own head for the first time in nearly a year.

"Micha?" My voice was swallowed up by the dark corners of my room, a weak croak that barely made it to the end of my bed before vanishing.

I called for him again, a little louder, but of course, no one answered.

I wasn't sure if that was a good thing or a bad thing, so I pulled the covers up over my head and tried to sleep.

And if there were salty, wet marks on my pillow, then I have no idea how they might have gotten there.

Chapter Twelve
Necromancers, Cats, and Other Dangerous Creatures

As promised, Maddie picked me up at exactly eight the following morning. I was still tired, but felt a lot better. Most of the sensitivity in my arms and hands had gone away, though my wrists were still sore and covered in bandages.

"How are you?" she asked, announcing her arrival with a light tap on the door frame.

"Hey. I'm fine, I guess."

"I brought you a change of clothes. Ian told me what happened, and I thought you might need them."

"You are amazing," I said, gratefully accepting the plastic grocery bag. I'd gotten into my jeans, which only had a little blood on them, but was still staring my shirt, sweater, and coat, trying to decide if I could get the stains out. My magic didn't seem to be working well that morning; the fibers were reluctant to follow any commands, though I was able to flake off a little of the blood on my sweater.

I changed into the new outfit and followed Maddie

out, stopping briefly at the nurses' station for my discharge paperwork. Maddie had to help me with some of it, since I'd never had to deal with an American hospital or insurance before.

"I got your insurance number from Ian. It should all be taken care of through the Night Shift. One good thing about working for a shadow organization— *fantastic* health and dental." She checked off the last box with a flourish, handed me the clipboard and pointed to the spot I needed to initial, and then we were out the door.

"You should know you're some kind of celebrity now around the dorms. Everyone is talking about you."

"Why?" How did they even know what happened?

"Well, it *might* have gotten out that you're the reason security got beefed up. And that you were working on a super-top-secret magic project with Ian. Which of course, means everyone has heard about it. Or at least, they think they have." She winked at me.

"You've been making up stories about me and spreading them around, haven't you?"

Maddie grinned. "Maybe."

I rolled my eyes, but I wasn't mad. It was hard not to get caught up in Maddie's sense of humor.

Much to my surprise, someone had decorated the door of my room while I was gone. "What's this?" I asked, pinching the paper streamer forming a border around the cards and notes tapped to the heavy wood door.

"Duck put that together. He got a couple of guys from his floor to help him. You made quite the impression. Something about dealing with a certain ghost?"

Get well soon.

We miss you! Good luck.
Good luck to you and Micha.

A surprising number of the little notes had Micha's name on them. Suddenly able to communicate to more people than just me, he'd started making friends, too, talking to other students in the hall while I was studying or in class, giving me a chance to be on my own for a little while every day, while still knowing all I had to do was think about him, and he'd be there.

I hadn't even realized the change, much. He usually picked times when I was distracted by something else. The whole time I'd been focused on getting us to the point where we could have separate lives, he'd been concentrating on the after, making it so we would have solid foundations away from each other, but still be able to come back to that middle ground, that place where we existed so well—that space between wakefulness and sleep, the one where it was just the two of us.

"Oh, now don't you go crying on me," Maddie teased gently, reaching into her pocket for a tissue.

"Sorry. Just...no one has ever done anything like this for me before." I was the kind of person who had maybe one or two close friends, if that. It was strange to think my classmates had even noticed I was in the room.

"Come on, Bambi. You're not going to sit out here in the hall all day and admire them, are you?"

"...Maybe." My voice *might* have been a little higher than usual.

Maddie finally got me into my room, ordering me to sleep until lunch time. "I'll come back, just to make sure you eat something. You're too skinny."

"Thanks."

"I'll see you then." She sighed. "Too bad we can't

all get day passes for PT."

***

Despite strict orders to rest, I never quite made it to my bed. No sooner had I hung up my coat on the hook behind my door than my cell phone rang. It took me a minute to find where it was hiding in the pocket of my dirty jeans, way at the bottom of the grocery store sack.

"Hi, Uncle Mike."

"Hey, Ginny-bug. I'm downstairs, at the front gate. Can you come down so we can talk?"

I tried to hide my sigh, but I think he heard it anyway. "Yeah, I'll be right down."

I made a second attempt to remove the blood from my coat, this time managing to convince the nylon to shake off most of the reddish stains, and exchanged my gray sweater for an over-sized angora one I'd picked up with Maddie in royal purple and pearl gray stripes. I glanced in the mirror, made a face at my reflection's pale face, shadowed eyes, and messy hair, then grabbed a hat to cover the worst of it. I was pulling on my coat before I remembered to snip off the hospital ID bracelet.

Mike waited in a white rental car just outside the front gate. I waved at the two Night Shift officers on guard, huddled in their thick winter coats and clutching steaming buckets of coffee. I winced a little when I remembered they were supposed to be there to keep *me* safe.

"You're the Cappelli kid, aren't you?" asked the man, looking up at me as I passed.

I thought briefly about pulling a *these are not the droids you are looking for* on them, but then reluctantly nodded.

199

"I'm sorry, but we can't let you out without an escort. Ian's orders."

"Look, I'm just going to talk to my uncle. See that guy in the car there? He's family. He's a cop. I'm not going far."

He frowned, and then leaned over to discuss it with his partner, a woman who was bundled up in so many layers I could only make out was her dark face, framed between a chunky black scarf and a fleece-lined leather aviator hat with the ear flaps pulled down. "What do you think, Mills?"

"You say he's family?"

I nodded again.

"Well, if he's an Adder, then I suppose you'll be safe enough. Just make sure you stay close, and don't be long, okay?"

I nodded, biting my tongue. It didn't really matter that Mike was from the *other* side of the family, did it?

Nah, why would it?

Mills and her partner opened the gate and I slipped out, ducking gratefully into the warm interior of the sedan.

"What was all of that about?" Mike asked.

"Nothing. Just saying hi. Why don't we go get some coffee?"

It wasn't like I was the type of person to spend all day out and about, or partying all night or anything, but after nearly a week of being stuck inside Station House Five, with nowhere to go that didn't involve another member of the Night Shift, I was more than happy for a chance to go someplace else. Maybe if I was *really* lucky, I could talk Mike into taking me to a yarn shop. I'd found one online that looked promising, but hadn't had a chance to ask Maddie to take me.

I directed Mike to the little cafe where Brianna and I had our ill-fated meeting. If the two guards had been concerned about us, they really needn't have bothered. I spotted Dan May, my L&R instructor, in one corner with his laptop, and four or five other trainees from the regular track going over essays at one of the larger tables, exchanging notes on telekinesis and other forms of psychic ability.

We got our drinks and claimed a table near the back, continuing the shallow conversation from the car—how cold the weather was and how bad the traffic; the way cab drivers always drove like they had a death wish, no matter what city they were in, and the annoyance of being caught behind a city bus.

Mike leaned back in his chair, sipping a cup of black coffee—two sugars—cradling the mug for a moment before setting it down on the table—effectively laying out his cards at the same time. He reached into the pocket of his coat, producing his cell phone, and slid it toward me.

"Call your mom."

I sat rigidly with my cup, inhaling the fragrance of cream and caffeine and trying to take comfort from the warmth.

He sighed. "I know you're angry. You have every right to be. But your parents are worried about you." I started to object, but he cut me off. "I don't care if they gave birth to you or not, they raised you. They took care of you. I remember when you were two, and you came down sick and had to go to the ER. Whooping cough. Your dad took you to the hospital and stayed up all night with you until the doctor said you were okay to go home. Your mom was down visiting her parents in London, and was so worried. She took the first train back."

I stared at the phone between us. I had no memory of the incident, though it had been recounted from time to time. There was an enormous plush rabbit—the squishiest rabbit on the planet, as I had dubbed it— sitting on my bed back at my parents' house, a gift my mom found at the London train station. Well, it was sitting on my bed the last time I saw it. If they hadn't turned my bedroom into a man cave or a craft room or something in the year I'd been gone.

"Everything they've done, they've done because they thought it was the best thing for you in the long run. Maybe they were wrong. Maybe we all were. But believe me, Evie, we've been trying to protect you. Even Izzy knows that. She was angry at first, but she came around, eventually. We love you."

I could feel a dangerous prickle in my eyes. I wasn't sure I knew the words for what I was feeling, and suddenly found myself missing Micha with a terrible ache, like my entire chest had been hollowed out.

"Then why aren't they the ones here?" I growled at last. I put down my drink. I was clutching it so hard I could almost hear the ceramic groaning under the strain.

"They didn't think you would talk to them."

"Damn right." I pushed the phone back across the table.

"Evie, you have to understand. They're in a rough place right now, too. After everything, they're trying to do what is right. To respect your space. But they'll still be there when you're ready."

I turned away, folding my arms protectively over my chest. I didn't want to talk about this. I didn't want to deal with it.

They kept saying they were trying to respect my space, but that was a first. They'd been so concerned about where I went and who I was with, what I did, how I spent my money, how many hours I worked or if I did my homework, but they had never once asked how I felt about anything. The moment I started to object to anything, to voice an opinion they didn't like, then I was just complaining. The last six months I'd been home, how many times had I been told to just grow up? To just act like an adult? To stop *whining* about everything?

Because that was all it was to them. I'd been less than five minutes away from bleeding out on the kitchen floor, but I was just complaining. Just trying to get attention, instead of acting like the grown woman I was suddenly supposed to be, based on my birth date.

Less than a month at home, and my dad was cracking "jokes" about how they needed to replace the linoleum in the kitchen because of the blood stains. But no, I was the one who was taking trivial concerns too seriously.

All of this spun through my head, and I didn't know how to articulate any of it in a way the Mike could understand. When I'd been at St. Mary's, and later in my sessions with Dr. A, I'd been able to describe what I was feeling and thinking, and they were able to make sense of it. But the doctors were trained in that kind of thing; my family wasn't. My family had a completely different view of mental illness, and they weren't willing to change it. Regardless of the cause, I was supposed to be able to flip a switch and "handle it."

I put down my drink, pushing it away. Maybe I wasn't doing the right thing by ignoring my family. But it was the only thing that kept me moving forward.

Talking to them made me revert back to who I was before St. Mary's, the girl who hid in her room, who didn't speak out. The one that didn't have any hope or ambition for the future.

I might still be struggling, but at least I had things to hang on to now.

"You've been gone a long time," Mike pleaded. "We all miss you. It's time to come home. What were you thinking, coming all the way down here without telling anyone?"

I'd been staring absently at a stain on the table, but my head shot up at his words. "I was thinking I needed to get away. That there's an entire part of my life I didn't even know about. That I *can't* go back home. I can't do it again, Mike. You of all people should know that."

Winter break, the year before. The dull period between Christmas and New Years when nothing happens. Home alone for the fifth day in a row. Nowhere to go, no one to talk to. Everything building up inside. Realizing just how little I meant to the people around me.

I didn't expect anyone to find me until my parents returned at the beginning of January, but Mike had stopped by with Chinese food to find me bleeding out on the kitchen floor. One more red light, a traffic jam on the way, and he would have been too late.

Sometimes, in retrospect, I wondered if Micha had something to do with his timely arrival.

He hung his head briefly. "Evie, you have to understand—"

"No. I've been trying to understand for my entire life. I've tried it their way, and *it doesn't work*. I'm not going back to that." I pushed myself away from the table, backing toward the door. "We don't have any common ground anymore. I've been trying to build bridges since I could speak, but no one bothered to meet me halfway until I moved to Montreal."

"Now that's not fair—"

"No. It's not. But nothing ever is, is it?"

I turned on my heel, striding toward the door. Mike grabbed his coat, hastily stuffing his arms through the sleeves as he called after me.

I hated fighting with him. Mike was one of the few people I'd been able to turn to growing up. He *had* been through a lot. I knew it hurt him to find me. I knew it had been difficult.

But not once had anyone ever asked how I wound up on the linoleum in the first place.

The bell over the door chimed when I opened it. The cold air was a slap in the face, one I needed desperately. The wind dried up tears that hadn't had a chance to fall. I sucked in a deep breath of it, and then I ran.

I was still tired from the ordeal the night before, but adrenaline kept me moving. Maybe PT was actually working and I was getting stronger. I don't know.

Mike's voice echoed behind me, his words carried away by the wind. I ignored them and ran faster.

I rounded a corner and stopped to catch my breath, needles of cold stabbing into my lungs and the back of my throat. For a moment, I doubted my own actions. Was I right in all of this?

I was distracted though, when I caught sight of a familiar face, leering at me from across the street.

Phillip Dare, necromancer, stood in front of a red brick apartment building with boarded up windows, watching me.

A chill that had nothing to do with November in Chicago ran down my spine. I reached into my pocket for my cell phone. Hadn't Ian said they were all arrested? Or at least brought in for questioning?

If Dare was out on the street, that meant they didn't have probable cause, right?

My hand relaxed. I checked traffic and then jogged across the street to him.

"Genevra Cappelli."

"It's Evie," I corrected him.

His lip curled slightly, and I got the impression he wasn't very happy to see me. "I haven't seen you out and about lately."

It's not like we have regular coffee dates or anything, I thought. "I've been busy."

"Yes. I'm sure you have. I was just looking for you. I have something of Brianna's you might be interested in."

I looked at him in confusion, but he only smiled, gesturing for me to follow him.

He led me up the walk to the apartment building, unlocking the grated iron door with a little brass key.

Inside was gloomy and damp. It smelled a bit like mold, and somewhere water dripped. Spray painted tags covered the peeling wallpaper.

"This used to be a lovely old house. Single family," he said off-handedly, leading me up the stairs. "Then, in the seventies, it was chopped up into these horrid little apartments. That was around the time the neighborhood started to go downhill."

"I'm not sure what you mean. It seems pretty nice, to me." Well, maybe not the building. I heard something scuttle away on the next landing and suppressed a shudder. But the neighborhood was pretty cute, and there were a lot of mom and pop shops—an Indian grocery, a Japanese bakery, and an amazing Jewish deli where Maddie liked to get sandwiches.

When I spoke, my breath formed a white cloud in front of me. *Some landlord. Is the heat even on?* I wondered.

"Yes, well. It's gone through many changes in the last forty years. But it was once a grand old house. Lovely wood floors. Stained glass." He pointed to a high window, just visible at the very top floor. "Just like that one. All of these were the same." Dare gestured to the little octagonal windows bringing light to each of the landings. Some were boarded up. All were filthy. Some were missing panes. Most of them were just a single piece of clear glass. "The neighborhood children don't have any respect for property. Every year, another window breaks, or someone decides to deface a wall."

A particularly foul odor hit me as we climbed the next set of stairs. At the top, something that might once have been a raccoon was decomposing in a corner.

"Do people still live here?" I gagged, covering my mouth with one hand.

"Not many. Here we are." He took out another key, unlocking the door at the very top. The bright colors of the stained glass window fell on his back, painting him in a jewel-toned floral motif speckled with the shadows of dirt and grime.

The door opened on an empty apartment, banging back against a broken refrigerator in olive drab. Beside it was a matching oven that would have been only just large enough for a casserole dish. A small one.

The floors creaked as he strode across them. In places the wood curled up hazardously, and in others there were entire strips missing.

I looked around, taking in crumbling plaster and the hole in the living room window. "Why did you bring me here?" I asked, suddenly afraid. I should have paid more attention. This was going to end very badly.

Dare spun suddenly on his heel to face me. "Because I need you."

Then he pulled out the Taser.

***

The next time I opened my eyes, I was laying on my side on the filthy floor, trapped inside a circle ringed with black, red, and white candles. The circle was drawn in charcoal, and ringed in something red I really didn't want to think about.

Dare stood over me, chanting in Latin. My Latin wasn't the best, despite Catholic school and years of Mass, but I was pretty sure I caught the words "drawing out of the soul," which did not bode well for me at all.

Already weakened, I could barely move my fingers. I tried to concentrate on my powers. Maybe I could tie his shoelaces together, or make his pants unravel or something. Something that would distract him from the spell long enough for me to escape. It was no use, though. The circle cut off my powers.

Dare's voice changed pitch slightly, rising to a crescendo. The inner circle, the red, began to glow ominously. When he opened his eyes, they had the same feverish light.

At each of the compass points of the circle lay a golden drachma, just like the one Brianna had given me. Two of them shone with spiritual energy, the ethereal glow of a ghost. When I reached for them, I

208

sensed the souls trapped inside. One was unfamiliar, but the other, I was sure, was Brianna.

The third coin was dull, but as I watched it began to glow as well. The weaker I felt, the brighter it became. I started to panic, struggling to rise, but I couldn't even lift my head.

He was using them all along! I realized. The *drachma* weren't a gift of friendship to his fellow Ferrymen. He was using them, leeching out their souls. He'd been the one behind everything—the murders, Micha's fit in the mausoleum. Maddie seemed genuinely afraid when I told her what he was, and suddenly I understood why.

I squeezed my eyes shut, concentrating all my energy on getting up. I had to get out of here, but I could feel him draining off my soul, all my life force, into that stupid coin.

I am not going down like this. Not in some disgusting, condemned apartment building. Not to some psychopath who steals souls.

When I opened my eyes again, I was no closer to escaping, but there was something else in the room with us. Behind Dare's legs, I could see something lurking in the shadows. It came toward us languidly, as though it couldn't care less about Dare and his spell, or what it was doing to me.

It stopped just outside the circle. Though it was less than a meter from Dare, he didn't seem to notice the black and white cat seated beside him, calmly cleaning one white paw.

Dracula?

The cat lowered his paw and stared at me with that grumpy glare all cats have. He seemed to say, *look what you've gone and done now. I just can't leave you alone, can I?*

There was no mistaking the semi-feral cat. At least twenty pounds, solid black except for his bib, paws, and the three "buttons" running down his stomach, I'd fed him every morning since I came to live with Izzy.

He gave a wide yawn, displaying a pink tongue and his over-long canines, then leaned forward in a massive stretch, digging his claws into the floor and reaching his tail and back end to the ceiling. As he pulled himself back up again, he left little gouges in the wood that sliced right through both the inner and outer circles.

With a *snap*, the magic retracted. Dare stumbled backwards, falling as the power recoiled. Suddenly I didn't feel so weak anymore.

Scrambling to my knees, I grabbed for the three coins, his source of power. But Dare was already recovering. On all fours, he lunged at me. "Give those back!"

His hands on my throat, I tried to remember what we'd been taught during the self-defense portion of PT.

I did have one advantage: I was taller. With the coins still closed in my fist, I drove it into his jaw. He bounced back, driven away by my longer reach. I kicked out and landed both feet on his stomach, winding him as he tumbled away.

I managed to get my feet under me and sprinted for the door. Dare howled, but I had to get out of range of that Taser.

He hadn't bothered to lock the apartment door during his set up. Who would bother breaking into an abandoned building?

Clamoring down the stairs, I jumped the last three steps to the landing, pivoted with the aid of the rickety banister, and then continued down the next flight of stairs. On the floor above came the pounding footsteps of my pursuer. I was halfway through the second floor when there was a shrill scream, then a deeper yell followed by a series of loud bangs as something heavy tumbled down the top flight. Three seconds later Drac streaked past at roughly the speed of sound. I caught up to him in the entryway, where he crouched by the door. I barreled through, letting him out with me, and crashed right into Mike's arms.

"What—"

"He's right behind me!"

Maddie pushed us both out of the way. An instant later Dare skidded to a halt, bracing himself on the doorframe. Before I could blink, Maddie reached out, shocking him as effectively as any Taser.

"That is...a very cool trick," I panted. My wrist throbbed and I shook it gently, wincing.

"Are you okay? Did he hurt you?" Mike asked, holding me at arm's length to get a good look.

"I'm fine," I replied, and was instantly crushed to his chest again.

Maddie knelt next to Dare, locking him into a zip-tie. When he regained muscle control, she hauled him to his feet and started reading his Miranda rights. Somehow, I thought that was more of a show for Mike than anything else. Dan had made it pretty clear that when you worked for the Night Shift, the bulk of suspects did not survive long enough to get arrested.

In daylight, restrained and being led away by Maddie—who continued to give him light shocks if he struggled or dragged his feet—I couldn't help but feel a little bit bad. He was a little old man, and seemed surprisingly weak and vulnerable.

But then I remembered the coins clutched in my

fist. This little old man had murdered two women in cold blood.

"Why? Why kill them? They were your friends," I asked as he was marched past.

Dare shot a vicious glare in my direction. "They were a means to an end. They could have brought back my wife and daughter, but you had to go and spoil everything. I wouldn't even need Basara and Jin if I had you and that ghost. It would have saved lives."

"Yes, killing people sounds like a great way to save lives." Maddie rolled her eyes and nudged him forward again with a spark to the lower back, just as a nondescript black SUV that could only be law enforcement pulled up to the curb. She helped the newcomers load Philip Dare into the back seat.

"There's one thing I don't understand," I said, putting a hand out to stop her from closing the door.

He looked up at me through narrowed eyes. I licked my lips. "The others were trying to recruit me. Why didn't you just wait? Why didn't you just wait for them to gain my trust, instead of sending those zombies to kill me?"

Dare only blinked, snorting. "You really are just as stupid as I first thought. I didn't send anyone or anything after you. And I don't make zombies. Don't you even know what a necromancer *is*?"

I opened my mouth, but nothing came out. Maddie pulled me back. The car door slammed shut, and the SUV pulled away from the curb.

"You're sure you're okay? He didn't hurt you?" Mike asked again. He looked a little confused. I took *are you okay* to mean *Zombies? Did you hit your head?*

"I'm sure." I was pretty sure I was still in shock or

something, and in about twenty minutes I'd collapse in a heap and have a good cry and maybe freak out a little bit because someone had tried to kill me, but it was hardly the first time that had happened this week. I came out alright on the other end, so for the moment, the freak out could wait.

Something rubbed against my ankles. I looked down to see Dracula waiting patiently for his reward. I knelt down and scooped him up, snuggling him affectionately. He was good enough to tolerate it, for once.

"You are such a good kitty. You're getting tuna tonight," I cooed. The big cat purred like a Harley, though from his expression it was clear he resented such a flagrant display of affection. I promised not to tell the other cats back in Montreal; his reputation would remain unblemished.

Mike stared at the cat. "Did you bring your cat with you?"

"No. He brought himself." I had no idea how, but for the moment, I was grateful.

Maddie finished talking to the officers, who drove away. She paused when she saw me holding the cat. "Is that...?"

"This is Dracula," I said, introducing them. I wasn't stupid enough to try the cute little paw wave with Drac. He was not that kind of cat.

"Dracula," Maddie deadpanned.

"Yep. I don't know how he got here, but he's definitely my cat. See the fangs? And look, he's even got a little bowtie." I pointed to the black mark in the middle of his bib.

"I...well...Yes, I definitely see the fangs," Maddie said. Why did she look so exasperated?

I told them how Drac had saved me by breaking the power circle. It was still strange to talk about those kinds of things in front of Mike, but if Ian had told him everything...

"And you have no idea how he got here?" Mike asked.

"None."

"I can think of a few ways," Maddie mumbled.

"Well, he saved you, so I won't complain," my uncle said, reaching out to scratch Drac's ears. Before I could warn him, the cat lashed out with teeth and claws, leaving puncture marks on his hand.

I winced. "Sorry, I forgot to warn you. He's a biter. I'm the only one that can pick him up. Sometimes." Really, Drac was being remarkably patient. He must have missed me.

"I'll just bet he is," Maddie said, a strange expression on her face. I looked at her in askance, but Mike was already ushering us back toward the rental car. Maddie quickly agreed, and asked him to drop us off at Station House Two.

Fifteen minutes later—and a lot of swearing on Mike's part—we were parked in front of the decrepit Municipal Utility building.

"What is wrong with the drivers in this city?" he asked the universe at large as we climbed out.

"Still not as bad as Montreal," I replied.

Mike snorted. "We aren't going to talk about Montreal."

I was about to suggest someone stay behind with Drac, but before I could open my mouth he'd leaped down and trotted up the steps to the front door where he sat and waited patiently for us mere humans to catch up.

"What, you think you're coming to this meeting?" I asked, following a few meters behind.

"I honestly don't think you'd be able to stop him," Maddie said.

"Of course not. He's a cat."

"That's not...that's not what I meant..." she mumbled.

Drac led the way to Ian's office with the three of us following behind like over-sized ducklings.

The officers on duty who noticed the cat invariably stopped to look. Some chuckled. Others tilted their heads quizzically while others simply stared, unable to believe their eyes. When we reached Ian's office, someone else was coming out. The man had black hair and gray eyes, and was carrying a sports bottle that seemed incongruous with his leather jacket and worn out jeans.

He stopped and stared at Drac. Drac stopped and stared at him, and then let out one surprisingly high pitched meow.

"Hi," the man said, addressing the cat. He blinked a few times, an absent look coming over his face. "I always wondered what happened to that cat."

That made me pause. "How do you know my cat?"

He seemed to shake himself out whatever world he was in long enough to spare me a glance. "Hm? Oh, me? No. Nope. Never. Vampire cats? What a ridiculous thing to mention. Never seen one before. Silly idea."

"Vampire cats? What about vampire cats?"

"I didn't say anything about vampire cats. Definitely never seen one before." He took a quick swig from his sports bottle that made me wonder what exactly was in it.

"Hi, Caspian," Maddie said as she blew past.

Still pulling on the bottle he raised his hand in a wave and then vanished around the corner.

"What was that about?" I asked.

Maddie just sighed. "Sometimes, Bambi, I think it's better if you just don't ask."

Chapter Thirteen:
Extremely Stupid Decisions

Our meeting with Ian was short. Once the other Ferrymen were cleared of helping Dare, Ian assured me Basara, Harmony, and Jin would be released. Since Dare planned to kill them eventually, too, it made the interrogations go a bit faster.

Though there was still some debate on the origin of the zombie attacks, the guards were removed from Station House Five during daylight hours. Ian still insisted Dare or another Ferryman could be behind it since there were different types of necromancy, but he also said the budget and their personnel were stretched too thin as it was. With the number one suspect in custody, he had to pull the guards. Even if I still had an angry cult after me. Still, there would be security at the front gate and he warned me not to leave the premises without an escort.

"And if they don't have a Night Shift badge, they don't count as an escort," Ian said pointedly as I turned to leave.

I nodded sheepishly.

And so began five of the dullest weeks of my entire life. Through the rest of November and into December my life followed a routine: wake up at six to get ready for PT; shower, change, and eat lunch before the more academic courses of the afternoon. Three days a week, and on some weekends, I and some of the other trainees also trained with Night Shift officers in how to use any special abilities we might have. Though Ian initially intended for me to train with Howl, that changed at the last minute and I wound up working with a telekinetic named Alexander. At first, he was flummoxed by my ability to control fibers, but eventually he decided to just roll with it. Even after five weeks, I still wasn't sure if Alexander was his first name or his last name.

At the encouragement of Maddie and Duck, I started studying in the common room on the second floor, where some of the other accelerated students gathered for a study group, as well as some of the others. I found out the three former cops in the class were a wealth of knowledge when it came to Law & Order, and Raimes knew more about magical beings than almost anyone, even Maddie.

Sundays were Adder family dinners. Every week the crowd seemed to get a little bigger. Shannon and her husband weren't regular features, but came when they could. Connor's parents flew in from Columbus to meet me. My newfound grandmother barely looked old enough to have adult children, let alone grandchildren, which was a far cry from Grandma Roberta, who had been complaining she was too old to do anything for nearly my entire life. Olivia Adder reminded me a bit of my mom's mother, Granny Siobhán: comfortable, feisty red-haired women (though Granny Siobhán's came from a bottle) who would gladly bake cookies and feed them to their grandchildren until they exploded. I supposed it must be an Irish thing.

It was at one of these dinners that I finally convinced someone to take me to a yarn shop. I was going insane without something to do with my hands, and suddenly finding myself without my constant companion was not helping. Fynn, who also turned out to be a knitter, offered to take me. When he showed up wearing an illusion knit scarf that read *Fuck you!*, I made a mental note of the pattern. Izzy, I knew, would wear the hell out of one.

I studied. I knit. I even made a few friends. After a while, I could feel myself leveling off—my anxiety started to even out, and I didn't have such a strong urge to hide in my room all the time.

Still, something felt off.

It didn't help that I was bored out of my mind.

Which goes a long way to explaining why I let Duck talk me into something incredibly stupid.

It was Friday night, the end of our second-to last week of training. Monday would begin a rigorous series of exams in everything from firearms, self-defense, and physical fitness, to the laws and protocols we would be expected to follow and uphold. There would even be a written and a practical for dealing with the paranormal.

"If I study any more my brain is going to explode," I sighed, collapsing onto my notebook. We were seated at our usual table in the library, the one in the back by the window. It had the best light and was conveniently located between the bathroom and the law section.

"I can't believe they even made you take this class, since you're Canadian," Duck said, taking another shot of his energy drink.

I mumbled into my notes. "The worst part is my boss will probably send me to another training program as soon as I get back so I can get the Quebec version."

"Yeah, but you'll just have to take the law portion again, right? And I'm sure a lot of it will carry over."

I raised my head just enough to give him a disbelieving look. "Clearly, you have never been to Quebec."

Duck smiled, raising the black and green can in my direction before drinking. "You know what we should do? We should take a break."

"Yes. That sounds like a fantastic idea." I pushed my chair back, slapping my notebook and text closed.

"We should get out of here."

Wait. "What do you mean, 'get out of here?'"

"I mean, get out of here. We've been cooped up in this library for ages, and when was the last time you just went out and had a little fun? You didn't even come with us last weekend when we went to Tony's." Tony's was the pub down the road. While the early birds hung out at the cafe, sipping double espressos, the night owls went to Tony's. I'd gone once with Duck, Maddie, and the others, but loud, crowded bars weren't my hangout of choice. I preferred quieter places where actual conversations could be had.

"I'm really not in the mood for Tony's," I said. I wanted to do something, sure, but not that.

"What about a movie?"

"A movie?" I checked my watch. It was almost ten o'clock. "Is anything playing this late?"

"Sweetie, this is Chicago. We're the city that never sleeps."

"I thought that was New York?"

"Fine, we're a close second."

"Aren't you from Columbus?"

"Stop splitting hairs."

I was about to object, but Duck was already piling

up our books. He gathered them all into his arms and started walking briskly toward the door, leaving me to catch up.

"Hey! I need my stuff back!"

"Nope! I'm holding it hostage until you loosen up a little!" he called over his shoulder, nudging the library door open with a hip, then broke into a run

I jogged after him, boots crunching in the thin layer of newly fallen snow. The wind had kicked up while we were studying. It jerked the end of my scarf and threatened to pull off the beret I'd just finished the night before. I clamped it down with one hand and swore at the cold as I added an extra burst of speed. For the first time, I was a little bit grateful for all of that extra PT Hamm made me do.

I finally caught up in the entryway of the dorm, crashing into Duck and punching his shoulder. "Give me my stuff back!"

He held it high over his head with a grin. "Your notes will be returned to you after you agree to go do something fun. Outside of campus."

I dropped my arms. "Duck, I already told you. I can't. Security is too tight. We'd never get out of here."

He made a sound like a buzzer. "That, my friend, is incorrect! There is a way out without tripping the wards or alerting our jailers."

"They aren't jailers. They're just doing their jobs."

"So are jailers. Now, go get your purse or whatever you girls take with you when you go out, and meet me in the cafeteria in five minutes. No more! Or else you'll never see your precious notes again!" He gave me a crazy-eyed stare, like he was some kind of serial killer with a vendetta against spiral bound notebooks.

Finally, I caved. I might be a homebody by nature,

but even I was going stir crazy. "Fine. But we're not going to that post-apocalyptic thing that just came out."

"Why? What's wrong with explosions and end of the world terror?"

"Nothing. But the main character is supposed to be Asian, not Texan, and they butchered the book."

"You read the book first?"

I gave him another Look. "Of course I read the book first. What do I look like, some kind of heathen?"

He laughed. "Okay, okay. We won't go to that one. Now hurry up and get ready!"

***

As promised, we met at the specified place a few minutes later. Though there were still plenty of people awake, most of them had retired from the stiff-backed chairs of the dining room to the worn out upholstered ones in the common areas.

The cafeteria was eerie without the bustle of starving, exhausted trainees, illuminated only by the light in the various vending machines and a single bank of fluorescents at the back of the room.

"Why here?"

Duck grinned, gesturing for me to follow him. He pulled out a mini flashlight, shining a path through the maze of appliances and stainless steel counters in the kitchen, until we came to a locked door, half hidden behind a metal rack of canned goods.

Well, I *thought* it was locked, until Duck pulled the latch right off.

"Raimes found this place a couple of weeks ago, when security was really tight and they were enforcing the curfew." The curfew period had been brief, and was lifted once Dare was arrested. Not that I'd needed anyone to tell me to be back on campus by midnight. I was usually asleep by then, anyway.

I peered around his shoulder at a long, dark descent. There was a narrow staircase on the left, and on the right, a slide. "What is it?"

"Our escape. Now hurry up."

I started to take the stairs, but Duck was having none of it. "Come on!" He grabbed me around the waist, and then we were both careening down the slide into the depths below.

I screamed bloody murder the whole way. The deeper we went, the stronger the chills running up and down my arms got; my sweater and coat did nothing to drive them way. It came from a deeper cold than mere air temperature.

It wasn't until we tumbled off at the bottom in a heap that I realized where I'd felt that penetrating cold before before—Hekate's cave.

I landed in a heap on the concrete floor, with Duck half on top of me and a lot less air in my lungs than I'd started with.

Duck rolled off, laughing. I coughed until I could breathe again. "M-Morgue. We're in the freaking morgue." Death hung all around us in the air. It didn't cling and linger the way it did in the hospital. This wasn't a place where people had died; this was only a place where the dead had been. Like a cemetery, there was a stillness in the air, like the particles themselves were reluctant to disturb the space. It was a less oppressive atmosphere than spaces that held the dying. The difference between *dead* and *dying* might be subtle, but it's a very important distinction.

"Yeah," Duck gasped, still catching his own breath.

"I didn't want to freak you out."

Standing, I brushed myself off. "It doesn't freak me out. Not really." I'd spent the summer talking to ghosts and patrolling nursing homes, hospitals, and graveyards so I could meet Hekate's quota.

"Oh, good. You had me worried there for a minute, with all the screaming."

"I was sliding down a creepy tunnel in the dark. Of course I was screaming!"

Duck retrieved the flashlight, and led the way toward the exit. I followed behind, rummaging in my bag.

"Do you have another flashlight?" he asked curiously. His was bright for the size, but it wasn't quite enough for two people.

"No. But I think this will work." I produced a large needle from my bag—an eleven millimeter straight needle.

"I think it's a little late to be whipping up a scarf for this trip," Duck said, raising an eyebrow.

It was my turn to grin. Holding the shaft in one hand, I twisted the knob at the base. "*Lumos!*"

When he finally finished laughing, Duck asked "Why is there a light up knitting needle in your bag?"

"Well, you said we're going to the movies, and these are kind of meant for knitting through movies..."

"Do you knit *everywhere?*"

"Not in PT," I said defensively. "But most other places. I've actually been doing a little less of it the past few weeks because of training." Training kept me occupied and exhausted, neither of which was good for learning a new kind of heel turn, or trying to keep track of a lace pattern.

"Less? This is less? I've hardly seen you without

yarn since we met."

"It's part of my therapy."

"Therapy?"

"Never mind. Let's just get going before we miss
our movie. What are we going to see, anyway?"

Gamely ignoring my awkward segue, Duck
shrugged and turned back in the direction of the exit
again. "I don't know. There's a little independent
theater a few blocks from here. They have one screen
that's dedicated to classics and cult films. For
Halloween they had a Hitchcock marathon, but I'm not
sure what's running right now. Probably something for
the holidays."

I'd nearly forgotten how close we were to
Christmas. I guess I'd been trying not to think about it
too much, since it looked like I'd probably be spending
it alone. I swallowed a hard lump in my throat and
clutched my needle a little tighter. I'd come so far in
just twelve months, but I wasn't sure I could go through
another Christmas like the year before.

Our lights bounced off abandoned equipment and
crumbling brick walls festooned with spider webs. The
webs, more than any knowledge of what the basement
used to hold, made me shudder.

"Where does this lead, anyway?" I asked, ducking
under a dangling web. We'd abandoned the larger main
room where we came in for a long, damp passage that
smelled strongly of mold and dust.

"This comes out by the back gate. There's an old
outbuilding there where they used to take deliveries,
then bring them down here. It's locked up now, so they
don't really add much extra security there. As long as
the werewolves aren't the ones on guard duty tonight,
we should be able to get out without a problem."

Werewolves. Of course there were werewolves.

The cobwebs were thicker now, clinging to my sleeves and catching in my long black ponytail.

The goosebumps got thicker, too. My heart began to race. I stopped trying to peel off the webs, raising my light high to see around us.

We were surrounded. Just at the edge of the weak circle of illumination, the spiders crouched, shoulder to shoulder—if arachnids even had shoulders—hemming us in.

The dusty, moldy smell of the basement was suddenly overpowered by something new. Something fetid and sour, like rotten meat thrown on a grill and left too long. Gagging, I reeled back. "Duck?"

"Yeah?" he was still trying to peel off the web stuck to his sleeve.

"You need to run now."

"What?"

"Run. Get out of here. Get Ian. Or someone. Just go!" As I spoke, the threads seemed to become sentient, snaking their way up my arms and legs. By the weak beams of our lights, a huge shape loomed up at the end of the hall.

No way am I doing this again! I thought. I'd been wrapped up in the cocoon from hell way too many times, but the spider silk was beyond my control. Someone else was commanding the fibers, and I had a sneaking suspicion I knew exactly who that person was.

My warning was too late, however. No sooner were the words out of my mouth than the spider silk began to multiply, growing like an uncontrolled lichen up Duck's legs and arms, pinning them together. I tried to pull it back, to reel it in before he was smothered, but the silk was not under my command.

Duck dropped his flashlight, flailing and fighting but unable to break the strands. Terror froze on his face and he screamed as it covered his head, encasing him completely.

The shadow lumbered toward me. With a shove, the zombie threw Duck's cocoon against the wall, where it slumped and slid to the floor slowly, sticky fibers clinging to the concrete wall.

I screamed, but he didn't seem to notice or care, merely grunting as he hoisted me up by a fistful of spider silk. My feet left the ground. He leaned in close, the rank smell of him filling my lungs as he bared his teeth.

Footsteps. I glanced up just long enough to see Anaïs Traverse materialize out of the shadows. She had traded in her '50s style skirt suit for black slacks and a pea coat, but the cat-eye glasses were exactly as I remembered. She looked way too put together for someone who had spent the last six months running from the cops.

"Now, now. Don't go breaking her yet," she said in French.

"Stop it! Let me go!" The closer she got, the stronger the silk wound itself around me. I was starting to lose ground. I pleaded with her again, this time in French, but when it came to super villains, Traverse wasn't a very good one, despite her powers. Or maybe she was excellent—she didn't indulge in those speeches about how she was going to beat me, revealing her entire plan. She let Madge Kelly handle all of that, preferring to watch in silence with an almost bored expression on her face while I struggled. The spider silk tightened uncomfortably, layer upon layer adding to the shell, as fast as I could peel it back.

A door opened, echoing down the lonely passage. More footsteps, and then Kelly and the other zombie were there with Traverse. The former literature professor looked just as smug and arrogant as the last time I'd seen her. Her gray pixie cut was hidden under a knit cap, and her hands buried deep in the pockets of her trench coat. She looked like she was out for a winter stroll.

The zombie holding me turned, walking a few paces to drop me at her feet. Kelly *tsked*. "Genevra Cappelli. At last we meet again." She said it pleasantly, triumph smoothing down the rough edges of her voice.

"It's Evie," I snapped. For a moment, my bonds loosened, several meters of silk uncoiling and falling to the floor before Traverse could stop them.

Kelly *tsked* again. She walked around me, examining her quarry like a cat pondering a mouse in a trap, like she couldn't decide the best method for ripping off my head.

"You really do need to work on your manners. I'm actually very glad you turned down our offer of membership. With an attitude like yours, you would have given us a bad name." She scowled a little.

"Oh, trust me. I can come up with quite a few bad names for you right now." *Damn it!* I'd never had so much trouble controlling fibers before. Traverse was definitely way more powerful than I was, but at least the three weeks of magical training I'd been putting in with Alexander weren't going to waste.

Kelly scowled. "So unpleasant. And I'm not the only one who thinks so. I found a few…old friends of yours." She gestured to the two zombies, and I finally realized why they looked familiar.

The fire in Hekate's temple. The soldiers who killed Micha. Just before I'd pushed them into the flames, I'd laid a curse on them. It was an impassioned speech; I didn't know it was an *actual* curse.

In the name of the Shadow Goddess, I curse you. May your feet ever wander, finding no rest, that you be as homeless as the innocent people that you have deposed. May the shadows grow around you until they consume you, making your path so dark that even Hades will not find your souls!

Well. It was certainly a more potent spell than I would have expected.

"I never would have expected to have such allies. I never would have found them without Athena's help. But they've been useful, even if they are horribly slow."

I coughed, gagging on the stench. The air was still and stale, and the smell of rotting flesh clung to everything. "Why the hell would she do that?" I didn't really care much about the answer; goddesses would do whatever the hell they wanted. Sometimes it just worked out to our advantages as humans. But if I kept her talking for a few minutes, it meant I had a few minutes to find a way out.

Kelly's grin was feral. "She's come to me in the past. She knows I am her loyal servant. I want what she wants. It has always been this way. In every life. I am only lucky that we have finally been reincarnated so close together. In the past, it made Arachne's daughter impossible to find. A needle hidden in a thousand haystacks. But for both of us to be in Montreal? It was a stroke of luck I haven't had in two thousand years."

Two thousand years? I searched Evadne's memories, but couldn't find anyone who reminded me of Kelly. I'd found Micha's former incarnation immediately, and even recognized Isaiah and Adam, but no one from my past life bore even a passing resemblance to the woman before me.

She cackled, watching me squirm as I tried to place her. "Don't strain yourself. You wouldn't know. We never met. Of course, I heard stories of the girl who made the magic amulets. The girl who saw the future in Hekate's tapestry. I wanted the tapestry for myself, but if I couldn't have it, I'd take you, instead. But these morons got there first. They killed you." She glared at her muscle, wrinkling her nose as if she'd finally noticed the smell.

I was still struggling against Traverse's hold, but I couldn't make any headway against her. The silk continued to wrap itself around me. I was starting to lose the feeling in my fingers and toes. It crept up my neck, up to my face.

"Now, let's not waste any more time. My friends here have waited far too long to kill you, and I would hate to deprive them."

"What, no ceremony this time?" I'd been counting on that as a stalling tactic.

"No. After further consideration, I have decided you would make a very poor offering to Athena. Oh, make no mistake—I'll still dedicate your death to her and burn your body in offering, but that's more of a post-mortem ceremony. No, I need something else from you."

Shit. I needed more time. If I could get a hand free, maybe I could get into my bag—a pair of scissors, or my cell phone, or something! "So you're just going to waste thousands of years of effort because *you* don't think Athena would appreciate me? Wow, I wonder what all of your predecessors would say about that."

The sickly sweet smile she'd been wearing collapsed instantly into a glare. "*No*. Our time, our efforts, will not be wasted. Thanks to that stunt you pulled, the other members of the order have decided our work is too *extreme*. They have abandoned me— abandoned our quest. But I still have a use for you. Just because I will not spill your blood to summon the goddess doesn't mean you will not be instrumental in her triumphant return."

That caught me off guard. For a minute, I lost my concentration. The silk sprang into action, covering me from ankle to shoulder.

"Leave her head free. We aren't done chatting yet."

Her little speech didn't make any sense. Why would the other branches of the Athenian Society suddenly back off, just because Kelly was running from the law?

"They realized you were twisting their mission statement, didn't they? They were never out to kill anyone. That was just you. And now they know what you're really up to, they've withdrawn their support," I gasped.

"They were weak! They were unwilling to make the sacrifices necessary! We are the chosen ones. We will complete the goddess's vision." Her face was livid, eyes wild. But then she inhaled sharply, regaining her composure. "Besides, it was *my* mission. The public may think we are just a *sorority*, but we are so much more than that. I never thought *my* vision would have such a lasting impact."

"*Your vision.* Wow. Somebody's got a big head."

She growled. Actually growled. "I started that temple. I made sure it would endure, for thousands of years. We hid, disguising ourselves as nuns when it was too dangerous to claim our true calling. Lifetime after lifetime, I have made sure our mission would be completed."

"Wait. You don't mean…you started the Athenians?"

Kelly smiled. "You know, you really aren't smart enough to do the goddess honor. All the better that we just kill you now.

"I've heard a very interesting rumor. It says you have an artifact that can give physical form to the incorporeal."

My lungs constricted. "What?"

She smiled again. "I see the rumors are true from your expression! Good. Then let's save time and skip the part where you deny everything and are disagreeable, and go straight to you telling me how to use it."

"I can't." Her eyes flashed. "I mean, it won't do you any good. You'd never get to it. And anyway, it can only be used once every hundred years."

"Well then, I suppose you'd better talk fast."

"I'm not telling you where it is."

Kelly laughed. "Oh, sweetie. I already *know* where it is. The Legion can go anywhere, remember?" She held out a hand and a trail of spiders scampered down her shoulder to rest on the back of her hand. Among them, I spotted the one with the red abdomen. *Izzy.*

"Now, I think we can reach a very agreeable bargain. You teach me how to use the sarcophagus to summon Athena, and I'll give dear Izzy that head start you were so eager for the last time we spoke. That's more than fair, don't you think?"

Staring down at the spider, I considered her offer. I'd been playing for time, and now it looked like I had it—years of it.

"Of course, you could always say no, and I could just squash her right here and now."

"No!"

I swear to god, as soon as I get out of this damn cocoon I am going to slap that smile right off her face! I thought, glaring at Kelly's smug expression.

"Good."

"But you turn her back right now. And let Duck go. I'm not doing anything to help you until I know both of them are safe."

"Duck?" She raised an eyebrow, then shook her head. "You always attract the most...*interesting* companions."

She turned back to Traverse, ordering her in French to release Duck. Like watching time-lapse footage in reverse, the cocoon unwound itself, coiling at his feet. Duck poured limply out of it, unconscious.

At the same time, the Izzy-spider spun out a thread, gliding gracefully to the ground. A moment later, my biological mother was laying on the filthy concrete floor.

Automatically, I tried to go to them, but I couldn't move. Kelly put a hand against my forehead with a laugh, which kept me from tipping over. "There. They're alive."

"I only have your word for that."

Kelly scoffed, rolling her eyes. "Someone will find them eventually. The paralytic will wear off soon." She gestured to one of the zombies, and he bent, about to pick me up.

I looked back at Izzy and Duck. In the low light from the abandoned flashlight, I thought I could see them breathing. Help wasn't far, if only they could wake up and get to it.

"You swear they'll wake up?"

Kelly rolled her eyes, deferring to her accomplice.

"*Quinze minutes*," the older woman grunted. Fifteen minutes.

I didn't have a choice. I was wrapped up tight in the spider silk, surrounded by two psychopaths and their pet spiders and a pair of zombies. The nearer one put spade-like hands on my shoulders, lifting me up, about to toss me over his stinking shoulder.

"Wait! I'll go with you. I won't run. Really. If they're alright, I'll do what you want. Just please, don't make me get any closer to *that*." I sneezed.

She stared me down, then nodded, a grin spreading over her features. She gestured again to Traverse, and with a wave of her hand the threads immobilizing me fell away. I breathed deeply, a tiny amount of relief seeping into my muscles now that I was no longer engaging her in a battle of wills.

The diminutive professor came closer, reaching out with one gloved hand. "Just one more thing, my dear, and then we can go."

She opened her hand and a large, hairy spider crawled out onto my shoulder. I screamed and tried to bat it away.

"Now, this is Drusilla. She's a Brazilian wandering spider. They're the most venomous in the world. One bite could stop your heart. Try anything funny, and the two of you will be getting much more intimately acquainted." She backed away, leading the way up the stairs. The zombies fell into position on either side of me, one more layer of protection for her as we made our way to the exit.

Miraculously, I was still holding the giant plastic

knitting needle, my tote bag over my shoulder. That didn't last long, however. Kelly held out her hand for the bag. Reluctantly, I slipped it off and passed it over.

She threw it on the floor next to Duck, spilling yarn and loose change all over. She raised my hand, inspecting the needle, chuckled, and then dropped it, shaking her head.

I get that a lot.

They marched me down the dark passage. Kelly took Duck's abandoned flashlight and led the way to the door. Traverse followed along in front of me. Though she didn't have a weapon, I knew the threat. As the leader of the Legion, the one who controlled the hoard of spiders, it wouldn't take more than a thought for her to kill me, and she would pick what was probably the most painful way possible to do it. And I knew she'd be much faster than their ham-fisted body guards.

My mind swirled, trying to come up with some form of escape. Running away, I could do. I was damn good at it, and I already knew I could outrun the undead. But I wasn't good at fighting. If I was good at fighting, in either a physical or a metaphorical sense, then I probably wouldn't have wound up in St. Mary's.

Extended my senses, I reached for the rags hanging from their bodies, but like the men themselves, they were so far gone they didn't even recognize what they were any more. A small scrap of what was once linen fluttered, but that was all. The cells were so degraded, so worn out, they wouldn't listen to me. I doubted they would even listen to Traverse.

I missed Micha. I'd been talking big, but my chest was tight with fear. Any moment, the scales would tip and I'd go into a full blown panic attack. I hadn't had one of those in a long time. Not since Kelly first took Izzy.

Keep calm. Deep breaths. You've got to keep it together. Keep it in.

That's it. I didn't need to find a way to get myself out—as long as I could keep *them* in.

I wouldn't get a second chance. I had to time it just right.

The door at the top of the stairs wasn't completely shut. A cold draft kicked up dust, mixing it with the putrid aroma of decomposing flesh. My nose itched.

Ahead, Traverse sneezed.

Not a little sneeze. No, this was one of those sneezes where you bend in half and have black spots in your vision.

I took my chance. Using the needle, I swept the spider off my shoulder. It flew off in Traverse's direction, landing on her head. I must have startled it, because a second later it reared up and buried its fangs in her ear.

She screamed. Kelly spun around, shining her flashlight on me. I closed my eyes against the sudden brightness. The zombies lurched in my direction, but I ducked. I didn't need to see to sense the fibers in her coat and jeans. I reached for them mentally, sensing a high quality merino in her coat, mixed with a hint of cashmere. There was also cashmere in her hat and scarf. It was soft and willing to do anything I asked of it, even though it wasn't the strongest fiber to work with.

Kelly hissed out words in Greek; one of her spells. One of the zombies grabbed the back of my coat. I kicked, the heel of my boot crashing into yielding flesh. I felt the crunch of bone and the zombie staggered to the right but didn't fall. Other than the loss of balance, it gave no sign it even noticed my attempt. Even though every fiber of my being insisted I run, get away, I concentrated on Kelly and her clothes, starting with her hat. The yarn began to unravel, sliding down her face to cover her mouth and eyes.

The coat went next. The sleeves began to lengthen, the fabric growing a little thinner as the material extended to cover her hands. It merged with her gloves, covering them until she looked like she'd put a pair of footie pajamas on upside down. As it squeezed her fingers together, she dropped the flashlight. It bounced down the steps, plunging us into near perfect darkness.

I grabbed Kelly by the collar, throwing her into the other zombie. The two of them fell, rolling down the staircase. An instant later, my winter coat disintegrated, falling into pieces of fiber fill and purple nylon. I slipped out of the first zombie's grasp, hitting the stairs on all fours and took off at a run.

I raised the needle to light my way, charging up the remaining steps and bursting through the door into the condemned outbuilding Duck had described. Pounding across the rotten wood floor toward the exterior door I shouted for help. I had to brace one foot against the wall to jerk the rusted door open.

Outside two Night Shift officers stood next to one of the guards, who was lying face down in the snow. Even in the dark I could see the ugly purple welt on his neck where one of the spiders had taken him down.

"What's going on?" one of the officers asked, shining a light in my direction. I recognized her as Mills, the one who had been watching the front gate on and off for the past two months. Her partner was a shaggy, bearded man built like a string bean.

Mills took one look at my traumatized, disheveled

state and reached for her sidearm.

"Get back up!" she ordered her partner, racing toward me. "Show me."

Chapter Fourteen: Underground

Babbling, I tried to warn Mills about the zombie. "Like the one at the gate. There's two down there."

We didn't have to wait long. Before we were even back in the building, one of them came lumbering out, scraps of my coat still clinging to his fingers. He looked at me, his one good eye burning with fierce hatred that belied his dumb appearance. He may have lost coherent speech, but if anything, he hated me more now than he had two thousand years ago.

Looking at him, soul trapped in a ruined body, I couldn't blame him. Panting, I paused. Mills raised her gun, firing rapidly. Three shots to the head, and his bad leg finally gave out. He collapsed onto the snow.

The second one was coming now, pulling apart the doorframe of the condemned little shack as he forced himself over the body of his comrade. Mills kept shooting until her gun clicked on empty, but this one was more stubborn. Even with three shots oozing on his skull, he remained standing.

This wasn't Dare. It wasn't a necromancer, or the Ferrymen, or Kelly, or Traverse.

This was me. This was the destruction my powers, my hatred had wrought.

They had tried to kill me—they *had* killed me. They'd killed Micha. But no one deserved this. No one.

I swallowed an angry lump and held out a hand. The door to the underworld unrolled before me.

"I don't know how to release you," I said.

The zombie didn't seem to understand or care. Realizing Mills was out of ammo, he strode toward me, gaining speed like a boulder rolling downhill.

"Please! Go! I—I release you from your curse!"

I don't know who was more shocked. Mills and her partner, as the zombie went rigid, or me as his soul began to glimmer around the edge of his body. Or the man himself, the former soldier, as his ruined body finally crumbled, falling to ash to leave nothing but the angry soul behind.

The door began to glow, a brighter, stronger light than usual. He turned toward it, staring, then back at me. For a moment, I thought he would dive at me instead, the most powerful of poltergeists, a vengeful spirit with two thousand years to catch up on. But the glow drew him in like a straw, sucking him into the glowing blackness before it winked out of existence.

Mills' mouth opened and closed several times. She lowered her gun. "What the hell was that?"

"Duck!"

I ran back down into the tunnel. The other zombie was already turning to ash, falling apart in the breeze. I leaped over it and ran back down the stairs, Mills hot on my heels.

She passed me and went straight to Traverse, checking her pulse with one hand, while the other pointed her gun and the light attached to it down the

long corridor. I followed at a distance, still clutching
that stupid knitting needle.

With a cold lump of certainty in my stomach, I
could tell Traverse was already dead. Below, a dozen
bodies were strewn over the floor like discarded toys.
Women, ranging in age from their twenties, up to
pensioners. Scattered between them in the dirt and dust
were black smudges, like burn marks, from the size of a
pin prick to that of a two-dollar coin. There was an
older woman in a crocheted mini dress that screamed
1960s, and a younger one in acid wash jeans and neon,
circa 1988. And those were just the ones I could see.

At the bottom of the stairs, Kelly, blind, mute, and
partially bound, stumbled for an escape, first on all
fours, and then pulling herself up with the help of the
wall.

Mills stood, aiming directly at Kelly's head.
"Freeze!"

Within minutes, backup arrived. Mills and her
partner helped coordinate. Medics were called. The
tunnel began to fill with people in uniform, and some in
plainclothes, Night Shift badges on chains hanging
from their necks. I was ushered out of the narrow space
to let the officers do their work. For all that my training
was nearly up, I was still a civilian, and happy to stay
that way.

The guard was taken away in an ambulance, along
with most of the women who had been released from
Traverse's spell. She herself was also taken away in
one, but in a black bag, and without the flashing lights.

Mills brought up Kelly, turning her over to the
officers above ground before going back down to
handle the victims. At some point, Ian arrived. I was
shivering by then, but when they tried to make me go

inside, I refused. "No. Please, my aunt is down there, and one of my friends. Duck Pizzuto. He's another trainee." The officer nodded, but I'd barely said the words when the two of them emerged from the dilapidated building. Izzy was on a gurney, pale as the snow around us. She wasn't moving.

I ran forward, but the medics pushed me back. "Is she okay?"

"We need to get her to the hospital," said the one closest to me.

"Please, I—"

Someone grabbed my shoulder. I turned around. It was Duck. He seemed like a shadow in the snow, hunched and exhausted. "I—My—are you okay?" I couldn't decide which statement was more important. What needed to be said.

"I'm fine." He smiled weakly. "I think I have a hangover. Did we do shots? Because that's kind of what this feels like."

I shook my head. "No. No shots. It was these psychos—"

The corner of his mouth twitched. "I know. I remember. I think I'm just not coherent enough to be making jokes. Sorry."

"I'm so sorry. This is all my fault." I covered my face with my hands, which were freezing and numb. I still hadn't gotten around to making a pair of gloves.

Duck folded me into a hug. Someone had wrapped him in a blanket, too, and he draped half of it around me, even though I already had my own. "Come on. Let's go find someplace warm. You can tell me all about it," he said, leading me back toward the dorm.

The commotion outside pulled the other trainees from their beds. Though they had been ordered to stay inside the dorm while the investigation was underway, they gathered in the common rooms to peer out at the chaos happening in the yard.

Maddie met us at the back door. "What the hell happened? What's going on?" she demanded. She glanced Duck up and down. Now that I could see him in proper lighting, I was pretty sure his skin wasn't supposed to be that color. "What the hell happened to you?"

"Let's get him to the infirmary," I suggested. It was closer than my room and more private than the common room, anyway.

The staff nurse wasn't there when we arrived, presumably helping outside. Maddie and I got Duck onto a cot, covering him with his blanket. Maddie checked his vitals while I talked. Duck tried to wave her off, but she just pushed him back down and gestured for me to keep talking.

"That was incredibly stupid," Maddie snapped when I was done. "Do you know how much danger you were in? What could have happened?"

"Yes, I think we got a pretty good idea," Duck grimaced from the bed. I had a feeling the only reason she didn't zap me like a dog with a shock collar was that I was out of reach.

Voices outside made us look up. I was closer to the door, so I stuck my head out into the hall.

Connor was jogging toward me. "Evie!" Before I knew what was happening, I'd been lifted off my feet in a bone-crushing hug. "Are you okay? Ian called and said you'd been attacked. Did they hurt you?"

I hung there, frozen, startled by the sudden contact and its fierceness. "I—I'm fine."

He put me down. "What happened?"

I gave him a condensed version of what I'd told Maddie and Duck, sanitizing it slightly. I'd gathered enough from our Adder family dinners to know that the idea of ghosts and magic still made Connor uncomfortable; he was willfully ignorant when it came to what Fynn, Michael, Jack, Ian, and Simon did for a living. Bringing goddesses into the mix might be a little much for him.

"So this crazy cult lady followed you all the way from Montreal?" I decided he really, *really* didn't need to know about the zombies.

"Yeah. But she's in custody now."

"I'm just glad you're okay," he said, leaning down to hug me again, a little more gently this time. After a brief hesitation, I returned the gesture. I couldn't remember my last hug before coming to Chicago. Was it my birthday, back in June?

Connor released me, exhaling slowly. "Do me a favor, would you? Don't tell Fynn I freaked out."

I cocked my head, and my father pulled a face. "He thinks it's absolutely *hilarious* that I had a daughter for nineteen years and didn't know about it. After all, it only took seven years for him to find out about Thomas."

"I promise I won't tell." I hid a grin. Behind me, I heard Maddie muttering, and thought she might be more of a wild card when it came to keeping secrets from his younger brother.

Biting my lip, I remembered something else. "There's one other thing you should know."

"What's that?"

"Izzy's here. They took her to the hospital with the other victims."

"Is she okay?"

"I don't know. They wouldn't let me see her."

"Well, come on then." He reached into his pocket, pulling out a set of keys. "Are you two coming? I think your friend there might need to be looked at."

"No, I'm fine, really—"

Maddie cut off Duck's objection with a light zap to the shoulder. "No. You are going to the hospital."

We all fit comfortably in Connor's SUV, with legroom to spare.

There were two officers with the nine pointed star displayed on their belts in the waiting room, talking to one of the doctors.

"I'll go see if I can find out what happened to the victims, and how your mom is," Maddie said.

That left Connor and I to get Duck checked in. He was barely upright by the time we got to the nurse at the reception desk.

Sometime later, Maddie caught up to us in the little curtained area where Duck was sleeping off whatever the doctors had given him.

"Hey," she said, parting the curtain. "I found her. She's at the end of the hall, if you want to see her. How's Duck?"

"He's fine. They think he got hit with a smaller dose of whatever toxin was used on the women." Spider venom. I shuddered, remembering Kelly's little friend Drusilla sitting on my shoulder, and wondered what type of venom they had been hit with.

Connor hung back, letting me be the first person to check on Izzy. "The doctor said she should be fine. They gave her something for the allergic reaction, but it wasn't bad. Mostly she's dehydrated and malnourished, like the other women."

"Have they been able to identify them yet?"

Maddie shook her head. "We'll know more in the morning. A few of them were coherent enough to give us names. Mills and her partner are going to run down the names and check the others against missing persons reports, but at least two of them don't even speak English. It's going to take some time." She stopped at another curtained cubicle, the second from the end. She gave me a nod of good luck, and then left me to enter on my own.

I took a deep breath and pulled the pale blue fabric back slightly. Izzy was laying with her eyes closed, as pale as I'd seen her on the gurney, but now the fluorescent lights added a new level of "What the hell happened to you?" to her complexion. Fluorescents aren't great for anyone, but they're worse when you have an olive skin tone.

Her eyes cracked open slightly. She squinted at me briefly before closing them again. "Hey, kiddo," she whispered through cracked lips.

"Hey." There was a big plastic cup of water with a straw on the bedside table. I nodded at it, even though she couldn't see. "Thirsty?"

She nodded slightly. I shuffled a little further into the cubicle, trying to ignore the beeps and the bustle of the ER going on all around, and instead concentrate on just what was happening right then, in that tiny room.

I held out the cup and she took a sip. There weren't any chairs; there was barely room to stand. I shuffled uncomfortably, aware that after months of trying to find her, to find a way to get her back, I had no idea what to say. I couldn't exactly open with *"Why didn't you tell me from the start that you were my mother?"*

Izzy opened her eyes again, reaching one weak hand to me. "I'm not sure what they gave me, but it's making me pretty tired. Sorry I'm not more fun right now."

"I don't know what you're talking about," I said, taking her hand. She could barely even squeeze my fingers. "This is right where I want to be."

A pale imitation of a smile crossed her lips. "They told me I was out for a while. Is it really December?"

"Yeah. Do you remember what happened?"

She hesitated. "Some of it. I think. I had this crazy dream about my old English teacher from university…"

Her voiced trailed away, and for a minute I thought she'd fallen asleep.

"I wasn't dreaming, was I?"

I shook my head. Her eyes were still closed, so I squeezed her hand. "We can talk about it in the morning," I said, leaning down to kiss the top of her head.

I held her hand until she fell asleep.

Epilogue

Izzy was released from the hospital on Christmas Day, along with most of the other women. Once they were coherent again, Mills and her team were able to track down some of their families. The others were sent to a safe house until friends or relatives could be found, and they learned how to live in the twenty-first century. Aside from Izzy, they'd all been missing for at least fifteen years, one for more than fifty.

Since I was still staying in the dormitory at Station House Five, and Izzy was still jumpy after her ordeal (I heard the words "PTSD" and "long-term therapy" tossed around when Connor and Ian thought I was talking to Simon at Christmas dinner), so Connor offered her the use of his guest room until the two of us could get back to Montreal. It was very sweet of him, I thought. Izzy was still pretty shell shocked by the whole thing—first with the Athenians, then winding up in Chicago, meeting Connor again for the first time in almost twenty years...and then we had to explain why I was hanging out in Illinois in the first place, and why I wasn't going back until January. Ian and Jack tried to explain it slowly, in small pieces. I was half tempted to ask Adam to fly down once Hanukkah was over, since he was an empath and good at that sort of thing, but decided it was better to take things one step at a time.

Either way, we had plenty of time for bonding. The beautiful snowfall that started Christmas morning turned into a blizzard by afternoon, leaving the Adders with a lot of unexpected house guests. It must have been kismet; Izzy and Connor seemed to spend a good portion of the evening talking in private, and I thought they were getting along pretty well by the time the snow plows showed up the next morning.

The day after Christmas, I was at Station House One tying up some loose ends with Ian. Fynn was supposed to take me home, but his meeting ran late. I was at the front desk with Steve, reading the comic strips and working on a new pair of socks when Dr. Peters came in, her four inch heels clicking loudly on the marble floor.

"I just came to return these," she said, handing a badge and some paperwork to the receptionist. He barely glanced up as he took them, shoving them in a drawer and going back to his game of solitaire.

"Are you leaving the Night Shift?" I asked.

She glanced over at me, smiling. "I'm just a private contractor of sorts. I've been on loan from another organization."

"Oh. Which one?" Were the other groups like the Night Shift and the Night Patrol? I racked my brain, hoping I hadn't slept through that part of L&R.

"Why don't you walk me out, Evie?"

I blinked, but stood, leaving my knitting on top of the newspaper as I followed her to the front door.

"I'm very impressed with the progress you made this term," she said. "I hope we have a chance to work together again."

"I…thanks." I wasn't really sure what she meant by

progress.

"I take it your friend will be returning shortly."

"Who—Oh, you mean Micha? Yeah. He'll…he'll be back next week."

"I'll admit, I'm glad it's finally over."

"Classes, you mean?"

She shook her head. "No. Two thousand years is a long time to wait."

We'd reached the front steps and I stumbled slightly. "Excuse me?"

Dr. Peters took off her glasses. For a moment, I was struck by the brilliant gold of her eyes. I couldn't look away. The way the sun backlit her—

No. It wasn't the sun. There was a bit of a glow. Not quite an aura. This was something else, stronger than the glow I'd seen around Brianna.

"I'm a little surprised it took you this long to figure it out."

I backed away, pressing myself to the hand rail. When Kelly said she was talking to Athena, I somehow pictured something much more one-sided.

Dr. Peters—Athena—held up a hand. "I'm not going to hurt you. I just wanted to say that I'm quite proud. I knew from the start you would be an asset. It's nice to be justified in that assessment, even if you've chosen to apply your talents elsewhere."

"You—you sent her after me!"

She frowned. "At first. But that's done now. In fair combat, you defeated my champion, with your own wits and skill."

My fists knotted around the handrail until my knuckles ached. Here came the sales pitch. Hekate had done the same thing.

Exasperated, Athena sighed. "I just wanted you to

know that I've lifted the curse."

"Curse?"

"The one on your soul, the one that prevented a peaceful ending. I've lifted it. If you meet a bad end this time around, it won't be my fault."

"You mean this whole time, it's been you?"

"I was somewhat rash. I don't forgive slights easily. After you evaded me, I charged one group of my followers to find you, no matter the lifetime. I'm rather disappointed it took them this long to manage it, but then, there is a reason Hekate is the goddess of shadows."

She slipped the glasses back on her nose and continued down the concrete steps. "If you ever tire of your position with her, you have one with me."

"Thanks, but I'm good where I am."

Athena laughed. "I thought you'd say that. No worries. I'm hardly lacking for servants these days."

"But no one worships the Greek gods anymore." It slipped out before I could stop it. I knew Hekate gained much of her power from new followers of witchcraft, but I somehow doubted that was where Athena did her recruiting. Weaving guilds, maybe?

But she only smiled. "My dear, I'm a goddess of war. We never fade."

Before I could respond, she vanished.

A few days later, Ian invited me to sit in on the interview with Kelly. "You are officially an officer, now. Eventually you'll be interviewing witnesses, victims, and suspects."

I shook my head. "No. I don't want anything to do with her. I just want to go back to my old job. My old life."

Ian raised an eyebrow. "You can't go back, Evie.

Trust me on that."

He did eventually demure, though. Despite now being field certified, it was pretty clear to everyone I didn't have the temperament for investigative work. Ian recommended me for a training program in dealing with magical artifacts—this one would be in Quebec, sometime next summer.

December 30, I was packing my bags, preparing to move out of the dorm when something in the hall caught my eye. I looked up, and through the open door I spied the pale form of the Soprano from room twenty-seven.

Her image was no longer crisp and bright; no longer could I mistake her for a living person. She was a pale shade of the performer I'd met a few weeks earlier.

Our nights had been silent. I'd hardly given her a second thought. Had forgotten our conversation entirely, to be honest. But watching her drift past aimlessly, I remembered the harsh things I'd said. Remembered what my anger had done to the Greek soldiers.

Dropping the clothes I was folding on the bed, I hurried after her. *"Signora!"*

She turned slowly, pivoting like a leaf caught in a lazy breeze.

"Signora..." I suddenly wasn't sure what to say. I reached for her hand instinctively, the way I would a friend with a broken heart. I remembered the horrible things I'd said at our last meeting, and my stomach seemed to drop through the floor.

"I'm really sorry," I said. "I was upset. But that doesn't give me the right to take it out on you."

She fixed her hollow eyes on me. I'd never been confronted with a visible manifestation of pain before, not like this. I'd lived through it myself. Disgust washed over me at the thought of inflicting it on someone else.

"He's not coming for me. I waited and waited, but he's not coming. He's abandoned me." Her transparent form shimmered, and she started to drift away.

"Wait! What if the two of you could meet again?" It was a desperate Hail Mary, but I hoped it would work for her the way it had for the little girl in the abandoned lot.

She didn't respond, but she did pause, watching me blankly over her shoulder.

"Just...think about him, okay?" I concentrated, pulling open the door to the underworld on a blank section of wall, right there in the middle of the hallway.

A spark came back to her eyes. "He's there?"

I bit my lip, hoping that I was right. "I think so. At least, if you go through there, you should be able to find him. He's not in this world anymore. He's in that one." All I could see through the doorway was light; What the spirits saw on the other side was a mystery to me.

As she stared into the opening the light seemed to fill her. Her spine straightened, her dull eyes brightened. "Paulo?" She reached out, her fingers just brushing the light.

And then she was gone.

The door winked out of existence. The hallway seemed oddly dark without it. Sounds I hadn't been aware of flooded back. I blinked a few times to regain my equilibrium.

My cell phone rang, pulling me the rest of the way back to reality. For once, it was in my pocket.

Mike's picture flashed on the screen, so I answered. "Hi."

"How are you, Ginny-bug?" He was trying to sound casual, but I still picked up on the wariness behind the question. Exactly a year ago, he'd found me laying on the kitchen floor in a pool of blood. After the tension marking his brief visit to Chicago, I wasn't surprised he was worried about me.

"I'm fine. Really."

"Good. That's really good. I thought about you at Christmas. I tried to call you."

"Yeah, I know. I was going to call you back tonight. I've been busy. We got snowed in on Christmas day, so I've been catching up on a few things since I got back to the dorm."

"I thought you were down south? Aren't they supposed to have palm trees or something there?"

I snorted. "Not likely."

"So how much snow does it take to shut down Chicago?"

"About forty-six centimeters, give or take."

Uncle Mike laughed, putting on an old man voice. "Only forty-six? When I was your age, I had to walk to school with three meters of snow on the ground."

"Uphill both ways?" I smiled, deciding to let the fact that I wasn't exactly school age anymore slide.

"Of course."

Something on the line beeped. I got so few phone calls that it took me a minute to recognize call waiting. I checked the screen.

Mom.

"Evie? Are you still there?"

I put the phone back to my ear. "Yeah. Listen, I need to go. I'm getting another call. But I'll talk to you later."

We said hurried good-byes and hung up. The phone

rang one more time; if I didn't answer, it would go to
voicemail. I held my breath and tapped the green button
with my thumb.

I held my breath; I couldn't speak, didn't know
what to say.

Timidly, my mother's voice came through the
earpiece. "Genevra?"

Licking my lips, I sat down on the bed. "H-Hi,
Mom."

"Genevra!" She dissolved into tears. I waited
silently for her regain her composure, reaching for my
project bag like it was a life preserver. Scooting back so
I could lean against the wall, I sat there and knit two
rounds on a sock before she was able to speak again.

"I've been so worried about you, honey. You
haven't taken our calls in so long, and didn't answer at
Christmas."

Was I supposed to defend myself here? Was I
supposed to come up with some excuse to make her feel
better? I wasn't sure.

"I didn't feel like talking." It was harsher and
blunter than I'd intended, but it was the truth. I didn't
want to talk. I still wasn't sure I wanted to, now. But I
couldn't blame them for not trying if I wasn't willing to
meet them halfway, right?

"Well, I'm glad you do now." She sniffled. I could
picture her in the living room, trying to find the box of
tissues in the end table drawer, the one that slid to the
back every time the drawer was opened.

And then neither of us said anything. I knit faster
and faster, until one of my double pointed needles
slipped out the back got lost in my wrinkled bedding. I
sat there, clutching the sock so hard I could feel the
1.25mm needles bending slightly under the strain.

"How are you?" she asked at last.

"Fine." More silence. "You?"

"We're good. Your dad is leaving for a conference in Seattle next week. I saw your Granny Siobhán at Christmas. She's not doing so well; she'd like to see you."

"What's wrong?" I asked suddenly on alert. I started to ask why she hadn't told me sooner, but managed to bite it back; I hadn't taken any calls from family except Mike since June. I hadn't even glanced at her texts before deleting them.

"Well, she's just old. She's been having some trouble lately with her memory, and her arthritis. Your Aunt Cathy is talking about putting her into assisted living." For a few minutes, she just talked about her mother, my aunts, and the O'Neil side of the family. I almost never saw the O'Neil relatives. They were two hours away, while the Cappellis were in Toronto, where I'd grown up. The Cappellis tend to steamroll anyone who gets in their way, anyhow. Mom had once told me she felt like there was some kind of competition between the two of them. If she mentioned going to visit her family on a specific date, then Grandma Roberta would plan something important for the same day that absolutely could not be missed. As a result, I only saw that side of the family once or twice a year, mostly when they came to see us. I barely even knew my O'Neil cousins. At the time, I don't think she realized I was old enough to understand what was going on, but it always stuck with me. Cappelli manipulation tactics went back decades.

But does it even matter? They aren't really your cousins. Granny Siobhán isn't really your grandma.

Like a guitar string that has suddenly snapped, I felt

a hard *twang* in my chest, and a hole opened up.

If there was one thing I'd learned in the past year, it was that the connections I made—not just the ones I was born with, but the ones I crafted for myself—were at least as important as the ones I'd had my entire life. Did I really want to stop being Granny Siobhán's granddaughter, just because there wasn't a blood link? Did that negate the precious little time we'd had together?

My mom was still talking but I wasn't listening. I snapped back into focus when she said my name.

"Did you hear me, sweetie?"

"Hm? Oh, yeah. I got distracted."

"Well, do you know when would be a good time? For me to come out? I thought maybe next week...Just for a couple of days. I could stay longer, if you wanted, but I'd like to see you. Once you're back in Montreal, I mean."

My throat closed up a little. "I'm not sure when I'll be back, really. I know it's going to be soon, but I don't have the exact date yet. I'm still going through the details with Connor and his family. And Izzy is still recovering."

"How is she? Mike said they finally found her, that she'd been kidnapped by some cult."

"She's okay. Still kind of shaken up. Crowds make her nervous, so we're putting off going to the airport. Connor mentioned taking some time off work to drive us home, make it easier on her, but I'm not sure either of us is ready to spend two or three days in a car with him."

"What's he like?"

I shrugged, even though I knew she couldn't see it. "He's a cop. He reminds me a lot of Uncle Mike, actually. Only he's a lot...taller." I wasn't sure I could convey Connor's size to her with mere words. Calling him a giant seemed a little rude, but "tall" was like saying the Titanic had a little trouble crossing the Atlantic.

I told her about the Adder Sunday dinners, and the coffee dates Connor and I started having on Wednesday nights. We were a little less awkward after the group gatherings, and it was good to talk to him one on one, too.

Hesitantly, she started to catch me up on my various cousins and aunts and uncles back in Ontario. Then her voice cracked. "I don't like that it's gotten this way between us. I know I may not have given birth to you, but you are still my daughter. And I have always done my best to give you what you needed. I…I know I wasn't always the best at it. I know I failed you. But that doesn't mean I'm going to stop trying."

My eyes stung. I rubbed my knuckles against closed lids and nodded. It took a minute for me to get my voice working. "I'm sorry, too. I know I'm not easy to get along with. It's really hard for me to ask for help. But I miss you."

"I miss you too, baby girl."

Then we were both crying. Ugly crying. For several minutes, all that could be heard on the line was sniffling and sobbing and a few mangled attempts at speech.

Finally, Mom managed to suggest that we hang up, and continue the conversation later, when we could both talk. I nodded again, then croaked out my agreement. I hung up, cried some more, and then got up, feeling a bit better than I had in a while.

It didn't escape my notice that my dad hadn't been in on that phone call, and Mom had intentionally scheduled her visit for a time when he would be on the other end of the continent.

But I didn't want to think about that. Not right now. I had other things to worry about, and hearing my mom's voice after so long was comforting. We had a lot to work on, but blood relation or not, she was still family.

***

With my training course complete, I moved from the dorm to a hotel—an actual hotel, with an *h*. One that didn't have coin-operated beds or a horrifying ecosystem living in the carpet. I didn't even have to redecorate.

It was there that I waited to be able to see Micha. Instead of dressing in sequins and heels to go out for New Year's Eve with Maddie and Simon, and Simon's new boyfriend, I put on comfortable boots and my thick, cozy sweater (now free of bloodstains), and prepared to take a cab to Station House One. I wanted to be there as soon as the sarcophagus opened.

I was just sliding my room key into my bag when someone knocked. "Evie?"

"Ian?" *What's he doing here?*

"I can't stay long," he said when I opened the door. He waved me off when I gestured for him to come in. "I'm on my way to Station House One. I'll be there with Howl and a few others when the spell is completed."

"I was just on my way there."

"I know, that's why I came.

"You can't come. I know how much you want to. But we've discussed it, and we think it's better if you wait. We don't know what the end result is going to be. We want to examine him first, to make sure everything is...as expected."

"What do you mean, 'examine him?'" I could feel my temper flaring dangerously.

"Howl and some of our other magic users will make sure Micha is just as he should be. And if the spell didn't work, well, it's best if you stay here."

No matter how much I argued, Ian wouldn't budge on his decision. After half an hour, he left.

I stood in the middle of the room, angry tears in my eyes. I threw myself onto the bed and took my frustrations out on one of the extra-squishy hotel pillows, alternately punching it and screaming into 400-thread count linens.

For two days, I stewed in that hotel room. In the mornings, I burned off my excess energy by running for miles on the treadmill. It seemed PT had at last made its mark; six months ago I never would have considered the possibility of running the equivalent of a marathon in two days.

After lunch, I watched too much TV and knit until I couldn't feel my fingers. I finished the sock I'd been working on while talking to my mom, and was three-quarters done with its mate before Ian finally called the evening of the third day.

"He's ready. Are you free?"

Is that really a question? "Yeah, I can be down in a few minutes," I said, oh-so-cooly, bolting out of my seat. I'd put on shoes and my coat and was halfway to the door before we even hung up.

I waited in Fynn's office. It was much more utilitarian than Ian's, a lot messier, and one of the desk drawers was open with something cabled and wooly spilling out, the needles jammed in at odd angles.

Nervous energy overwhelmed me. My foot bounced out of control; I couldn't even sit still enough to knit. I pulled out the sock, knit a few stitches, set it down, then stuffed it back in the project bag only to pull it out again a few seconds later. Anything to concentrate on, anything to distract me.

Someone was coming. I shoved my yarn back into the bag and stood up so quickly it tumbled onto the floor, rolling under Fynn's desk.

Before I could retrieve it, the door opened. Howl motioned for someone behind him to enter.

I felt him before I saw him: raw, coursing, energy; uncertainty and anxiety to match mine. Self-doubt. Confusion. Fear.

Micha.

It was so strange—in a way, he looked exactly as he always had. Reddish brown curls. Silvery eyes. Slightly taller than me, with an average build.

But for the first time since he'd shown up in my hospital room in Toronto, he wasn't wearing the dark brown leather jacket and blue jeans, or a tee shirt for some 80's rock band. Someone had provided him with some standard issue Night Shift sweats, just like I'd worn for PT. There was stubble on his chin, and the silver forelock was gone, which came as a bit of a shock, but even more startling was how uncomfortable he looked. His eyes had turned an unearthly shade of silver, flushing out almost any trace of green. It almost hurt to look at them. Even more startling was the way his soul seemed to be tied to his body like a helium balloon, the same way Michael's was. He turned away quickly.

"I'll leave you two alone for a minute," Howl said.

For a brief moment, I thought his arrogant face softened into something almost sympathetic. Then again, I could have imagined it.

The click of the latch sealed us in. The psychic link between us, though weaker than before, surged with our uncertainty.

For so long, I'd been depending on Micha. He'd always been something of an ice breaker; lightening the mood when things became uncomfortable, standing behind me when I was nervous. But as I sifted through what I was feeling, mentally labeling it *his* and *hers,* I realized he need me to be the one to make the first move.

I didn't know what to say. I stood there, watching him stare at his bare feet, fidgeting with the cuffs of his too-big sweatshirt.

Oh, no. He's regretting it, I thought. *That's what this is about. He's decided it was a mistake.*

"Well. Um. Hi?" I tried. *Oh, god. What do you say to someone who's recently back from the dead?*

"Hi."

I swallowed the hard lump building in my throat. *Keep it light.* "Wow. I... I can't believe they made me wait three days to see you. What happened?"

He shrugged, pulling on a loose thread. "Mostly they were questioning me, casting all kinds of spells, testing a bunch of charms to make sure I didn't come back as anything...unnatural, I think they said. Basically, to make sure I'm really me, and not some kind of demon or something."

"Now that's just ridiculous."

"They're also still debating other things, like if I should be allowed to go back to Montreal. They're talking about keeping me here for a few months, 'just to be sure.'" There was a bitter edge to his voice. "One of the administrators was even talking about having you reclassified as a necromancer, and having you permanently assigned to the Chicago Night Shift for supervision."

I was livid at the thought. "They can't do that!"

"Ian told them no. He said he'd be personally responsible for us. I think he's going to want to talk to you about that later. I think we're going to have a lot of visits from him in the near future, if they ever let me out of here."

"They will. They can't just keep you here indefinitely." I put a hand on his shoulder. He looked up for the first time since he came into the room.

For a minute, we just took each other in. I stared into those silver eyes, acclimating to them, getting used to the warm, solid body under my hand.

I reached up to touch his chin. "They have to let you out. Eventually you're going to need a shower and a shave. Actually, I think you might be a little past due for both."

That got a smile out of him finally, and I felt like I was coming home. He reached for me, wrapping me up in his arms. I breathed him in. Every muscle in my body, held tense for so long, relaxed. Forget sex, or kissing. The greatest physical act of love is a hug from someone you've been away from too long.

"I've missed you," I whispered.

"I missed you too." He squeezed me a little tighter.

When he finally pulled back, he rested his forehead against mine. Our emotions had gone from two churning seas that met, fighting each other, to a single calm shoreline, waves of affection rolling in every few seconds and washing us in sorely needed warmth.

He was still unsure, and I couldn't blame him. A lot of things had just changed very quickly. I was scared too, but it finally felt like things were *right*.

I reached up to cup his face, lightly kissing his lips. Micha hesitated for only a moment before returning the gesture.

When we broke for air, I took a step back, suddenly reminded of a scene, lifetimes go, when the two of us had stood on a hill in Greece, tugging at each other's clothes. I could still remember the feel of his hand on my thigh.

I coughed. Micha's face was inexplicably red, and I wondered if he was sharing the memory, or if that was just me.

"We should probably go," he said quickly. "I know Ian wants to talk to you. About the thing. The probation thing they were talking about. And Montreal."

I've never seen him flustered before. It's kind of cute. I slipped my arm into his. "Lead the way."

Micha took two steps toward the closed door, but instead of reaching for the knob, be walked right into it.

"Ow!"

I covered my mouth and tried not to laugh, more at the startled expression on his face, like he couldn't figure out how on earth the wall had gotten there. "Are you okay?"

"I... I can't walk through those anymore. I keep forgetting."

My stifled laugh turned into a snort. "I'm sorry!" I was trying really hard not to laugh. I really was. It just wasn't going so well.

He gave me a disgruntled glare. "Hey, *you* try breaking two-thousand-year-old habits. It's not easy."

"I know," I said, reaching for the doorknob. "I will try not to laugh. And in the meantime, I promise I'll protect you from the big bad door."

Micha rubbed his nose. "This is going to take some getting used to."

I smiled, squeezing his hand. He was right about that. But whatever happened now, we'd tackle it— together.

**National suicide prevention hotline (US):
1-800-273-8255**
The Trevor Project (for LGBTQ youth)
1-866-488-7386

**Suicide prevention hotlines (Canada):
1-800-273-8255**
KidsHelpPhone Ages 20 Years and Under in Canada 1-800-668-6868
First Nations and Inuit Hope for Wellness 24/7 Help Line 1-855-242-3310
Canadian Indian Residential Schools Crisis Line 1-866-925-4419
Trans LifeLine – All Ages 1-877-330-6366

National Domestic Abuse Hotline (US):
1.800.799.SAFE (7233)
https://www.thehotline.org/

**Domestic Violence Crisis Text Line (Canada):
Text CONNECT to 686868**
https://www.crisistextline.ca/

ABOUT SOPHIA BEAUMONT

Sophia Beaumont is an author of dark paranormal stories for young adults that deal with mental health, grief, and finding the magic in life.

Growing up isolated in rural Ohio, her childhood would not have been out of place as the plot for a Gothic novel, and provided the perfect backdrop for a developing author.

With a degree in fine art and art conservation, Sophia has a slight obsession with knitting, ghosts, and witches. In her spare time, she knits, crochets, sews, embroiders, and spins, among other crafty pursuits.

Her favorite thing about writing fantasy and paranormal is adding magic to every day events.

Sophia lives with her partner in crime and five little beasties that *might* be cats, or maybe just very fluffy genetic experiments gone wrong. She also writes Gaslamp mysteries for teens and adults as Sìne Peril, and nonfiction (including knitting and crochet patterns) as Sheena Pennell. Together, they make up KnotMagick Studios.

Find KnotMagick Studios Online:
www.KnotMagickKnitter.com
Socials: @KnotMagick
Ko-Fi: Ko-Fi.com/KnotMagick
Youtube: @SinePeril

If you enjoyed *Moreau House*, please consider telling others and writing a review.

You might also enjoy these books by Sophia Beaumont:
The Spider's Web (Evie Cappelli book 1)
The Ferrymen (Evie Cappelli book 2)
The Night Wars Collection (with Missouri Dalton)
Bind Off: The Evie Cappelli Bind Up Omnibus
All for One
Midnight Radio
Dru Faust and the Devil's Due

Don't forget to look for these titles by Sìne Peril:
Off the Rails
By the Grace
Colors in the Dark

If you enjoyed The Spider's Web, you might enjoy
Colors in the Dark by Sine Peril.

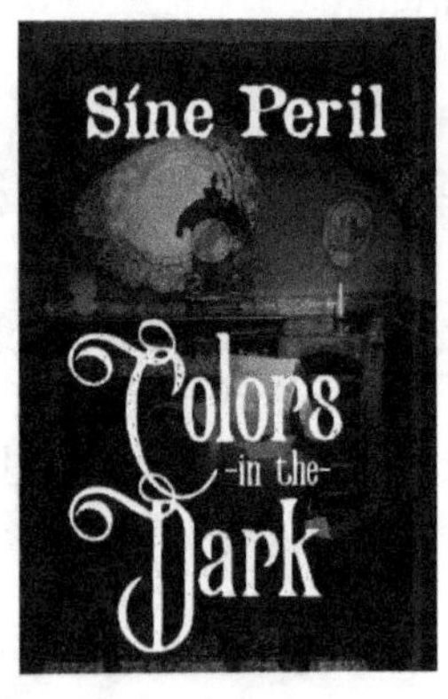